HAMMERED

"*Hammered* is a very exciting, very polished, very impressive debut novel." —Mike Resnick

"Gritty, insightful, and daring—Elizabeth Bear is a talent to watch." —David Brin, author of the Uplift novels and *Kil'n People*

"A gritty and painstakingly well-informed peek inside a future we'd all better hope we don't get, liberally seasoned with VR delights and enigmatically weird alien artifacts . . . Bear builds her future nightmare tale with style and conviction and a constant return to the twists of the human heart." —Richard Morgan, author of *Altered Carbon*

"*Hammered* has it all. Drug wars, hired guns, corporate skullduggery, and bleeding-edge AI, all rolled into one of the best first novels I've seen in I don't know how long. This is the real dope!" —Chris Moriarty, author of *Spin State*

"A glorious hybrid: hard science, dystopian geopolitics, and wide-eyed sense of wonder seamlessly blended into a single book. I hate this woman. She makes the rest of us look like amateurs." —Peter Watts, author of *Starfish* and *Maelstrom*

"Bear is talented." —*Entertainment Weekly*

"Moves at warp speed, with terse 'n' tough dialogue laced with irony, larger-than-life characters and the intrigue of a 3-D chess match. It's a sharp critique of the military-industrial complex and geopolitics—with our normally nice neighbors to the north as the villains, to boot . . . a compelling, disquieting look at a future none of us ever wants to see." —*Hartford Courant*

"Bear skillfully constructs the ingredients for an exciting, futuristic, high-tech book."
—*Dallas Morning News*

"*Hammered* is hard-boiled, hard-hitting science fiction—but it has a very human heart. The reader will care what happens to these characters." —*Winston-Salem Journal*

"A hard-edged, intriguing look at a near-future Earth that paints technology in some quite unique ways."
—*Davis Enterprise*

"A violent, compulsive read . . . [Bear is] a welcome addition—not only to 'noir sci-fi' but to sensational fiction in general. . . . Compulsively readable . . . Bear's greatest talent in *Hammered* is writing about violence in a way that George Pelecanos, Robert Crais and the

aforementioned Parker would envy. . . . Bear isn't just a writer to watch, she's a writer to applaud."
—*Huntsville Times*

"Bear's twenty-first century has some intriguing features drawn from ongoing events . . . desperate and violent urban centers, artificial intelligences emerging in the Net, virtual reconstructions of famous personalities, neural augmentation, nanotech surgical bots. Bear devotes admirable attention to the physical and mental challenges that radical augmentation would likely entail, and *Hammered* certainly establishes Bear as a writer with intriguing potential." —*F&SF*

"With Jenny Casey, author Elizabeth Bear delivers a kick-butt fighter who could easily hold her own against Kristine Smith's Jani Killian or Elizabeth Moon's Heris Serrano. . . . What Bear has done in *Hammered* is create a world that is all too plausible, one wracked by environmental devastation and political chaos. Through Jenny Casey's eyes, she conducts a tour of this society's darker corners, offering an unnerving peek into a future humankind would be wise to avoid." —*SciFi.com*

"*Hammered* is a tough, gritty novel sure to appeal to fans of Elizabeth Moon and David Weber. . . . In Jenny Casey, Bear has created an admirably Chandler-esque character, street-smart and battle-scarred, tough talking and quick on the trigger. . . . Bear shuttles effortlessly back and forth across time to weave her disparate cast of characters together in a tightly plotted page-turner. . . . It takes no effort at all to imagine *Hammered* on the big screen." —*SFRevu*

"An SF thriller full of skullduggery, featuring a razor-sharp ex-soldier who's on the run from her own government for fear they'll want to do worse things to her than they already have, and they've done a lot. . . . A tense, involving and character-driven read . . . A doozy of a ride." —*New York Review of Science Fiction*

"A sobering projection of unchecked current social, political and environmental trends . . . Without giving too much away, it can be said that the underlying theme of Bear's novel is *salvage*, in all its senses . . . how what we would choose to preserve and what we wish to discard are sometimes inextricable."
—*Green Man Reviews*

"It's rare to find a book with so many characters you genuinely care about. It's a roller coaster of a good thriller, too. . . . I, for one, will be looking forward to that next book. Elizabeth Bear has carved herself out a fantastic little world with this first novel. Long may it continue." —*SFCrowsnest.com*

"*Hammered* is a well-written debut, and Bear's deft treatment of the characters and their relationships pushed the book up to keeper level. . . . I would gladly hand it over to anyone who would appreciate a broader spectrum of strong female characters to choose from, particularly in the realm of speculative fiction." —*Broad Universe*

"An enthralling roller-coaster ride through a dark and possible near future." —*Starlog*

"Bear has done a bang-up job rearranging a few squares of the here and now into a future that's guaranteed to raise the blood pressure of readers in the present. Sure, we all want heart-pounding suspense, and Bear offers that in spades. But she also provides the kind of pressurizing prescience that doesn't exactly see the future so much as it repaints the most unpleasant parts of the present into a portrait of a world that knows and loathes itself all too well." —*Agony Column*

"[Bear] does it like a juggler who is also a magician."
—Matthew Cheney, *Mumspsimus*

"Packed with a colorful panoply of characters, a memorable and likeable antiheroine, and plenty of action and intrigue, *Hammered* is a superbly written novel that combines high tech, military-industrial politics, and complex morality. There is much to look forward to in new writer Elizabeth Bear."
—Karin Lowachee, Campbell Award–nominated author of *Warchild*

"A superior piece of work by a writer of enviable talents. I look forward to reading more!" —Paul Witcover, author of *Tumbling After*

"*Hammered* is one helluva good novel! Elizabeth Bear writes tight and tough and tender about grittily real people caught up in a highly inventive story of a wild and wooly tomorrow that grabs the reader from the get-go and will not let go. Excitement, intrigue, intelligence—and a sense of wonder, too! Who could ask for anything more?" —James Stevens-Arce, author of *Soulsaver*

"In this promising debut novel, Elizabeth Bear deftly weaves thought-provoking ideas into an entertaining and tight narrative." —Dena Landon, author of *Shapeshifter's Quest*

SCARDOWN

"Bear deftly creates believable characters who walk into your heart and mind easily. . . . [Her] prose is easy on the mind's ears, her dialogue generally crisp and lifelike." —SciFi.com

"For all the wide-screen fireworks and exotic tech, it is also a tale in which friendships and familial relationships drive as much of the action as enmity, paranoia and Machiavellian scheming. . . . Here there be nifty Ideas about natural and artificial intelligences; satisfyingly convoluted conspiracies; interestingly loose-limbed and unconventional interpersonal relationships; and some pretty good jokes. . . . I will simply warn the tenderhearted that Bad Things great and small will indeed be allowed to happen, but that those who come through the other side will have exhibited that

combination of toughness and humanity that makes
Bear one of the most welcome writers to come
over the horizon lately." —*Locus*

"*Scardown* is a wonderfully written book, and should be a
prerequisite for anyone who wants to write intrigue.
Although it doesn't reinvent the cyberpunk genre with
radically new science or philosophy, it uses the
established conventions to tell a thoroughly engaging
story, and tell it with a high degree of skill. It's engaging
brain candy with surprising emotional insights—and
some cool gun fights—and you won't be able to
put it down." —*Reflection's Edge*

WORLDWIRED

"By sheer force of will and great writing, Bear has
pulled off a rather remarkable feat without drawing
attention to that feat. That is, beyond the attention
you get when you nab a John W. Campbell Award . . .
What we didn't expect was that she'd manage to sort of
reinvent the novel and reinvigorate the science fiction
series. . . . [A] rip-roaring tale of detection, adventure,
aliens, conspiracy and much more told in carefully
turned prose with well-developed characters."
—*Agony Column*

"Elizabeth Bear is simply magisterial. She asserts firm
control of her characters, her setting, and her research
(for the novels). She creates flourishes of style and

excitement; not one time does this novel bore its characters or readers. . . . Run, do not walk, to your nearest bookseller, buy this book, and then sit back and enjoy." —Las Vegas SF Society

"Bear excels at breaking world-altering political acts and military coups into personal ambitions, compromises, and politicians who are neither gods nor monsters. . . . *Worldwired* is a thinking person's book, almost more like a chess match than a traditional narrative. . . . Hardcore science fiction fans—especially those who read David Brin and Larry Niven—won't want to miss it."
—*Reflection's Edge*

"The language is taut, the characters deep and the scenes positively crackle with energy. Not to mention that this is real science fiction, with rescues from crippled starships and exploration of mysterious alien artifacts and international diplomatic brinksmanship between spacefaring powers China and Canada. Yes, Canada!" —James Patrick Kelly, author of *Strange but Not a Stranger* and *Think like a Dinosaur*

"An enjoyable, thoughtful and above all fun trio of books. Elizabeth Bear's work is definitely worth sampling but you probably won't want to stop with just the one book." —SFCrowsnest.com

"A compelling story . . . Bear has plotted the global geopolitics of the next sixty years with considerable depth and aplomb." —*Strange Horizons*

CARNIVAL

Runner-up for the PKD Award for Best Novel, 2006
Nominated for the Lambda Literary Award for
Best SF Novel, 2006

"Bear has a gift for capturing both the pleasure and pain involved in loving someone else, particularly in the acid love story between Kusanagi-Jones and Katherinessen. While these double-crossed lovers bring the novel to a nail-biting conclusion, it is the complex interplay of political motives and personal desires that lends the novel its real substance." —*Washington Post Book World*

"Enjoyable, thought-provoking . . . Like the best of speculative fiction, Bear has created a fascinating and complete universe that blends high-tech gadgetry with Old World adventure and political collusion."
—*Publishers Weekly*

"Bear's exploration of gender stereotypes and the characters' reactions to the rigid expectations of a world of strict gender roles proves fascinating, as does her exploration of political systems gone too far in more than one direction. Her sense of pacing and skill with multifaceted characters prone to all sorts of confused motivations and actions also enrich this action-packed, thought-provoking story." —*Booklist* (starred review)

"Another great adventure of ideals, prejudices and consequences by one of the brightest new minds in speculative fiction." —Mysterious Galaxy

DUST

ELIZABETH BEAR

Bantam Books

DUST
A Bantam Spectra Book / January 2008

Published by
Bantam Dell
A Division of Random House, Inc.
New York, New York

This is a work of fiction. Names, characters, places, and incidents either
are the product of the author's imagination or are used fictitiously.
Any resemblance to actual persons, living or dead, events,
or locales is entirely coincidental.

Bantam Books and the rooster colophon are registered trademarks, and
Spectra and the portrayal of a boxed "s" are trademarks of
Random House, Inc.

ISBN 978-0-553-59107-1

Printed in the United States of America
Published simultaneously in Canada

www.bantamdell.com

OPM 10 9 8 7 6 5 4 3 2 1

This book is for Jaime, Leah, Steve, and Roger.
And you.

● acknowledgments ●

It would be physically impossible for me to thank everyone who needs thanking for the construction of this novel. However, I would like to thank my writers group/online chat gang—collectively known as the Bad Poets Society, a monicker that's becoming less and less convincing as they wrack up the Rhysling and Pushcart Prize nominations—for unrelenting moral support, butt kicking, and revision notes; my agent, Jenn Jackson, who is also a fabulous first reader; J.K. Richard and Ian Tregillis, for going over my physics homework and coming up with all the cool ideas I stole; Asha Shipman, who drags my sorry self to the gym and explains biology to me; my mother, who first inflicted Roger Zelazny, Mervyn Peake, and *Upstairs, Downstairs* upon me; my editor, Anne Groell, who keeps letting me get away with writing very odd little books and then works her butt off to make them work; my copy editor, Faren Bachelis; the approximately umpty-eleven people in the production department whose names I will never know, who work very hard to make nice books on tight schedules; my writing partner, Sarah Monette, for service above and beyond the call, because they won't let me award her a medal even though she richly deserves one; and Stephen Shipman, because.

contents

DUST

1

light from a high window

To know all is not to forgive all. It is
to despise everybody.

—QUENTIN CRISP

At the corner of the window, a waxen spider spun.

Rien's trained eye noticed the spider, the way her spinning caught the light. But Rien did not move her rag to break the threads and sweep the cobweb down. She pressed to the wall between that window and the door and held her breath, praying like the spider that no eye would fall on her, as Lady Ariane Conn and her knights brought in the naked prisoner from Engine.

Rien knew the prisoner was of noble blood by her chains. They writhed at her wrists, quicksilver loops of nanotech. An ancient colony, costlier than rubies and more rare, but forestalling any untoward transformations.

Nobody would waste chains like that on a Mean when cheap extruded would serve. And then there was the way the prisoner bore herself, strong shameless steps that swept the nanotech across the floor behind like silken swags, and there was the buttermilk blue of her complexion.

The girl was tall, almost sexless in her slenderness and anything but sensual, though she was naked except for streaks of indigo blood, and dirt, and manacles. Her bony face was square, and tired sweat stuck her dirt-brown hair to her cheeks and shoulders. The only breadth on her, other than across the jaw and cheekbones, was in the wiry muscles of her shoulders and her chest. Even her bare feet were narrow and elegant.

Rien could not see the prisoner's hands through the twisting chains, but judged they must be the same. Furthermore, she was escorted in by a half-dozen of Ariane's knights, beam weapons slung across ablative armor carapaces, faces concealed under closed and tinted helms. The girl—no older than Rien, though far more imposing—was Family.

Rien drew back among the other upstairs maids, twisting her polishing cloth between her hands, but started when Head's hand fell on her. Rien craned her neck around, catching a comforting glimpse of Head's craggy profile, the long furrows beside hir nose, and whispered. "Will there be war?"

Head squeezed. The pain was a comfort. "When isn't there? Don't worry, girl. We're beneath soldiers. It never touches *us*."

Rien's mouth made an O. "Who's *she* then?"

Head's hand slid down Rien's sloping shoulder and brushed her elbow when it dropped. "That's Sir Perceval. They'll want her well fed once she's in her cell."

The chained girl's eyes swept the room like searchlights. Rien lowered her gaze when the stare seared over her.

Head cleared hir throat. "You can do it."

Care for the prisoner. Not a job for an upstairs maid. Not a job for a mere girl. "But—"

"Hush," said Head.

And Rien had run clear of words anyway. For when the girl knight, Sir Perceval, passed—back still straight as a dangled rope, chin lifted and eyes wide—Rien saw what she had not before.

From long gashes between her shoulder blades, two azure ropes of blood groped down her back, across her spine. They writhed when they touched each other, like columns of searching ants.

Fruitlessly. The wings they sought had been severed at the root. And if Rien were to judge by the Lord's daughter Ariane striding beside the captive, her unblade bumping her thigh, the maiming would be permanent.

That sword's name was Innocence, and it was very old.

Rien raised her hand to her mouth and bit at the skin across the bones as the mangled demon of Engine was led through the hall, down the stair, and away.

At first Perceval thought the tickle in the hollow of her collarbone was the links of a silver necklace she always wore, kinking where they draped over bone. Then, as she came awake, she remembered that she was a prisoner of the House of Rule, and they had taken her necklace along with her clothes, so it must be a trailing strand of hair.

But she turned her head, and nothing slid across her

nape and shoulders. They'd shaved her head—one more humiliation, not remotely the worst.

Perceval's arms were chained over her head, and as her shifting weight fell against them, sensation briefly returned. The chains were not cold and hard, but had stretch and give, like oiled silk. Fighting them was like fighting the River, like a child wrestling adult power.

But she must fight anyway.

She bent her elbows, dragged at the bonds, tugged the sheets of nano that chained her feet to the floor. It hurt, though her weight was halved now, though her shoulders were shorn as naked as her scalp. Rule set the gravity high. Her muscles hardened reflexively, across her shoulders and her deep-keeled breast, and where translucent blood-warmed membrane should have cupped air, instead she felt the clean-cut rounds of bone twist in her new-scabbed wounds.

The tickle at her throat was a forlorn tendril of blood, still groping for the severed wing.

At least there was light here, light from a high window, falling warm and dusty across her scalp and shoulders. Perceval knew it was only to taunt, like the breeze that ghosted between the bars, but she found it a small mercy anyway. If she were to die, at least she would die in the sight of the suns, their strength soaking her bones.

She wrapped her fingers around the sheets of nano, straining to close numb hands, working her fists to move the blood inside. They came back to her in pins and needles, bursts of static along chastened nerves. The effort broke her scabs, and more blood ran from her wounds, dripped along her spine, outlined a buttock's curve. The blood was hotter than the sunlight.

She would not weep for her wings. She would not weep here at all. Not for anything.

She pulled at her chains again, and again, and only stopped when she heard the echo of a footstep on the stair.

Rien came down spiraling polycarbonate steps, one elbow brushing the wall for balance as she steadied a tray on her hands. Sunlight falling through the stairs cast her shadow on the welded floor seven stories below. Her shoes tinkled on the high-impact plastic, the sound ringing back from roof and walls.

The prisoner would know that she was coming, which of course was the design.

At the bottom of the stair was an arched doorway into a short passage. There was no door, nor any need of one; no one who could escape nano chains would be forestalled by anything as fragile as a material barrier. Rien passed the locked and trapped controls and stepped through into the spacious, well-lit dungeon.

Perceval hung in her bonds like a marionette from a rack, head lolling and fingers limp. She did not stir when Rien entered, but Rien thought she saw the quick gleam of a flickering eye. "I've brought food," she said, and set the tray on a folding stand beside the door.

The food was quinoa porridge, steamed and sweetened with honey and soy milk, and a jug of peppermint tisane. Simple fare, but nourishing: the same breakfast Rien had partaken of, though colder now. Rien picked up the bowl, a transparent plastic spoon, and an absorbent shock-wove napkin and crossed the chamber to where the prisoner hung, silhouetted by falling light. "Lift up your head," Rien said, trying to sound stern. "I know that you're awake."

Fortunately, the bowl was durable. Because when the prisoner lifted up her head, blinked eyes the same color and transparency as the peppermint tea, and said, "Hello, Rien," Rien dropped it.

Dust closed his eyes and leaned back in a chair beside the conjured fire. Of course real fire was an impossibility here, a terror that would devour irreplaceable oxygen and fill airtight spaces with killing smoke, but the flicker and warmth and light of the programmed counterfeit would serve him, who was a counterfeit himself.

He put his feet up and listened to the downpour flooding the battlements. It rushed over polycarbonate-paned windows and poured out the rough-beaked snouts of precision-molded rain gutters, beaded on mossy outcrops, and thundered down the ragged shoulders of his house.

The sky creaked overhead. Somewhere deep in the bowels of the world, a conduit had broken. The unseasonable rain would continue until the world's blood healed the wound; Dust's anchore would be washed with water needed, no doubt, in far holdes and domaines. There was no sunlight in the core, except whatever reflected through the long-lensed and mirrored channels from the skin of the world, but there was water aplenty. Half the rivers in the world twisted across his sky.

He breathed the chill air, and smiled. The rain washing his house tickled his skin, the memory of a caress on skin that had not felt such a thing in centuries.

He had lost much of the world when he lost the rest of himself, but all that occurred *here*, he knew. He retained that, though he was not what he had been.

His ring caught on the placket as he tucked one hand into a white-and-silver brocaded waistcoat and felt for his watch. The chain fell cold and silver between his fingers, as if the rain ran through them, too.

When he raised it to his eye, he neither lifted his eyelid nor exposed the crystal. He did not need the watch, the glance, or the gesture. He knew the time; it ticked out within him with atomic regularity. But the ceremony pleased him nonetheless.

"Nearing midnight," he said to an empty chamber, voice ringing on stone walls and hushed by hand-knotted carpets. Dust sat upright, opening his eyes, tucking his watch away. White sleeves billowed as he stood and walked to the window, where a watery light struggled: the reflected suns' doomed but valiant attempt to shine through the sheeting water.

"All but midnight already," he said, and streaked the condensation on the plastic with a casual finger. The house rubbed into his caress. "And so much to be done."

With a magician's gesture, he plucked a glass of brandy from the air, swirling the liquor under his nose. It smelled sharply of real rain—as the rain could not—and chocolate, atomized molecules tickling his receptors, and he smiled when he tasted it.

He spoke to the rain as if through it the world could hear him, though he knew the world had gone deaf long before. But memory was what he had, memory and ritual, and a flair for the melodramatic honed through centuries of study.

"By the elements, by the ten directions. I have not forgotten. My name is Jacob Dust, and I have not forgotten."

Dust could see through the rain if he chose to, stretch out his senses to the skin of the world. He could attenuate himself, reach broad, grow into mist and brush as if with invisible fingertips the transparent skin of the world, reach out beyond it, into the cold empty darkness beyond, where the light of the stars and the temporary suns burned. He could stroke the vast cratered hide, its twisted sun-shades and solar panels, the old wounds and injuries that there simply were not resources to repair. He could reach out into many the holdes and anchores and domaines, into the chambers and vaults of the world. If he were not prevented, in places, he could have extended that reach into its long-cold engines and rent reactor cores, through the homes of Mean and noble alike, into the courts of Engine and Rule. But not all paths were open; some of them his brothers watched over jealously.

He could, however, stroke the cheek of an exiled prince, and of a princess who would be Captain, and of Perceval in her dungeon chains.

And only the angels would know.

But world was vast, and vastly broken, limping in its desolate orbit around these shipwreck stars. And Jacob

Dust was not what he had been, when he and the world were whole. He could do these things, if he chose to. But the effort would exhaust him. And there were those to whom he could not risk being made vulnerable.

Not yet.

2

they know all, that dwell in the silent kitchens

In my Father's house are many
mansions: if it were not so, I would
have told you. I go to prepare
a place for you.

—JOHN 14:2, *King James Bible*

Some of the milk and porridge splashed out when Rien dropped the bowl. It spattered Perceval's ankle, and her chains writhed toward it, defensively. But once they tasted the spill, they withdrew again—Perceval could not help but think—nonplussed.

"I'm sorry," she said. "I did not mean to startle you. Was that for me, Rien?"

The girl stammered, staring. She was small, fine-boned, with delicate features and a wild froth of frizzy black hair chopped off shoulder-long and clipped back with jeweled plastic spiders that spun a transparent hairnet between them—something cheap and pretty.

She looked nothing like her mother, but then, who did?

"It is for you," she managed, bending down to pick up the bowl. It hadn't overturned.

She picked the spoon off the floor as well, and scrubbed it on the hem of her tan blouse. As if a little dirt from the dungeon floor could discomfit Perceval now.

When Rien looked up again, Perceval spread her hands, a gesture of helplessness. She could not feed herself bound up in chains, the strain like dripped fire down her neck and shoulders, a hurt even sharper than the missing wings. *Ariane Conn*, Perceval promised herself, feeling a little ridiculous. She could say the name a thousand times. It would not free her, nor put her in a place where she could fight Lady Ariane.

And in any case, Ariane was the eldest living and acknowledged daughter of Alasdair Conn, who had been Commodore since the death of the last Captain. Nearly five hundred years, nearly since the moving times. She was out of Perceval's league.

Except here unlooked-for was the child Rien, sent to serve Perceval in her captivity, apparently in all innocence. An Engineer's miracle. It might mean that even somewhere here in Rule there was a friend.

Perceval arched up on the balls of her feet to ease her arms and shoulders as Rien fussed with the spoon.

"I will feed you," Rien said, as if noticing Perceval's gesture. She dug the spoon through porridge and held it up so Perceval had only to push her chin forward to take it.

Of course the stuff might be drugged, but they had her in nanochains. If they wanted to poison her, or kill her, or interrogate her, there were easier means.

And Perceval had no doubt those means would be used.

Even such a small motion made her want to gasp in pain, though she schooled herself to let only a little air hiss from her nose. Rien noticed, however, and after Perceval had her mouthful, Rien walked around her to examine her back.

Mere nudity could not make Perceval naked, but standing spread-eagled while a servant of the House of Rule gawked at her stumps was a true humiliation. She lifted her chin anyway, and chewed the porridge before she swallowed it. The stewed grains popped between her teeth. She could taste the flowers in the honey. Thyme and lavender, she thought.

A mercy, that Rien did not touch her. But she did say, as if she would like to touch, "So why is it that your wounds aren't healed?"

Perceval shuddered, as if Rien's words had been a hand brushed across the fine shaved stubble on her nape.

Her wounds weren't healed because she could not bear to heal them. She could not bear to admit that she would never fly again. And that was the darkest kind of foolishness.

She did not need to close her eyes to heal herself. She just reached into the symbiotic web that interleaved her brain, pumped through her veins, laced her flesh and muscle, willing the wounds to heal. There was a prickle and itch; she felt scabs writhing, the cells growing, the wounds sealing closed.

She let the chains take her weight again, though the pain was dizzying. Healing exhausted her.

Rien still stood behind. Perceval could picture her,

mouth agape, watching the scars knit where the unblade had bitten deep. She wondered if she could actually feel the heat of the girl's palm hovering near her freckled back, or if she only imagined that Rien would want to touch, and barely restrain herself.

In any case, now Perceval needed food more than before.

"The porridge," she said, and Rien gasped an apology, scampering around to raise the spoon and bowl again.

Perceval ate it all, and drank the tea. And as Rien was leaving, Perceval stood up strong and stretched against her chains. If she had wings, they would have fanned for balance . . .

Instead, the tender healed skin broke, and blood trickled in quill-thin streams down her back once more.

Rien ascended the stairs, shaking. The empty bowl rattled on the plastic tray and her feet clicked on the transparent steps. The echo—through strangely silent halls—could have been the reverberation of Perceval's voice, as if the prisoner called after her: *Rien, Rien, Rien.*

When Rien came into the kitchen with the dirty bowl, Roger was there with Head, being trained to supervise the scrubbers. He was skinny and dark—a beaky, random-jointed man with a cleft chin, counterpoint to Head's stocky muscularity. Head glanced up as Rien came in, and with a flick of fingers gestured her closer. Rien leaned past Roger to slide the dishes into the scrubbers: pink and frothy, they reached up to cushion and coat each item as it dropped from Rien's hand.

Head stepped closer and pinched Rien's cheek to make her smile. "Why the worryface?"

Strange that sie should tease, when Head's own expression was taut. But that was Head. Sie had been castelan and householder to the Conn family since Tristen and Aefre were crawling babes, to hear hir tell it. Rule might have grown up around hir, as if sie were its rooftree.

Head had no need to prove hir authority through blows or remonstrations. And Rien, who was without family, could think of none she trusted more. "Head, she knew my name."

Head tched, and touched Roger's elbow to draw his attention to a place where the scrubbers were working over the same spot again and again, caught in a feedback loop. "They say demons know all sorts of things," Head said, without a glance at Rien. "And if what crawls out of Engine is not demons, why there are no demons in the world."

Rien snorted, and that *did* net her a jaundiced look. "You have opinions, Miss Rien?"

"No, Head."

But Head smiled, a quick flicker of lips, and Rien smiled back before she dropped her eyes to the scuffed toes of her shoes. And then Head dipped a hand into hir pocket and extended the closed fist to Rien.

What sie laid in Rien's cupped palms, though, was no gift, but a crumpled length of black crepe. "While you were in the dungeon, the Commodore struck Lady Ariane over the prisoner," Head said, "and the princess sent for a sharpening stone. You'll want to be ready with that."

•   •   •

At the sound of footsteps, Rien backed into the shadows of the portrait hall, wringing her rag between her hands. It was slightly greasy, aromatic of lemon oil.

If she closed her eyes and crowded the wall, she could convince herself that she smelled that, and not the acrid machine-oil scent of noble blood. She could convince herself that the burled gold-and-black ironwood frame of the Commodore's portrait—of the *old* Commodore's portrait—was deep enough to hide her, even as it shadowed the image of Alasdair I within.

There was no black sash across it yet, though the confrontation had been coming a long time. Rien had the crepe looped through her belt in the back, freshly pressed, and she had a hammer in her apron pocket also, and sixteen long framing nails.

Eight of the other twenty portraits in the hall were already crossed by mementos of mortality: those of the Princes Royal Tristen, Seth, Finn, Niall, Gunther, and Barnhard, and the Princesses Royal Aefre and Avia. Tristen and Aefre were the eldest, and Aefre had died in a war with Engine before Benedick or Ariane were ever born. There were songs about them, some of which Rien knew. They had been lovers as well as brother and sister, and Tristen was most recently lost, though he had been gone longer than Rien had been alive. So that was centuries of life without his true love, and Rien, who as a Mean could expect to live a hundred years if she were lucky, wondered what it had been like. Could you find other loves? Did you just endure alone, like in the songs?

That seemed, she thought, unnecessarily melodramatic. Of the other twelve portraits, nine smiled or frowned from the wall, unmarked: Benedick, Ariane, Ardath, Dylan, Edmund, Geoffrey, Allan, Chelsea, Oliver. Oliver was Rien's favorite. She gave his frame especial attention. Three final portraits were turned to the wall and nailed there. Whoever they memorialized, Rien had never heard their names, but she knew they had rebelled and been cut down.

The blood smell wasn't fading, no matter what lies she recited. And the footsteps were growing closer. Crisp footsteps, a woman's hard small boots, and the shimmering of silver spurs. Rien forced her eyes open, untwisted the rag in her hands, and began rubbing the scrolled edge of the frame, work smoothing the tremble from her fingers.

No gilt to concern her, just oil-finished wood from which a deep luster had been developed by centuries of polishing. Like the spider in the window, whose web had already been cleaned away when Rien went to see, she wouldn't look up, wouldn't pause, wouldn't seek notice.

Not until the jingling spurs drew closer. Then she put her back to the painting, lowered her eyes—closed her eyes, truth told—twisted that sorry rag in her hands again, and bowed so low she felt it in her knees.

The footsteps paused.

Rien held her breath, so she wouldn't sneeze on the stench of gardenias and death.

"Girl."

"My Lady?"

"Your rag," the Princess Ariane said, her spurs ringing like dropped crystal at the slight shift of her weight. Rien knew she was extending her hand. She risked a peek to find it, and laid her greasy yellow chamois across the princess's callused palm.

Lady Ariane Conn of the House of Rule could never be mistaken for a Mean. Her hair was black-auburn, her eyes peridot. Her collarbone made a lovely line over the curve of her velveted ceramic power armor, and her cheek would have been smooth as buttermilk had the plum-dark outline of a gauntlet's fingers not been haloed in chartreuse upon it, pricks of scab night-colored against the bruising where sharp edges had caught her.

The scabs writhed as she repaired herself.

Lady Ariane laid the flat of her unblade on Rien's chamois and wiped first one side, then the other. She scrubbed a bit where forte joined hilt, angled it into the light for inspection, picked with a thumbnail—careful of the edge—and scrubbed again. The blood she wiped was scarlet, not cobalt. The unblade had already absorbed whatever noble virtue had been in it.

At last satisfied, she handed the rag back, then sheathed Innocence almost without steadying the scabbard.

"Will there be anything else, My Lady?"

Ariane's lips pursed, and then she smiled. It closed her more swollen eye, but she did not wince. "The Commodore is dead," she answered. "Stop polishing the old bastard's picture and hang up the crepe."

Rien tried to look only at the princess's hands, at the pale celadon flush coloring her skin. Had she consumed the old Commodore's blood already? Were his memories prickling through hers, influencing whatever it was that she saw through those modified eyes? Rien knew the House of Rule did not see or think as the Mean did. Their sight, their brains, their hearing was as altered as their blood.

Before she turned away, Rien cleared her throat.

"Yes?" the princess said.

"I'm . . . Lady, it is I who is caring for the prisoner."

Silence. Rien sneaked a look through her lashes, but Lady Ariane gave her no help, only waiting impatiently with one hand on the hilt of her unblade.

Rien took a breath and tried again. "Lady, she knew my name."

"And what is your name, girl?"

"Rien."

Rien thought the princess tilted her head, as if surprised. And then her smile broadened, the swelling around her eye already diminishing as the bruise faded across her cheek. "Fear not, Rien. I'll eat her in the morning. And then after that, she can't very well bother you again."

3

the mute resurrected

Lear: Nothing will come of nothing,
speak again.

Cordelia: Unhappy that I am, I cannot
heave my heart into my mouth: I love
your Majesty according to my bond,
no more nor less.

—WILLIAM SHAKESPEARE,
King Lear, 1.1

Before anyone came down to the dungeon again, a
shadow panel had passed between the world and the
suns, and Rule chilled in the twilight between days. For
Perceval, unclothed and wounded and as necessarily slender as all her winged kind, the cold was a hardship. She
could not even cloak herself in the warmth of her wings,
nor curl her knees into her chest and trap some ghost of
heat.

She had spent her attention earlier on memorizing
each detail of her dungeon cell, figuring the steps to the

top of the tower by counting Rien's footsteps when she came and went. Even here in the darkness, Perceval could conjure the image and space into her mind. It was a spatial gift that accompanied her wings, but which had not left her with them.

So she stood, shoulders hunched and head bowed, shivering with everything in her, teeth clenched so they would not clatter. She heard the footsteps descend, and tried to lift her chin, but the locked muscles in her neck would not allow it.

This could be the Commodore coming for her, or Ariane again. Ariane, who had met Perceval as an equal on the field of combat, and then when Perceval surrendered, struck her wings away. Ariane was without honor, without mercy.

Perceval tried to believe that she would ever have the opportunity to teach her, at least, humility.

She sagged against her chains and tried not to cringe.

But the visitor was the girl Rien, with bandages—and food and drink that Perceval was not at first strong enough to take. The girl—a girl or a young woman; Perceval knew not how they figured such things in Rule— first touched on the lights, and then bathed Perceval's shoulders with warm water and stinging soap, and tched over the cracking, futile scabs. "I thought you healed these," she said.

"What's the use?" Perceval asked, surprised how a few short hours in chains had wearied her spirit. "Your Commodore's only going to consume me. And soon; he can't keep me chained like this forever."

Rien giggled, wringing out her rag. "There is no

Commodore," she said, and hiccuped. The hiccup was the clue Perceval needed: Rien's laughter was not nervous, but repressed hysteria.

There is no Commodore.

"But I saw him when I was brought in."

The soft cloth scrubbed at the tender edges of Perceval's wounds. And Perceval dropped her head down and tried to stretch out her neck, tried to soak up the warmth of that water and stop shivering for a little, until it would start to dry on her skin and more chill follow.

"He's dead," Rien said, in a tone that indicated she understood she'd already said too much. She dropped her rag into the bucket with a plop. Then Perceval felt warm towels drying her back, warm hands measuring tape and gauze.

Perceval breathed deep to steady her hearts, racing in sudden terror in her deep, broad chest. If Alasdair was dead, it was because Ariane had killed him. And if Ariane had killed the Commodore, there was no chance at all that Perceval would ever go free again.

"Don't bother," Perceval said, flinching away from the bandaging.

But Rien ignored her protest, or such protest as she could manage, and continued salving, measuring, taping. There was something possessive in the touch, and Perceval thought she understood it, and Rien's awkward kindness, too.

Perceval sighed. "How long before she comes for me, then?"

"She said in the morning."

Against the protest of her aching neck, Perceval

arched back and glanced at the high window. More torment than darkness, that she could see her life slipping away like the ticking of a clock. The edge of the shadow panel was a limned knife-line, the sky behind still black, but alleviated.

Rien patted her on the back below the bandages, and came around to face her again. Using her numb and burning arms for leverage, Perceval forced herself to stand tall. "But you waste food on me anyway? And air and bandages and water?"

"Air is cheap," Rien said, incredible arrogance for a serving-girl, a sentiment to make an Engineer sign herself and shudder. "And sometimes the Lady doesn't get around to things as soon as she means to."

Meaning she might not get around to destroying Perceval in a timely fashion.

"Can you lengthen my chains?" Perceval asked, when Rien had at least given her the soup and was cleaning the chamber while it worked its restorative magic. "So I may sit upon the floor, or else lie down?"

If Ariane truly was so distracted—and she might be, if she was attempting to wrest control of her father's government—Perceval might linger here in chains, in growing pain, for days upon days, while Rien stolidly washed her filth from the floor and down the gutters with a steam hose. There would be no interrogation; no point, if Ariane meant only to consume her, with due ceremony.

Perceval almost wished it over with.

"I will ask," Rien said. At least the room was warm now, and moist from the cleaning. Rien draped a blanket over Perceval's shoulders, tucked it around her, and clipped it across her chest. It was soft and white. It would show the blood.

There was bread and oil in addition to the soup, and soy cheese. Rien broke it all carefully into bite-size pieces and fed it to Perceval, and Perceval ate like a tame bird from Rien's fingertips. If she was to die, then let her die in whatever comfort she might take.

When Rien gave her another fragment of food, Perceval kissed her fingertips in thanks.

Rien jerked her hand back and jumped a step away. She stared at Perceval, and Perceval stared back. The difference was, Perceval could feel herself smiling faintly. She licked her lips to get the last of the herbed oil.

Rien said as if through a tight throat, "How did you know my name?"

Perceval blinked, and knew she looked just as taken aback. "And why should I not? Are we not sisters?"

It was not Rien who carefully set the plate of bread and oil aside. Nor was it Rien who dabbed Perceval's lips with a damp cloth and brushed the crumbs from her cheek. Some other did it, some other who wore Rien's body.

Some other whom the demon of Engine called sister.

She didn't speak, but she could not leave, and eventually Perceval cleared her throat and spoke again. "Rien? Are you angry? I would not mean to presume . . ."

Rien was not angry. She was nothing, chill and breathless as if a stone sat in her throat.

"Well? Are you struck dumb, are you resurrected? They cannot speak either."

Rien had heard such legends, but she had never met a resurrectee. She was not certain she believed in them.

She busied herself, staring at her hands, and when the tray was ordered and the dirty towels folded, she gulped twice and made herself turn to face Perceval. "You lie."

"I do not," Perceval answered, and her affronted dignity—as if she did not stand in a dungeon, nude and stretched and hollow-eyed with pain—was convincing. "You are the daughter of my father. How in the world is it that you don't know that?"

Rien fled. Without dignity, without grace, leaving the tray on the rack beside the door and finding her way up the stairs in the dimness only by the luminescent strips of edge-lighting.

Supper was over, thankfully. Rule lay quiet under the shadow of evening, and there was nothing expected of the Mean, these eight hours, except sleep.

Rien did not think she would sleep.

But she could retire to the cell she shared with Jodin and Shara and the woolly-haired scullery girl who almost never talked, and clamber into her own unsealed coffin-bunk—the others were closed up tight, the women within sleeping or seeking their own little privacy—and pull the lid down close. The light was on a timer, in case she drifted off while reading or playing games, but she set it to the longest interval and folded her hands behind her head and stared at the whorled greeny-blue translucence of the coffin-top.

Of course there were reasons for Perceval to lie; Rien

was Perceval's keeper. Not that Rien could do anything to save her. Or would, even if she could.

What was Perceval to her?

But she thought of the freckled back, the bloody wounds, and the dark hollows under Perceval's brown transparent eyes, and wondered. What *was* Perceval to her?

Not a friend. Not a sister, whatever Perceval said.

No, but . . .

. . . but what else did she own? It was like finding a wounded bird, which Rien had done. And binding its wings with yarn so it could not flap and injure itself, and bedding it in fleece beside the hearth until it either died, or was fit to fly again.

Except the odds of one of those straggly wrens or juncos ending up in the stew pot had been slim.

There was no profit in dwelling on it. Perceval was condemned. She would die in the morning, and all her lies would die with her. And so, too, would Rien's fantasies of possessiveness and protectiveness.

It was the way of the world.

Still, she stared at the roof of her coffin until the light clicked off, and then she stared into the dark.

The darkest part of night was not very dark in Rule. Even in her dungeon chamber with its lone high window, enough light filtered past the shadow panels to let Perceval pick out the outlines of things, once the timed light flicked off in Rien's absence. Whatever her jaunty words about air, they did after all think of conservation here.

And as she had suspected and intended, her words

brought Rien back to her. In the coldest hour, when even the white blanket thrown over her shoulders could no longer defeat her shivers and her slow-dripping blood clotted and cracked down her rib cage and thighs, she heard a hesitant step on the stair.

Not the purposeful click of the daylight hours. This was a hurried, scuttling movement, soft-soled and shoeless. But still Perceval knew it. She'd heard it descend twice already, and that was enough.

"Hello, Rien," she said, softly, before Rien rounded the corner at the bottom of the stair.

"Don't you think they're watching you?" Rien asked, without stepping through the door. "I mean, don't you think they're observing everything you do and say?"

"Of course they are," Perceval answered. Her chains had not been loosened, and she could no longer stand. She slumped, knees bent, her slight weight all pulling on her shoulders and her wrists. She did not lift her head.

It would be over in the morning.

Maybe.

"What does it matter? I will tell them nothing they do not already know."

Until Ariane ate her. Then Ariane would know anything Perceval could not purge before she was consumed.

Rien stood framed in the doorway, a small awkward shape, one hand reaching for support. "What did you mean when you called me sister?"

"I meant that we are sisters," Perceval replied. "I am the daughter of Benedick Conn. And so are you."

The stick-narrow shape came through the darkness, and though Perceval could not bear the pain to lift her head, she saw the gray-on-gray shape of Rien's hand come up to touch her cheek quite plainly. The touch was human and soft, a kind of blessing.

A benediction, she might have thought, if she were prepared to pun so terribly even in the privacy of her own mind.

"Then how came I here?"

"Servant in a great house?" Perceval's voice rasped, though, and when she coughed the pain in her neck and over her kidneys was unbearable. Rien brought her water, steadied her head to help her drink. "They've been kind to you?"

"Head is fair, and generous," Rien said, which Perceval supposed was a sort of answer. "Tell me how."

"Hostage," Perceval answered. "As I was hostage in Engine, you see. Your mother is a woman of Engine. We were born to be a set. A matched and balanced pair."

Rien stroked her hair, and lowered Perceval's head to let it hang again. "And now?"

Perceval could not shrug like this. Just the thought of it, reflexive, caught her breath in a sob. "Ariane wants a war despite you, doesn't she?"

"Is that what you're for?"

"Oh," Perceval said, "when word gets back to my mother how I died, don't you think it will suffice? Have you met our father, Rien?"

"No," Rien answered. "He does not come to Rule."

"Hmm," Perceval said, and did not trouble herself to say also, *I do not wonder why.*

4

of course she fell

The sceptre, learning, physic, must
All follow this, and come to dust.

—WILLIAM SHAKESPEARE,
Cymbeline, 4.2

Rien awoke to the pulse of her coffin, surprised to find
that she had slept at all. She released the catch and
fumbled her way upright—still before her roommates—
stripped down in one awkward elbowy motion and so was
the first into the cleanser. It polished the dirt and dead skin
away while the sonics made her teeth rattle, and then she
stepped out and rubbed herself down with an astringent
cloth.

She took her time dressing, dawdling really, hoping
that by the time she came into the kitchen, the execution
would be over. Then she would have the cold comfort of
nothing-she-could-have-done.

Then she could tell herself, as orphans do, that she was
a forgotten princess, that it was all a case of mistaken

identity, and her real parents would be along momentarily to rescue her.

But Head was looking for her, and there was a tray waiting, eggs and toast and coffee cooling by the door. "You're late," Head said, and thrust the tray into her hands.

Rien balanced it, practiced and deft. "Must we feed her today?"

"We must," Head said. "The execution is postponed. Lady Ariane has been called away." Sie hesitated, which was unlike hir, and scrubbed broad-palmed hands over the legs of hir white kitchen coveralls. Sie lowered hir voice and glanced over hir shoulder, stalling just long enough that Rien wondered *why* in the world sie was about to reveal whatever could be so dangerous. And then sie said, "You were right, child, and the old Commodore was right. Engine has come to avenge the prisoner. Ariane has brought us to war."

Rien lowered her voice as well, and ducked her chin so her hair and shoulder would hide the shapes her mouth made. "So she'll let Perceval go."

But Head's mouth was a hard line. "I do not think so. I think she'll . . . when she comes back, I think she'll do what she always meant to do. She means to rule Rule, but more. She means to try to conquer the world, to become Captain as well as Commodore, if you ask me. And her brothers and sisters won't like that either, once they see what she's up to."

Rien's mouth made an O, like her eyes. She felt them, felt the tissue stretch and shape itself, felt her lungs stretch around the deepness of her breath. "You said a war wouldn't touch us here. You said we were beneath it."

"I might have been wrong," Head admitted. Sie patted Rien on the shoulder. "Now go. Feed the prisoner. She has to live until—"

Until Lady Ariane wanted her.

"Head," Rien said, before she turned away with the tray, "the chains have her in great pain. She can't sit down, or move from where she stands."

Head—because Head was like that—thought about it carefully. Then sie nodded and reached into hir pocket and pulled out a control box and a key. Sie put the key into the box, and held it close enough to Rien that it could get a sniff. Then sie took the key out again and held the box over the tray.

"Leave it outside the door," Head said. "Then even if she gets ahold of you, she can't make you release her."

"Yes, Head," Rien answered.

Head put the box down beside the coffee and the eggs.

The dungeon had begun to stink, and Rien was at a loss, at first, on how to proceed. She left the tray by the door, of course, but if she just lengthened Perceval's chains, the Engineer would fall in her own filth, and with the un-healed wounds, Rien did not want to risk being able to scrub them clean enough. She did not think that even Head in hir kindness would waste antibiotics or intra-venous fluids on the enemy.

Rien closed her eyes. She was thinking, she realized, as if Perceval would live out the week.

But by the way Perceval hung in her chains, Rien did not think she would live out the day. And if Rien could not come close to her while holding the key, Rien could not cushion her fall.

She would clean the cell first, she decided, and bring in bedding. If it meant leaving Perceval in suspension a little longer . . . well, Rien wasn't entirely certain that she was conscious.

Perceval did lift her head while Rien was cleaning, and tried to stand straight. She wept, though, when she got her feet under her and straightened, and the weight came off her shoulders. "I am fortunate I am, I was a flyer," she said, licking the tears from her mouth. "I am not as heavy as some. Have you come with my last supper, Rien?"

"Just your breakfast," Rien answered. She had to go back up two levels to get bedding when the floor was clean, but that would give it a chance to dry and it wasn't as if the food could get any colder.

Still, she hurried.

Perceval watched with a faintly puzzled expression as Rien laid an open-celled foam pad and fiber-filled comforters at her feet, but seemed either willing to trust, or too befuddled by pain and exhaustion to question Rien's action. "I'm going to put you down," Rien said, returning to the door for the key. "Try to fall on the mattress."

Perceval spread her feet as wide as the chains would allow and centered herself. "I won't fall," she said.

But of course she did. The nanotech relaxed, the chains stretched, and Perceval went down like a sack of wet laundry. She fell across the mattress, and got her hands before her to break her fall, though Rien didn't think the joints were working as they should.

Blue blood and yellow pus, leaking from under the

clipped white blanket, had matted its edge to Perceval's skin, and Rien flinched to see it. But she came to her and carefully lifted the blanket away, though Perceval moaned and stirred. The bandages under were saturated with seepage, and when she peeled them back, all the scab and tender proud flesh was torn.

"Your bones keep moving," she said. "This hasn't healed at all." But at least if it was infected it was open, and not abscessing. And once she got the bandages off and the wounds aired, the smell was less awful.

She disinfected the wounds and irrigated them, thinking it was useless if they wouldn't scab. And Perceval bore it all stolidly. Or perhaps she was lost in some hallucinatory fever-dream, her arms stretched uselessly, awkwardly at her sides. The chains trailed like swags of drapery now, rather than stretching taut with her weight.

Rien had brought clean bandages, too, and with Perceval's muscles soft she could do a better job of it this time. By the time she had finished, Perceval was strong enough to sit, and with Rien's help to steady the spoon she managed her breakfast half by herself.

"I am surprised to be alive," she said at last, between sips of cold coffee. She rubbed her lips together, as if working the fat from the creamer into the chapped skin. "Why are you wasting food on the condemned?"

Rien didn't know, exactly. And she could have lied, to comfort Perceval, and told her it wasn't certain that she would be condemned. But after she thought of that, she shook her head and said, "Because Head is softhearted."

"So I see she is," Perceval answered, and after setting

the molded cup aside, stretched out on her side on the pallet.

"Sie," Rien said. "Head is a kant. Ungendered."

"Sie," Perceval echoed. "Softhearted. And so is Rien."

"Rien is known for it," Rien said. Her own stomach grumbled; she would have missed breakfast by now, but she could probably beg something from Head, or—if Head were not in the kitchen—from Roger, or whoever was. Rien stood, just as Perceval reached out, as if by accident, and brushed fragile fingertips across her knee.

"Come back, Sister?" Perceval asked, very softly.

Rien bit her lip until she thought she could speak without her voice cracking, but it turned out she was wrong. "If you live to suppertime," she said, "I'll be back to care for you."

But she wasn't.

Lady Ariane had called her brothers and sisters home, and they arrived with entourages, or at the very least Dylan, Edmund, Geoffrey, Allan, and Oliver did. Ardath came alone, tall and well muscled, her black hair twisted into a single long queue and a pirate emerald winking in her lobe. Chelsea was nowhere in evidence, and—though Rien held her breath—neither was there any sign of Benedick. She only knew him from his painting: a hollow-cheeked man whose hair hung lank and black to frame a lantern jaw.

That space-black hair and the piercing eyes were the look of all the Conn family, except Tristen, who had a mutation. Of course, they were Exalt, and could look exactly

as they chose. That they chose, within certain limits, a resemblance to their father, was a telling thing. As telling,
Rien supposed, as that the eldest son and the youngest
daughter wanted nothing to do with Ariane and her
games.

The family reunion was also a council of war, and so
there was to be a feast. Preparations took up the after-
noon. And Rien was better at table than Roger, so it was
Roger who was sent to tend Perceval. Rien knew better
than to protest; it could only make Head suspicious, and
then Perceval would be taken away from her for her own
good.

She tried not to think of that happening anyway, as she
tried not to think of Perceval's wounds. Instead she waited
table, and pretended not to hear what the House of Rule
said as they dined.

Ariane sat the head of the table, not in her father's
chair—not yet—but with his chair pulled aside and
draped in red velvet so none would sit there, and a smaller
one set in its place. On her left was Dylan, the second-
eldest present, a tall man and strong. His titanium exo-
skeleton lay flush to his skin, an elaborate filigree of
rainbowed gilt. It made no sound at all when he moved,
but loaned an eerie floating grace to his movements, as if
he had no more substance than Perceval.

Then, down each side of the table were the middle and
younger brothers: Edmund in his brown and crimson, a
beard cropped close to his cheek; Geoffrey slender and
small and debonair, eating with skewers and a knife; Allan
in a white jersey shirt under a blue embroidered vest, his
hair cropped close to show the delicate bones of his skull;

and Oliver, the youngest. Oliver winked at Rien when she placed his plate in front of him, and Rien winked right back. He'd still been home when Rien grew old enough to work outside the kitchens and realize who it was they served, and he'd also always been dismissive of any boundary between Exalt and Mean.

He didn't believe himself any less *worthy* than the rest of his clan. He was just nicer about it.

Ardath sat alone, at the foot, and seemed most inclined to argue with Ariane's insistence that it was time—time the Conn family took back Engine, time they captured and consumed the Engineers. Time for a Remaking, time to bring all the Exalt back into the Family. Time, Ariane said, to get the world under way again.

Rien thought Ardath raised good objections. What about the moral issues of conquest? What about the logistical issues—which of the House of Rule would serve as the locus of the Remaking? Who, in other words, would devour the enemy, take on the responsibility of consuming their memories and program and keeping that online? And what about the free elementals, the wild nanotechnology, artificial intelligence, or artificial life? Who would track all that down, and how would they capture and collect it? There were domaines and holdes and anchores all through the world, some inhabited, some not, and no reliable communication or passage between most. They would have to fight chamber to chamber, cabin to cabin.

They would have to conquer the entire world.

What would happen if they won, when they had collected everyone? How then would they heal a world that even the first Engineers and the first Conn had declared unrepairable? How would they reconcile the angels, without whose assistance they stood no chance at all of getting the world moving again?

How would they choose a destination, when all was said and done? Wars had been fought over that in the past, as well.

These were excellent questions.

But Ariane answered each one. And in the end, when Ardath asked her last and hardest question—*how can we fix something even the Captains of old could not mend?*—Ariane smiled, and shrugged, and said, "We'll see what our resources are when we come to it. Perhaps they simply were not ruthless enough. In any case, we have no choice."

"No choice?" Ardath asked, leaning on her elbows, over the damask tablecloth.

"No," Ariane answered. "We go to war whether we want to or not, dear sister. You see, Engine is marching already."

5

outside rule

Tell it not in Gath; weep not at all.
In the House of Dust roll
yourself in ashes.

—MICAH 1:10,
New Evolutionist Bible

The kitchen was tight and silent as they tidied after supper. There should have been lessons in the evening, but Head, fingers knotted about hir belt, instead dismissed the younger servants to their rooms. Rien had never, she thought, seen Head look frightened. She would not have believed such a thing, had it been told.

Later, in her coffin, Rien could not sleep. She turned and turned again, stretched on her back and curled on her side, pressed her hands against the spongy lid and felt it fill the spaces between her fingers. She counted backward from a thousand—or tried: she kept losing her train of thought in the eight hundreds.

And she kept snaking one hand over the top of the kit pouch that ran along the back edge of the coffin, groping out the sharp-cornered cube of the code box to Perceval's chains, and running her thumb across the controls.

It was her responsibility, wasn't it? Even if tonight Head had said that Roger could do it for her.

Roger couldn't even get the scrubbers to work right. Head didn't trust him to care for the ship cats. And Rien was worried about Perceval's wounds, which had been getting infected. Would Roger know to change the dressings?

If he knew, would he care?

She closed her fist around the key and counted twenty. Forward, this time, and this time she made it.

And then she unlatched her coffin-lid, disabled the light (just in case one of her roommates was awake in her own coffin), and opened it up with great stealthy care. She slid on soft full-legged black trousers, a hand-me-down stretch tank (she'd knotted the straps to make it fit), and a green cardigan. The night would be chilly, but she didn't dig out her shoes, which were safely tucked into the coffin's storage nets.

She didn't want to look as if she were going anywhere.

The chill from the decking made her arch her feet and mince, at first, until her soles and toes went numb. The lift would be too noisy; she just came up the stairs into the courtyard, limping slightly, the box in her pocket swinging against her thigh. Jodin had the night watch, and Rien waved as they crossed paths under the eucalyptus in the courtyard, its heavy breath scenting the air.

She could almost feel the sting of its astringent on her skin. She concentrated on that. She wasn't doing anything wrong. Just going down to check on the prisoner, who was her responsibility, and Jodin would know it.

Jodin wouldn't think anything at all of Rien being up late and wandering. Once in a while, they even wandered together.

It was as dark as it ever got under the sky of Rule. The shadow panel was centered over the suns, its back side soaking up needful solar energy, its front side shading the world's windows for a time. In the latticework of the world, Rule was at the center of sunside, and it would have been bright-lit by day and by night if it weren't for the shadow panels. Instead, Rien moved through a blue kind of twilight, where shapes blurred together and edges grew indistinct.

She let her fingers trail through the broad leaves of grapevines as she passed along the wall, startling some small bird that shot away through the darkness. She'd heard that in the great Mall, swallows nested and sailed across its empty spaces in flocks and flights, but she had never seen such a thing.

She'd never been outside of Rule.

Two olive trees stood guard on either side of the door into the tower, the fruit on one green and on the other, ripening. She stroked the ropy gray trunk of the nearer, feeling it damp with condensation, and wiped her wet fingers on her nape.

She didn't believe at all what Perceval had said, about them being sisters. It was a child's fantasy, a prisoner's ploy. She held that thought as tight in her mind as she held the key in her hand, as she padded down the stair.

No ringing echoed this time. Bare feet made no sound on the polycarbonate, only adhering slightly with each step, the stickiness of moisture and skin oil. Rien paused at the bottom, though, for she heard rustling within.

She peered around the door frame, and found Perceval pacing, wearing a circle at the limit of her chains. She'd redraped the white blanket, and either Roger had changed the dressings or Rien had done a better job the second time, because no fresh matter stained the cloth. But when she turned her shorn head to the door, and bit her lip—apprehension, perhaps? Had she heard Rien on the stair?—Rien saw the blue shadows under her eyes, the skin stretched taut over the bones of her face.

And then she said, hesitantly, "Rien?"

"It's only me," Rien answered, understanding—abruptly—her fear. A silent observer in the early morning could mean many things, for a prisoner, and none likely to her benefit. Rien stepped into the light, tugging her cardigan straight, and went to Perceval.

"Oh," Perceval said. "I wondered, when I didn't see you." She sat down on the pallet, wrapping her arms around her knees, wincing when she moved. Somebody had made it up tight, and Rien did not think Roger would have done so.

Rien crouched beside her. There was enough cloth in the trousers to make a pair of skirts, and they puddled on the floor around her feet when she squatted. She laid her left hand on Perceval's arm, without looking at the prisoner, and was shocked to feel her skin so dry, crepey and hot.

"If you got back to Engine," Rien said, "do you think that they would stop the war?"

She hadn't understood her plan until she spoke it.

For a long time, Perceval did nothing. Then she turned, tendons stretching in the long line of her neck, and said, "It depends, don't you think? Tell me what's going on."

Quickly, softly, Rien told her. That Perceval's capture and mutilation had been the trigger of Lady Ariane's plan. That she had meant, no doubt, to overthrow her father and bring Rule to war with Engine, from the start.

That Engine had obliged.

Fever-bright, Perceval listened. And then she folded her bony forearms one over the other and rested them on her knees, the chains a long silver-blue sweep framing her on either side, her chin pillowed on her bony wrist. "It doesn't matter," she said, after chewing her lip a little. "I'm never getting home, am I?"

Not believing what she was doing, Rien reached into her pocket, down into the depths of the soft swinging dark cloth, and drew out the control. "But I don't know the way out of Rule," she said, when Perceval's eyes finally focused on it.

"Oh," Perceval said. "That's all right. I do."

When the chains slid from her wrists and ankles, Perceval thought the sting in her eyes would blind her. She shuddered, forehead on her arms, and almost wept.

And then she gathered her courage, tented her fingers on the pallet, and pushed to her feet. "We'll go to Father," she said, decisively. "Rien, may I have the key?"

Rien hesitated, but seemed to have made up her mind. She gave Perceval the box, and Perceval used it to tweak the draped chains into a sleeveless column dress, something to hold heat against her skin. She shed the blanket without a glance, and though she winced when she raised her arms to wriggle in and the touch of the fabric made her skin crawl, it was good to have something between her and the world.

"Father," Rien said. "Lord Benedick."

"Who else?" For a moment, Perceval considered crushing the controller, locking the dress into that shape unless and until the colony could be reprogrammed. But there was the risk that someone in Rule had another control for this colony, and it was far too useful a tool to abandon.

"Isn't that . . ." Rien, when Perceval turned back to her, stood with her face screwed up, seeking the right word. ". . . presumptuous?"

Perceval bit her lip. This was probably not the best of times for her to admit how distant her own acquaintanceship with Benedick was, but she would not lie. So she said only, "For his daughters to call in time of need?"

There was a pause. A lingering contemplation. And then Rien shook her head. "You meant it. That we are sisters."

"Yes," Perceval said. And when Rien just stood, staring and shaking her head, she grabbed the young woman's wrist and dragged her along.

Climbing was anything but easy. Perceval was fevered, and her blood—still shocked by the unblade and the amputation of her wings—was not fighting as it should. She must haul herself ten or fifteen spiral steps and then pause, resting one hand on the wall, reeling. But after the third time, Rien seemed both to understand and come back to herself, and begin steadying Perceval up the stairs.

It went faster then.

When they came to the courtyard level, everything was still the indigo of evening. Rien stopped Perceval with a hand on her shoulder and stepped forward first, just to the edge of the door. She glanced cautiously each way—about as nonchalant as a stalking cat, but Perceval wasn't about to tell her so—and then stepped forward.

If there was a night watch—as there would be in any sensible holde: who would wish to trust his breath *only* to automatic alarms?—it was elsewhere.

Or so she hoped, until they crossed between a massive tree that must have been planted when the world was made, turned down a side corridor, and found themselves face-to-face with a young woman with a stunner at her hip and a lightstick in her hand.

"Rien—?"

The girl was a Mean, pink of skin and slow to move. In pity, Perceval only broke her wrist and struck her once hard over the sternum to silence and disable her. She pushed past Rien—she had merely reached over her before—and snatched the stunner from the guard's belt. A quick reversal, the ozone scorch of a bridging spark, and the guard went down.

A good technology. So much safer than anything equally incapacitating Perceval could have done with her hands.

Briefly, she thought of murder. Her hands itched for the wash of blood. But this blood was not the blood she wanted.

"Run," she said, and grabbed Rien's wrist again. "Run! Lead me to an air lock. *Run!*"

Rien stared at her, blinked, blinked at the woman on the floor—then caught her hand in turn and pulled her on.

Good. Good, because Perceval needed it. Needed the hand and the tug, needed the other woman's strength to keep her moving. She had no momentum of her own. Every lifted foot was dragged as if through porridge. The gravity pulled like hands.

They had been running some ninety-three seconds by Perceval's atomic clock when the shriek of alarms began.

"Oh, space," Rien swore, and then covered her mouth with her hand. Were they so strict of their speech in Rule, then? Perceval forced her feet to lift, fall, lift again as fluid soaked her bandages, slicked the inside of the imporous dress. "They'll turn off the hydraulics. We won't be able to open the lock. And I can't go Outside anyway. I haven't a suit. We haven't a go-pack."

"We've my dress," Perceval said. "It'll do."

"I can't breathe vacuum." Rien let go Perceval's fingers, slumped against the corridor wall.

Perceval staggered two steps past her, turned, and caught herself on a twist of ductwork when she almost fell. But she lifted her eyes to Rien's and met them. "Where's the *lock*, Rien?"

"Aren't you listening?"

"Rien."

Rien rolled her eyes, shoved her frizzing tangles off her face, and jerked her chin down a side corridor. "Here."

"Come on." Perceval was dragging Rien again, but

once she turned the corner she could see the massive vault door of the air lock. It gave her strength. They were alone in the corridor, though the wail of the siren and the thump of emergency lights on her retinas made her shudder with adrenaline.

Perceval grabbed the great old use-polished wheel on the air-lock door and twisted. Rien, surprising her, grabbed and strained as well. "Told you," she said, when the weight resisted them. But then she gasped, and leaned into it harder, as—under Perceval's strength, even without mechanical assistance—the lock began to turn.

Perceval might be light as a ghost, made of twigs and wire. But she was Exalt, daughter of Engineers and the House of Conn, and there was machine strength in her blood. From behind them, she heard running footsteps. She ducked her head and covered Rien with her body as a needle-gun sprayed the bulkhead.

The flesh of her palms broke open on the steel. But that steel yielded and, by inches, the door—thicker than her waist—cracked open. She dropped one arm around Rien and pulled her through and in.

Sealing the door was easier. She thought she felt hands fighting her as she dogged and locked it, but there was an emergency override, and she slapped it. Spring-loaded, ceramic bolts shot home, the impact shivering through the walls of the world.

One would need to cut through to open the interior door.

"Safe," Perceval said, and sagged against the wall for a moment. The pain of the contact shocked her back to her feet; she had forgotten the wounds. When she lurched forward she tripped and would have fallen if Rien had not steadied her. Without her wings, she was awkward and easily overbalanced.

"Trapped," Rien replied, turning to look at the exterior door. Her shoulders hunched. She knotted her hands together. "We don't keep suits in the locks. I told you."

"You won't need a suit," Perceval said, "if you will trust me."

"Trust you to what?"

"Exalt you." Perceval stroked Rien's arm. The flesh felt cool under the cardigan, but Perceval thought that was just her own fever.

"Infect me?" Rien turned, abruptly, light on the balls of her feet, and backed away from Perceval's touch. "You want to colonize me."

Perceval shrugged. "You've the blood to sustain it. You're old enough. You should have received a colony years ago. And it will keep you alive"—a gesture at the exterior air-lock door—"Outside."

Rien had put her back to the Outside. And on the inside door, Perceval now heard rhythmic hammering.

"What if I'm not?"

"Not?"

"Not your sister." She shook her head, her hair moving on her neck the way Perceval's once had. "Not Benedick's daughter."

Perceval could not help herself. She spread out her hands, palms toward Rien, and tilted her head. "Then it will kill you, Mean."

Rien gestured over Perceval's shoulder. "And so will they."

"Yes."

"Fine then," Rien said, all hollow bravado, and stepped forward into Perceval's arms.

Rien thought it would hurt. She imagined it would be hard, the initiation, that there would be some sense of transformation or wildfire intimation of change.

Not so.

Perceval embraced her, and she smelled the blood and the antiseptic, and when she lowered her mouth over Rien's, Rien tasted the faint sourness of uncleaned teeth. One would think her colony would take care of that for her, but then, it had perhaps been busy.

The kiss was long and soft, fever-hot and gentle, although holding Perceval in her arms was not unlike embracing a rope ladder. Her lips were soft and cracked over the firmness of her teeth, and it seemed as if Rien expanded on her breath like a blown balloon. Rien was reminded that she had always preferred young women.

She giggled, embarrassed, and stepped back—

—and felt, of a sudden, not outside herself, but rather *inside* herself as she had never felt before. It snapped in, as a whole, abrupt and perfect, the image and awareness of every nerve and every cell. She felt the colony engage her, accept her, rush with each beat of her heart on oxygenated blood to every extremity.

It felt curiously natural.

"Oh," she said.

"Breathe deep." Perceval was fiddling with the key, reshaping her dress into something else. A propulsion pack.

"Let the colony get as much oxygen as it can. We should have about fifteen minutes. I can get us out of Rule in fifteen minutes, and safe back inside."

If it was bravado, Rien would rather not know. "What about the cold?" she asked. "And ebullism?"

"Don't worry; your colony can maintain pressure. It will keep your eyeballs from freezing or your fluids from boiling until long after we run out of oxygen."

"Oh. Good to know."

Perceval laughed. "Hold onto my harness. I'm going to break the door open now. I won't be able to talk to you once we're outside, so just—for the love of all your ancestors, when we get out there—*hang on*."

Hold on. Breathe deep.

Simple enough.

When the massive door swung open, though, and the puff of escaping air sailed them grandly into the crooked sunlight between the world's vast webworked cables, Rien forgot anything but the cold black fire-pricked vault of the universe stretching out forever, and the wheeling world that framed it on each side.

6

the beast in the heart
of the world

In the sweat of thy face shalt thou eat
bread, till thou return unto the
ground; but out of it wast thou taken:
dust thou art, yet absent dust shalt
thou be exalted.

—GENESIS 3:19,
New Evolutionist Bible

Everyone else had forgotten, or was forbidden from remembering, which came to the same thing. Dust had never been human, but he remembered.

He remembered more of being human than the humans did. He contained novels and dramas, actors and singers, stories long untold. He contained histories dead a thousand Earth years. Dead to the world, anyway.

The same thing. The same.

No one in the world had seen a single yellow sun, dug fingers into crumbling natural earth, felt an acid rain trace down her face. Dust had never seen, felt, tasted any of these things either. But he recollected them.

In proper terms, he could not see, feel, taste in any case. But he could approximate. Smell was only a matter of detecting and sorting drifting molecules. Seeing was only a matter of detecting and sorting bounced light.

And what he could not approximate, he could remember.

"The world is mine," said Jacob Dust. "Mine. It has my name on it."

No argument.

No answer.

He hadn't expected one.

Dust hung in soft threads all through the atmosphere of his domain. It was mostly water vapor now; the world had healed its wounds, and as Dust's need for the luxuries necessary to carbon-based life was small, he did not trouble himself to normalize.

Too much oxygen would only encourage the mortal and unmodified to seek him, anyway.

Dust believed in conserving resources. Energy came from the suns, a vast crimson sphere and a tiny white dwarf that whipped about their common center of gravity with a rotational period of only hours, tethered by a luminous banner dragged from the former, accreting to the latter. Material resources were more limited: only what was in the world, and what the world was made of. But Dust's years were long, and the suns burned bright.

By that brightening, he knew the hours of his safety were numbered. The dwarf star had entered its period of convection. At any point, it might commence a deflagration phase, fusing carbon and then oxygen.

Because the integrity of a dwarf star was dependent on the quantum degeneracy pressure of the core, it would be unable to expand and cool to maintain stability in response to an increase in thermal energy caused by accretion, as a main-sequence star would.

Within seconds, a considerable portion of the carbon and oxygen within the star would be fused into heavier elements. Because the star was supported by degenerate pressure rather than by thermal pressure, this thermonuclear event would cause the core temperature to skyrocket—to employ an entirely inadequate metaphor—by billions of degrees, causing further fusion.

The sun would unbind.

The white dwarf would explode, its outer layers hurled clear in a single apocalyptic paroxysm, a shock front moving at nearly 3 percent the speed of light. In a flare of brilliance that would outshine entire galaxies fiftyfold, the world would end.

The sunlight that warmed Dust, which fed all his inhabitants, heralded the furnace that would burn him. And through that sunlight hurtled a pair of half-grown women, whom Dust watched with amusement and a bit of approval. When the angels were otherwise occupied, he could still use their thousands of eyes, all over the skin of the world.

Those eyes showed him Perceval, Rien clutched in her arms, gliding soundlessly across the hub of the turning world. The go-pack on her back trailed wisps of vapor, a trickle of reactive mass. The sort of thing one usually avoided sacrificing to the great cold Enemy, but then, one made exceptions in an emergency. A sacrifice. A burnt offering to Entropy.

Which, like most gods, took no notice.

Dust was different from other gods. And he was not particular about the intended consecration. It attracted his attention—well, to be fair, his attention had been held already—and that was enough.

Dust could not reach Perceval's colony. It would not see him; it would not hear him. It was blinded and deafened to any of his blandishments. He could not see through her eyes, speak through her lips. She possessed it fully, and all its service, and Rien's new daughter-colony was likely forbidden to Dust as well, and would only grow more so as Rien mastered it, and imprinted it with her personality.

But the chains that had become a dress and which now were a simple propulsion device, trickling pressurized atmosphere—that colony had no guiding intelligence.

Dust reached out through wireless connections, through the constant soft hum of telemetry in which the world floated, embedded. He saw as the colony saw—not that it was seeing, exactly. He tasted Perceval's skin, felt her fever-heat (she was very brave, and very ill), felt the bones and skin pressed to the go-pack like a man might feel a lover's spine pressed to his chest. He felt Rien's hands clenched on his straps as she clung against Perceval's chest, shivering and awed.

Like a man waking a child who must not cry out, Dust tickled the edges of the go-pack colony. It was stupid, lobotomized, an idiot system. He made it whole, alert, aware. It was fit only for following orders. He gave it autonomy—of a sort.

Perceval and Rien passed under the stark shadows of the cabling, which with no atmosphere to refract or soften the light remained razor-edged upon their skin. They passed by the hub of the world, where Dust's house was, and where the abandoned bridge moldered. Rien's eyes moved as she read the gold and black lettering upon the hull.

Jacob's Ladder.

Behind the words was painted a double helix, green and yellow, red and white and blue.

"This is my world," said Jacob Dust, as they passed the skin of his domaine, Perceval and Rien in the arms of his newborn son. "My world. My name."

Phantom pain.

It was only phantom pain. Except it wasn't pain, exactly, because it didn't hurt. Rather, Perceval thought she felt her wings stretch and cup, pulling against the knotted, insulted muscles of her chest and back.

It must be only the cold of space on her unhealed wounds, the severed nerves and the reprogramming damage of the unblade. It was still bleeding, she thought, her blood and her colony still groping for lost members and severed flesh. She would have to make it stop bleeding somehow. She would have to heal the unhealable wound.

She wasn't self-deluding enough to imagine she could ever replace what a weapon like Innocence had pared away.

So she concentrated on Rien, shivering, huddled, but craning her neck to see. She concentrated past Rien, too, on the far wall of the world, to which they had come halfway. There must be a hatch, an air lock. There must be a way inside.

Blood or no blood, Exalt though she was, she might be able to half feel wings she didn't have, but her fingers were already going numb. There was no warmth trapped between her and Rien, as there would have been in the coldest imaginable air. There was nothing there but the Enemy, surrounding them, stealing their heat and strength. The great emptiness waited for them all.

It couldn't have her now.

Rien's jaw worked, her lips stubbornly pressed together. Not that she could have said anything—the Enemy would steal her words, and more of her warmth with it. So Perceval was pleased that she had the sense to shut her mouth and cling to the harness straps.

They needed more acceleration. A fine balance; she didn't want to strike the far side of the hub with too much of a difference in inertia. And they could not afford to overshoot and try to come back. Perceval might survive it, but Rien's colony was fragile and new.

She'd freeze solid if they missed, and even if Engine could bring her back, there was a risk of brain injury. Or of resurrecting only the body, the person within long fled.

Perceval found she was fond of Rien's voice. She did not care to have her lose it.

As an additional problem, Perceval thought, as they approached the towering shadow of the far rim, there was relative motion to consider. The world rotated in a stately fashion, but as they crossed the hub, the direction of that movement appeared to reverse. In other words, if the wall they had exited—a wall kilometers in breadth, and they had emerged by the top or sunward edge of it—was spinning to the left, the wall ahead spun to the right, and they were drifting the wrong way to match velocities.

Perceval hoped they had enough reactive mass left to make a difference. Perhaps she should hoard it . . . but when they came gliding among the silent, waist-thick, spinning cables of the far side, she needed the maneuverability, and she needed to be ready. Slowly, so as not to startle Rien, Perceval loosed her clasp on her sister's shoulders. Rien's fingers whitened on the harness— Perceval risked shifting her attention from the onrushing hull and saw the skin crack where they tightened—but she held on and huddled close.

Perceval could not feel her fingers. Ironic cruelty, that the cold stung along the ghost bones of her wings.

The cables spun slower, covered less distance, near the center of the hub. Easier to catch, safer to brake yourself against. But it would take too long to crawl along them to the rim. *I am on the horns of a dilemma*, Perceval thought, and almost giggled, picturing a spiky-horned, two-headed animal. It was all the evidence she needed of oxygen deprivation.

It was all so silent. Perceval heard her own blood hum in her ears, a kind of ringing she thought was just the firing of unused nerves. She reached out before her, both arms and her curved flyer's toes on their long legs, and now the hull was rushing at them like a spinning saw blade, each protrusion or projection another chance at death.

She didn't have time to reprogram the go-pack on the fly, but reversing the thrust was easy enough. All she had to do was use the attitude jets to turn herself, to put her back to the rim of the world, and face away. Rien was looking over her shoulder, Rien with her eyes so wide and weeping tears that crazed with ice and froze to her lashes and had to be shaken away.

Perceval hoped she understood.

They were slowing, though; that, Perceval could feel in her inner ear, in her bones, in her teeth. Now? No. Now?

And then Rien gave the harness straps a yank, and Perceval felt something skip past her toes, bang her foot hard and spin her, but as she whirled like a throwing star, a flat spin with limbs extended, she saw some kind of antennae or mast as it glided past.

It was Rien who grabbed it, and held onto the harness with the other hand, and then with a skull-rattling jerk they were moving, and Perceval got a knee hooked around the thing, and they turned with the ship until it seemed that they moved not at all. Instead the universe wheeled around them, while they hung on the edge of the world, motionless and sublime.

Perceval might have hugged Rien and kissed her, but she felt the ice crystals growing in her own skin, her colony losing its battle. Hand over hand, she pulled them down the mast, and hand over hand, along the grab bars set in the hull. Ahead was an air lock, round, outlined in green paint and the dark sockets of long-dead lights.

It was locked, but Perceval was Exalt. The world opened its doors to her.

And then they were inside, in the heat, in the moisture, and the air was freezing to their skin, cracking off in great flakes when they moved, the sting of thawing flesh too much to be borne. Perceval's knees folded and so did she, knees everywhere and forehead on the heels of her hands, slumped forward automatically as if she still had wings.

Rien coughed up blood. Bright, frothy, oxygenated. Lung blood, and still more red than blue; she must have tried to hold her breath. It didn't matter; they were inside now. Whatever she had sustained, her colony would heal.

Except she was staring at Perceval, not her own blood on the floor. Her voice cracked and raggedy, she rasped, "Perceval. Your wings."

And by some luck, before Perceval called Rien any of those perfectly appropriate names that sprang to mind, she glanced past her and saw them reflected in the inside air-lock hatch. Spread out behind her, no hollow bone and soft membrane but seemingly wrought of shadow and mist and silk. Pearl and charcoal and silver, raddled this way and that like a colt's thin legs.

A pair, indeed, of ghostly wings.

7

the beat of parasite wings

When the white flame in us is gone,
And we that lost the world's delight
Stiffen in darkness, left alone
To crumble in our separate night.

—RUPERT BROOKE, "Dust"

The air-lock decking was cold under Rien's feet, her own blood seaweedy, meaty-sharp in her mouth, overlaid with an unfamiliar bitterness. Even after speaking to Perceval, she spat and spat. The blood made a streaked puddle by her feet.

She started when Perceval touched her shoulder. "Don't spit it out," she said, the gauzy wings stirring behind her. "Swallow it. You're spitting out your symbiont."

With an effort, Rien did as Perceval instructed. Her throat was raw; it felt like swallowing scrubbers. When she could make herself stand straight, she looked at Perceval and spared herself speech by lifting her right hand, wrist bent, and making a spinning motion.

Perceval seemed to understand. She turned in place.

Rien noticed that the tips of the half-material wings lifted slightly to miss the puddle of slime on the decking. She, too, picked her way around it, cautious about stepping too close. Although, she considered, anything in the air lock was within range, if they lashed out.

The go-pack had vanished. Perceval's pale freckled back was naked from the base of her stubbled skull to the cleft of narrow buttocks. And the wings—translucent, whispery—grew from where her wounds had been. "What do you see?" Perceval asked. When she craned her head over her shoulder, the tendons stood out along her throat all the way up to her ear.

"Are we in Engine?"

"No," Perceval said. "I don't know exactly where we are. The world was spinning. But not in Rule, that's something. What do you *see?*"

"It's the chains," Rien said. "The nanocolony. It's turned into wings."

"And?"

"And fused with you," she finished, reluctantly. And spoke the next words on a rush, wishing she dared to touch Perceval just then. "Come on, we need to get out of this air lock and figure out where we are."

"And how to get to Father," Perceval said. She turned, decisively, and the wings missed thumping Rien as deftly as if they had been real. With one hand, the Engineer struck the air-lock release. Into the other, she produced the control for the nanotech colony, and was already fussing with it as the air lock cycled.

It had, Rien noticed and did not say, no visible effect.

She walked through the lock behind Perceval, distracted by the distinct, minute sensations of her lungs and skin repairing themselves, or being repaired by her new symbiont. Rien had split her scalp when she was a child, as children do, and the sensation reminded her of the tug of stitches in anaesthetized skin, on a micro level. The lock closed behind her, and they stood in the warm air of the corridor.

Perceval reached up over her shoulder and ran her fingertips from the base to the joint, as far as her arm would reach. She grasped the bone—what would have been the bone, in a living wing—between thumb and forefinger, wrist bent tortuously. She pulled, muscles flexing in her forearm, wiry biceps taut, her breast lifting as her pectorals tensed.

The wing did not budge. Perceval only succeeded in pulling her own shoulder forward. "Ow," she said.

Here in the corridor Rien could see it better. And see how the light did indeed fall through it, as if it were a three-dimensional rendering made real. She let her hand drop by her thigh, defeated. "I think it's engineered out of nanoscaffolds. And it's bonded to my stumps."

"Can you feel it?"

At first, Rien thought Perceval would not answer. The question, on second thought, was quite rude. She winced an apology. But Perceval didn't seem to find it presumptuous. "Yes," she said. Her lips looked thin. A muscle twitched along her jaw, a rhythmic tic. "It doesn't hurt anymore."

Rien thought about raw bone, naked to air, chafed by bandages. Bile rose up her throat.

"I hate this."

All Rien could do was put her hand on her sister's arm. "We need to find out where we are."

"It's warm," Perceval said. "So it's populated. There are a lot of parts of the world that I know nothing about, though. Have you memorized any of the world plans?"

"I've never been out of Rule," Rien said. Even that was overstating the case. She'd never been out of the Commodore's household, not even as far as the algae tanks.

"Well, no matter." Perceval craned her head back. She still held the key box in her hand, clenched like any other useless talisman. Were even Engineers superstitious? And then convulsively, she turned and slammed it against the wall. It shattered, and she let the pieces fall. And then turned away, head jerking as if startled.

Rien opened her mouth, still tasting blood and that machine-oil funk. But a frown of concentration drew down the corners of Perceval's mouth, and she held up one impatient uplifted hand. Whatever Rien had been about to say, she hushed herself.

And so heard the pad of running feet.

Perceval heard them, too. But she could not afford the time or the break in concentration to look. They were un-armed, alone, barely dressed.

The pull of skin across her cheeks told her she was purs-ing her lips as she concentrated, a habit her mother always teased about. It helped distract her from the weightlessness of her shadowy new wings, which generated a deep and re-pellent terror.

No one had a schematic of all the world. Not since the moving times, as far as Perceval knew. Not since the engines and the world brain failed, leaving them with partial maps and hard copy. But she knew her history, the stories of the world ships sent out like groping fingers across the Enemy's empty sea, better charted but no less gallant than any unevolved raftsman braving the Pacific. It was a kind of superb blindness, the human push for exploration, for growth.

Or maybe it wasn't. After all, any virus could do the same. Her symbiont, engineered and unintelligent, was even now colonizing the unknown shores of Rien's body.

Still, Perceval was human. She could be forgiven an ethnocentric value judgment. And she was a human with a carefully bred and force-evolved body and a highly engineered prosthesiotomy. She had seen maps. Thus, she could recollect them. And—it was just possible—figure out where they were, at least in the broadest of terms.

Images flickered, turned, shuffled across her inner eye. Sharp and precise, machine-learned: unlike her father, she was not a bred eidetic. But she had a trick he didn't, and she layered and turned and compared. She had her natural spatial sense, heightened for a flyer, and she had the sound of the echoes along the corridor, closer, rounding the corner now. It all built an image, a geography. A *map*.

She knew where they were.

And then, when she would have expected a hail or a challenge, came the flat hiss of air guns.

Perceval's reflexes were accelerated to the edge of diminishing returns. In a stress situation, thinking chips made her limbs' decisions for her; it could take too long for electricity to flow along nerves. She could assess and act faster than any unengineered creature could dream of, if it could not be precisely described as thinking.

She had no time to react.

Her parasite wings flared wide; they spun her. The sensation was as a child swung around in a strong man's grip, and Perceval was as powerless to hold her ground as that child. One wing cupped Rien, drew her close, and with that Perceval could assist. She caught her sister in her arms and clutched her inside the curve of her body, her nose buried in Rien's greasy dark hair. Rien screamed, or started to scream, and they were slung around again. Perceval felt the vibration of Rien's cry through her rib cage, and could think only how it must hurt to shout like that, with vacuum-stressed lungs.

Perceval wanted to close her eyes. But were she willing to admit cowardice, she barely had the time.

There were four in the corridor: a crossfire, two at each end. They wore coveralls, black with bright patterns in ultraviolet, which made Perceval think they were Exalt.

Without asking questions, without a word, they fired, and continued to fire. And air darts sailed all around Perceval and Rien, slivers of drugged or deadly plastic that were no threat to the world's fragile hull. No one would risk an explosive weapon inside. Mean or Exalt, everyone feared the Enemy more than anything save fire.

The darts made little sound when they struck the parasite wings—no melodramatic clang or thud. Just a patter like the drip of condensation from a conduit. They did not pass through. And wherever the darts flew toward Perceval or Rien, there in advance were the wings.

And then they were moving, again, not flying—the corridor was too narrow and too low—but the jerk at Perceval's shoulders was like flying. The wings—she *felt* them, felt them spider along the bulkheads and decking, felt the pinion-tips bend, tension between them holding her feet from the floor, felt the strain along their struts. It felt nothing like flesh and membrane and bone.

There were four wings, then, six, nine. The darts sounded like a hard rain. All Perceval could do was cling to Rien, whose forearms were locked over her own, legs trailing, and press her mouth into Rien's hair.

They came among the defenders. One dived aside; Perceval's retina photographed her, arms reaching, weapon thrown aside.

The other one, the wings went through.

If Perceval had a hand free, she would have covered Rien's eyes. They might be of an age, but she could not help but think of her sister as a child, in need of protection. Rien's fingers dug into Perceval's wrist, and there was blood, blue and bright, darkening in atmosphere, the sharp stink of it. Rien sobbed.

The defender was meat, and they were through.

The patter of darts against the parasite wings stopped abruptly when they turned the corner. They passed through lock doors, into abandoned portions of the world where the air was stale and chill radiated from the bulkheads, and it was no longer any effort for her wings to hold her feet from the floor. No gravity and no light: she saw in infrared, and by the faint chill radiance of the greeny-blue fungus that grew in the welded seams of the walls.

No pursuit followed; they were away. Perceval felt the last blood sliding as if frictionless from the wings that weren't hers. It flicked free, shivering globes that struck the corridor walls and stuck, food for that fungus. The wings folded together again, encapsulating Perceval and Rien in a warmer chrysalis.

"Who was that?" Rien said, finally, her voice thready but admirably calm.

Perceval wondered if it was a pretense.

"I don't know anything about them," she admitted.

"Oh." After a silence, though Rien cleared her throat and continued. "I do."

"What?"

Rien was shaking, and her fingers bruised Perceval's flesh against her bones, but Perceval wasn't going to say anything. She waited until Rien organized herself enough to say, "They're on a war footing, don't you think? Expecting invasion."

"Yes," Perceval said. "I think so. I think it's not just Rule and Engine that are fighting. And I know something else."

"You know where we are?"

Perceval nodded. Rien would feel her face move against her hair. "We're a really long way from home."

One of Dust's relics of remembrance was the fond old ideal of gallantry. In watching Perceval and Rien, he recollected it.

He was too much a gentleman to insinuate himself into the awareness of Perceval's wings when they wrapped her and her sister so tightly. They seemed to be functioning as intended.

It was enough.

He held the maidens in his attention for a moment, then released them. Left them huddled in his gift, and turned away.

He could not be distracted by his darling girls when he must be about seducing villains. Something might show, some hint, or texture. Some glimpse, and it would never do for Perceval and Rien to be unsafe, even for a moment.

Dust's guest would be with him shortly. And beyond the girls' safety, Dust couldn't afford to let his rival guess from whence the blow would fall.

Chimes announced a visitor. Not Dust's bells, however. Samael, damn him, selected his own clarion. He chose to be piped aboard like an admiral. Was it any wonder Dust found him unbearable?

The chime was only a courtesy. Samael began to resolve in Dust's chamber almost instantaneously: not a full manifestation, but still something more concrete than a hologram. Real politeness would have waited for an invitation, but Samael was arrogant.

Dust flattered himself that he could have prevented the entrance. But perhaps it was better to appear less than one was, to keep something in reserve—

That he had lost his last argument with Samael did not mean that he would lose them all. Surely not. Still, politeness was a virtue.

With a half-breathed sigh, he resolved a tendril into a concrete state, meeting Samael halfway.

Samael's avatar was cleaning his nails when Dust stepped out of air beside him. It was an ostentatious nail-cleaning, involving a facsimile of a pearl-handled pocketknife, and the parings that fell to Dust's deck spread hairy roots and grew into some creepery vine heavy with fragrant, waxen flowers.

Dust ground it under his polished black boot. "This is not the place nor the time to stake claims."

However mildly he spoke, wherever Samael seemed to be looking, Dust knew his sibling's attention focused on him—at least as far as the current interaction went. He folded his black-sleeved arms over the silver brocade of his vest, aware that it glittered in the light like mail or scales, and let his stare rest on Samael.

Dust's sibling affected a pale and ascetic aspect, long white-blond hair trailing in locks around a narrow basset-hound face. He frowned, and it made him look soft-eyed, but Dust knew it for artifice as surely as the band-collared shirt worn with blue jeans and bare feet and an emerald brocade tailcoat with velvet lapels.

Self-consciously, Samael folded the knife away, and then picked lint from his shoulder. He did not flick that to the floor, but tucked it in his pocket. Which was something, Dust supposed.

He thought Samael would counter with some comment on Dust's lack of sibling hospitality, but Samael hooked his thumbs in the waistband of his jeans. "I want to trade," he said.

Dust stared. He brushed invisible fringes over the edges

of Samael's avatar, but for all Samael's reaction the caress—or test—might have been a breath of wind. "Trade?"

"I'm the Angel of Death, aren't I?" The knobby hands turned palm-up now. "And you're the Angel of Memory. So trade me a little knowledge for a little life. A little withholding of death, if you will."

"Don't be ridiculous," Dust said. "You're not the angel of anything."

"That's what they call us. And not just us. Some of them call the old crew angels and demons, too."

"Ahh," Dust said, willing his fingers to stillness when they wanted to worry his sleeves, "but we know better, don't we? Besides, if you were the angel of anything, it would be the angel of . . . life-support services." He scraped his boot across the deck, leaving a green smear of chlorophyll like a punctuation mark.

"Not very poetic," Samael said, disappointed.

Dust shrugged. He only cared about his *own* poetry.

"And anyway," Samael continued, with a sweeping dismissal that pulled shirt and coatsleeves up his bony wrist, "in the midst of life support we are in death, o my brother."

Dust kept his attention spread through his anchore, for he suspected that Samael would have liked him to concentrate and neglect his boundaries. "Your trade sounds more like a threat than an equal exchange."

Samael's shrug, one-shouldered with disingenuously tilted head, was disturbingly reminiscent of that of a twelve-year-old girl. "I think there's an Engine girl you've taken an interest in," he said. "What if I could help her?"

"An Engine girl?" Dust thought he could give Samael

fair competition when it came to disingenuity. Once upon a time, they would have held this meeting in the channels of the world's analytical engines, but those were long unavailable. They met in the metal if they met at all. And Samael kept all his parts tucked in, like a cat tea-cozied on the rug, so Dust couldn't even brush microsurfaces with him and see if any stray electromagnetic intelligence was seeping free.

"Perceval Foucaulte Conn," Samael said, and if he couldn't trim his nails, he could study them. How peculiar it was, Dust thought, that a century since any of them had had much cause to interact with their creators, they still wore human guise. "She's trapped with her half sister on epsilon deck, and she could be fumbling around down there for a good long time. She's also suffering from septicemia and a viral infection, and her symbiont is heavily stressed. She needs warmth and food. And medical attention."

"And you're offering that assistance?"

"It is," Samael said, "what I was built to do."

"And the recompense?" That was always the rub, wasn't it? They all dealt from a position of strength; they all had their unique fields. When the Core died, the world had shifted as many of its functions into its symbionts as possible. It had saved itself, against future need. But none of those symbiont colonies could hold the entire mind of the world. They were fragments. Specialists. With differing agendas.

They rarely got along.

"Navigation logs," Samael said. "Starmaps. Tell me where we had been, and where we were en route to."

"Useless," Dust said. There were no engines. There was no way to *move*.

"I want to know where we are," Samael said. "Give me that, and I spare your pet."

Then it was Dust's turn to fiddle his fingers. "She's not a pet."

"Cat's-paw," Samael said. "Dupe. Whatever."

The fragment of Dust that rode along with Perceval's gift-pinions stayed in coded contact with his main colony. He could feel her huddle tighter around Rien, shivering within the thin warmth of the wings. If she had been closer, if he would not have had to withdraw the fragment from contact with the suborned colony, Dust might have stroked her shaven head.

No doubt, he thought, the child could use a little love. "Creator," Dust said, fondly. "Inventor and the daughter of inventors."

"Heresy."

"Nevertheless," Dust said. "Her kind invented ours."

"How could something like *that* invent something like me?"

"Nevertheless," Dust said. "It is what happened."

"You lie."

"No," Dust corrected. "I remember." He turned away—his avatar turned away. His own hovering attention never shifted. Not from Samael's sock-puppet, not from the boundaries of Dust's own domaine. "Navigation logs."

"Yes."

"That's all you want."

"For now."

"Help the maidens," Dust said. "I'll share the logs."

In all fastidiousness, he would have preferred not to touch Samael. It was less risk to his own system to chip off a packet and hand it over—but he did not wish to lose that much of his colony, would not take any of Samael in return, and didn't want to give his sibling that much insight into his program.

Instead, he bent down and "kissed" Samael on the "mouth."

A meshing of programs, but only a surfacy one. A quick handshake and transfer of data, nothing more.

As they broke apart, the information safely handed over, the memory of the kiss left Dust full of an aching emptiness, everywhere his airborne nanoparticles drifted and spread.

8

poison angels

Let the dwellers in emptiness bow
down before him; in his presence, let
his enemies lick up dust.

—PSALM 72:9,
New Evolutionist Bible

No matter how she tried to pull them under the covers, Rien's feet stayed cold. She wrapped her arms around her knees and hugged her face down tight, except then it was strange that her back was so uncomfortably warm. And she couldn't breathe. The air was still and stale and tasted of sweat. Perhaps her coffin was malfunctioning. She opened her eyes, expecting energy-saving darkness, and reached out left-handed to grope for the timer switch.

Her fingertips brushed the cool nanomesh of Perceval's parasite wing, and she jerked it back with a gasp, sucking her fingertips as if she'd burned them. "Perceval?"

Yes. Once she was awake, even half awake, she was unlikely to forget again where she was. Her pulse hammered in her throat, a panicky adrenaline reaction, but as soon as she identified it her new internal senses—her colony, her symbiont—adjusted the level of worry to something more sensible and appropriate.

"Oh, space," she said, and pushed at Perceval's arms. She had to get out. It wasn't her. There was an alien holding her, but worse, there was an alien in her, and it was making decisions for her. *Don't be scared*, her symbiont whispered.

Which, predictably, scared her even more.

Perceval's skin felt wrong. Fragile, papery. Hot. Rien thought if she pulled at it, it would slip and tear like the friable skin over a blister. Perceval moaned. Her breath smelled cloying.

She was sick, and Rien didn't know what to do. She struggled free. Perceval's parasite wings held her in place in the corridor, but Rien kicked too hard and went tumbling. She smacked one wall, smearing fluorescent fungus across the plating, her left arm first numbed from wrist to shoulder and then searingly alive. Tears stung, swelled in the corners of watering eyes, broke from acceleration and spread. But she got her right arm and her legs out, spread them wide—though it was counterintuitive—and slowed her rate of spin.

Rien was half competent in microgravity. But this was different. She was better, faster, seeing trajectories and velocities with her inner eye as if they were projected on a screen. And something was building in her awareness: a model or structure, a schematic of surrounding corridors that stretched beyond what she could immediately perceive. Echoes, she thought. Like a bat.

She bounced off another wall, redirected to the far end of the corridor, and managed to hit with bent knees and take the edge off her velocity. And then she was coming back up the hall at Perceval, but slower now and in a more controlled fashion.

And Perceval was braced.

Rien struck Perceval's pinions with both palms. The left arm buckled, but that didn't matter; it had helped absorb some of the energy. The pinions were not hard, not like hitting the decking, and Rien managed to catch hold of an edge and hold on. "Space and ashes," Rien said.

Perceval hung in midcorridor, suspended between extended pinions, her body curled into a fetal huddle and folded inside another pair of wings as if in a translucent clamshell. They looked like smoke, but when Rien braced herself against the extended wing and reached out to touch her sister, the surface was smooth and quite cool.

Even through the cocooning colony, Rien could see Perceval's face shining with sweat, though, and the inflamed red streaks like spiderwebs surrounding the attachment points of her pinions. She tugged, but she had nothing to leverage against except Perceval's other wings—of which there were currently in total six, the four spanning the corridor and the two within which she slept—and it was useless.

"Oh, please," Rien said. "I have to get her someplace with water and food."

The pinion shifted, relaxing under Rien's hand. Abruptly, she realized how cold she was, the sweat of too-warm sleeping chilling on her skin, the ends of damp hair freezing. Perceval's pinions might have trapped the warmth when Rien was inside them, but they were themselves as cold as the corridor's frigid air. And Rien was wearing nothing but the sweeping knit trousers, cardigan, and strap-shoulder top.

"Please," she said again, fearful she had imagined the response. "Perceval, you have the map. I need you. Open your damned pinions."

When the shell cracked open, the warm air within escaped in a scroll of mist and flaking frost. Perceval floated limp as the third pair of pinions silently merged into the mass of the parasite wings. Rien stretched out from where she clung and touched Perceval's cheek.

Hot and moist, and Rien's fingers smelled of sickness when she pulled them back.

"Perceval." Her own pleading voice might have belonged to another. "That's good, sweetheart. Now open your eyes."

It was what Head might have said. What Head *had* said, when Rien was little and she was sick. And whether it was Rien's tone of abject fear, or some virtue in the words, when Rien touched Perceval's face again, she turned her cheek into it.

Slowly, the pinions relaxed further, and with unhurried motions unlike last night's frantic scuttling, began to bear Perceval and Rien forward. The feathertips—well, what would have been the feathertips, if the pinions had real feathers—bent against the corridor bulkheads, and they glided along as if borne by a giant, mechanical, four-legged spider.

Rien released her grip on the leading edge of the wing and instead caught Perceval's shoulder, floating beside her, huddled close to share warmth. It was easy in the microgravity.

The parasite wings paced along the corridor for some fifteen minutes, during which Rien's dark-adapted eyes saw nothing but Perceval and deck plates and the teal and lime bioluminescence of various kinds of fungus. And a school of ship-fish, a half-dozen of the oxygen-breathing scavengers floating midair, glass-transparent except for eyes and guts and teeth and streaks of blue and vermilion neon. They hung momentarily in a cloud, and then were gone in a flicker of winfings.

Rien, light-headed from cold and poor oxygen saturation, wondered if they had come through whatever crevice the atmosphere and spores had entered through. She would not like to be the sparrow hawk whose dinner depended on catching one.

Eventually, the pinions paused before a hatchway like a dozen others they had passed. The burning pain in Rien's left arm had dulled to the sharp occasional twinges of a bone bruise, but without releasing Perceval's shoulders, Rien was able to grab and shake her face. "Here?"

Perceval's eyes were crusted yellow along the lashes. She shivered, and Rien's clothes were wet with Perceval's musty sweat. Whatever the infection, her symbiont was having a fight.

"Open it," she said, her voice cracked and sticky. "We might be safe in here."

Rien tried the palm panel, but the hatch—like the previous ones—was dead. Instead, she undogged it manually, made sure Perceval's pinions would hold her in place, and—with one hand holding her sister's—pulled the hatch open.

At least she knew it wasn't the Enemy on the other side. Overpressure pushed the door into her hand. Her ears popped painfully, and Rien made a small sharp noise.

The atmosphere that rushed out to surround them was warm and moist, scented pleasantly of chlorophyll and richly composted loam. Birds sang; the interior of the hatch cover trailed vines heavy with unripe slipskin grapes, and a drone of insects broke what Rien now realized was the humming, mechanical unsilence of the cold corridor. There was gravity beyond the door, and she swung forward half deftly to get her feet into it and feel the strength.

The ship-fish had not come from here.

Rien swung again, using Perceval's pinions like monkey bars. She generated enough momentum to carry her over the threshold and landed barefoot on mossy soil that squished water over her toes.

She pulled her injured arm against her chest, hugging it for comfort, and stepped forward. "Perceval," she said. "You found it."

There was no sound behind her. She turned; Perceval still floated amid the charcoal sketch of her parasite wings. Her eyes were only glassy slits behind her lashes.

"Pinion," Rien said, feeling foolish, "please follow."

They moved forward, smooth and graceful, with the speed and assurance of a giant spider. The trailing wing brushed the vine-hung hatch closed again, and Rien heard the thump of bolts as it sealed.

Then she also heard a flurry of wings, not Perceval's,

but smaller and soft-feathered. Something white as star-shine and bigger than a rooster descended before her, fluttering hard.

The wings were so pale the blood tinted the light shining through them blue, the span a little more than the length of one of Rien's legs. The animal had fishhook talons like a hawk, a long neck leading to a cockatoo-crested head with a heavy, curved, lacquer-black beak. But the eyes were tight-shut, eyelids like the crumpled crepe of an old man's throat, and the tail that coiled around the branch it landed on lashed, scaled and patterned silver-on-blue-white.

"I am Gavin," said the basilisk. "Welcome to this Heaven, daughters of Benedick."

Rien did not know what Perceval would have done, but she could imagine it.

She stepped between the basilisk and her sister.

The branch still swayed under its sudden weight, its wings fanning lightly for balance. Rien had seen a mountebank's parrot on a swing, and she thought of that now.

She didn't know what she'd do when it lunged. Its toes and talons measured together were as long as her pinky finger; its beak looked strong enough to snip that finger off. When it turned its head side to side, she was certain it was measuring the distance between them, and no matter that its eyes were closed. She crouched under its gaze, extended her right arm—the left still stung numb—and groped in wet earth and leaf litter for a stone, a branch . . . anything.

"I greet you politely," the basilisk said. "And you fumble for a rock. Is this how you meet a stranger on the road in Rule? I would worry about your courtesy to guests."

The oddest thing was its beak, moving like a hand puppet's mouth. Exactly as if a beak and a thick black tongue could form the sounds of human speech—

Rien remembered the parrot, and shut her gaping jaw. She didn't straighten, though, or drop a knee. Fair words or not, after the past few hours she was not eager to trust a stranger. "I beg your pardon," she said. And pointed back, with her elbow like a bird's bent wing, at Perceval. "This is how we treat guests in Rule. I would not recommend you go there."

"Indeed. I am your guide to this Heaven, though, and if you come with me I will see what we can do to aid you."

"And if I don't come with you?"

The basilisk flipped its wings closed, flight feathers crossing over its back. The sequiny scales on the tail, she saw, made a reticulated pattern in unpigmented white and silver, the bluer, grayer scales showing the color of the blood beneath.

"Your sister is sick," it said. "If you do not come with me, what will you do?"

It waited a moment, as if it actually expected her to answer. And when she didn't, its tail uncoiled from the branch with all the sleekness of a heavy-bodied snake, the undersurface hollowing, pulling broad scales into an arch. It launched itself into the air, circled—over Rien's head, but not passing over Perceval—and reversed direction.

It beat away on heavy wings, ten meters along a bare root-raddled trail and then a pause, ten more and then another. Rien watched it.

It never glanced back.

Rien stood. She reached back among the parasite wings and took Perceval's limp hand, and stepped forward. The construct shivered, and seemed as if it would edge back. It leaned away from the basilisk like a cringing dog, she thought, hoping not to be noticed.

She said, "Stop it. Hurry up. Come on." And the parasite wings—more spider legs now—reluctantly stepped with her, as if Perceval were a leash and she led them at heel.

Another step, and another. And then, if she wanted to keep the basilisk in sight, she was committed. *If you're walking, you might as well walk,* she thought, and strode out as if she meant to get somewhere.

Under trees and beside the vine-hung wall, following the blind monster. The pinions—Pinion, Rien told herself firmly; giving it a name of its own could only help to separate it from Perceval, and Rien wanted to keep them separate in her head—minced along, the girl dangling beneath them like an overripe fruit from the tree. In gravity, Perceval no longer floated in a loose fetal position. Now her arms and legs dangled, her head bouncing on her neck no matter how smoothly Pinion moved.

The earth was level once Rien was on the trail, packed and warm, the bark worn from the roots by many soles. Still, bare feet were not the best for this, and the second or third time she stubbed her toe, she whimpered.

And then bit her lip, as the basilisk turned back to her.

Perhaps the stop had roused her slightly, but Perceval made a mewing sound and pushed petulantly at Rien's hand.

"She's so sick," Rien said, as the basilisk stared with tight-shut eyes.

It nodded. "Then please hurry." And set off again, twice as fast this time.

Perceval still hurt: a different kind of hurting now. It was not the pain of ongoing injury, but the ache of abused muscles at rest, a reminder of recent damage rather than the thing itself. And she was warm in the mantle of her wings, and lying peacefully in shade.

Vaguely, she remembered a march, dizziness and nausea and shaking chill. But not now; now there was a soft pallet and green leaves and the clean scent of air in a planted habitat.

Rien must have brought them somewhere safe. The pain was almost pleasant, when Perceval thought of it that way.

She rolled onto her back, and recalled doing so that the wings wrapping her weren't her wings. Her belly clenched. She wondered if it would ever stop hurting like that, every time she remembered.

But she was dressed now, loose trousers and a long-sleeved halter top that tied at the waist and kept her blessedly warm for the first time in . . . the first time since she had been captured. She was in a clearing, on a pallet on soft moss, and woven sunshades were suspended above her from cords strung to tree limbs. Chips of light fell through them. A cicada droned. Underneath it, Perceval heard faint strains of music, flute and guitar.

And Rien was nowhere in sight.

Heart pounding, Perceval sat up. And almost vomited, a thin flavor of bile filling her foul-tasting mouth. Her eyes were crusted and gummy, her teeth disgusting. She couldn't imagine what might keep her symbiont colony so busy as to neglect hygiene. Her skin was clean, though, and she smelled soap; someone had bathed her. And there was water beside her, a pitcher on a low tray, room temperature but—by the smell—laced with crushed mint leaves.

She dabbed her fingers in the water and scrubbed her eyes, her face, the crusted lips. She picked out the mint leaves and chewed them, and then, crosslegged and hunched between the straggle of her parasite wings, she cradled the pitcher on her shins and bent forward to drink from the edge until she'd gotten enough out of it to lift the entire thing and drink. It was heavy, the metal surface dewed with condensation.

The water inside didn't taste of aluminum, though; the pitcher was lined in glass. It all went into her, except rivulets that ran down her chin on each side and spattered her shirt.

She could have drunk more.

Feeling better, Perceval set the pitcher down. She gathered herself and stood, feeling attenuated and rickety. When she wobbled, the wings fanned and caught her.

Strange, to realize that they did so and caused no pain. Perceval reached over her shoulder and felt the root of the stump, where her own warm wings had grown. They seamed imperceptibly into her flesh, flexible at the point of contact, only growing cool and hard by stages as she ran her fingers as high along the leading edge as she could reach.

Wounds dealt by an unblade were not amenable to regeneration, and they were not supposed to take a prosthesis. They healed only with difficulty, and often bled like stigmata intermittently for years. Sometimes, a deeper amputation would provoke better healing. Sometimes.

The unblade's program was designed to disrupt symbionts. They were colonies themselves, and from what Perceval had heard, ones with dark and aggressive personalities. She was lucky the wound hadn't become toxic.

The thought triggered a contrary memory. Poison *had* gotten into the wound, hadn't it? She'd been fevered. There had been a gunfight. She couldn't actually recall.

That would explain why she felt so achy and sluggish, like a Mean the morning after a beating, and why her symbiont had failed her.

Trailing her inexplicable wings behind her, either still thirsty or thirsty again, she went in search of the musicians. She would panic later. She would remain calm, now.

The trees bore bud, flower, and fruit on the same branches. She recognized peach, olive, almond, the tallest more than twice her height. The trunks were thicker than those at home. Gravity here was heavier, and as she craned her head back to stare up through the leaves at the crystal panels far above that let the suns shine in, she wondered if she would be able to fly here, even with mechanical wings. The holde would be big enough.

The sound of the flute carried better, but it also echoed more. The guitar told her where its player sat. Perceval followed the music until she saw a camp identical to the one she'd left, only occupied by two figures.

No, she realized. Two humanoid figures, and a big white bird.

One of the humans, cross-legged on a pallet like the one Perceval had left, was Rien. She held a guitar in her arms, her fingers sliding up and down the neck half awkwardly. She lifted her head as Perceval's motion caught her peripheral vision, and flubbed a chord.

Beside her sat the person with the flute. Perceval had a confused image of mahogany hair, as curly as Rien's but softer, all twisted in ringlets instead of wooly and wiry with frizz, of slender arms and narrow shoulders. And then the flautist stood, turning to her, and she saw bare feet and bony ankles, an ankle sheath on the left. The face was a woman's—angelic and sweet and rounded—with great dark eyes that looked kohled. But though small breasts stood from a boy's shirtless chest, tight trousers left Perceval in no doubt as to the masculine arrangement of the more intimate anatomy.

She tried not to stare.

The flautist balanced on each foot in turn, slipping on soft boots. Rien was not rising. She did let the guitar fall silent, though, as the stranger said, "Perceval, this is Mallory, who helped us. Mallory, this is—"

—*my sister*, Perceval coached, inside her head, but she could not force the sense of the words into Rien's head or the shape of them into her mouth.

"Sir Perceval Foucaulte Conn," Perceval said. "Of Engine. I am trying to reach my father, with urgent tidings."

Rien gave her a look, and from it Perceval gathered that Rien had not, perhaps, told this person everything.

Or even much of anything. Perceval bit her lip; of course, they were fugitives, and anyone could be in the pay of Rule.

She thrust out her hand, and waited for the mahogany-haired flautist to take it. But before that could happen, a voice spoke from the stump on the other side of the clearing.

"A pleasure to meet you in better circumstances," the white bird said, and when Perceval glanced up she saw that it was not a bird at all, but a basilisk.

It was worrisome, to find herself missing details. "Oh," she said. And then she sat down hard on the moss as her knees failed her.

Rien did jump to her feet then, almost tripping over the guitar. And sat back down hard herself. Mallory crouched, sliding the flute into a boot, and laid hands on her face. "You're both sick, children. And exhausted. Stay where you are."

Even the voice was androgynous, not for neutrality, but for flexibility. One moment, Perceval imagined it echoed a man's deep sonorous tones of authority, then a woman's chiding.

She did as she was told and sat.

A little later, as their host fussed with a self-heating kettle and water and pills and packets of herbs, she gathered her energy enough to take an interest. Deft hands sorted and sifted and poured. Perceval was fascinated.

"Are you a healer, Mallory?"

"No," Mallory said, and lifted a pair of cups. "I am a necromancer. Here, drink up."

9

what it means to be
a princess

This dust was once the Man.

—WALT WHITMAN

So that's what it is to be a princess, Rien thought, watching the perfect unconscious arrogance with which Perceval gave away her name and their goal, as if it were nothing. Or—arrogance was the wrong word, wasn't it? Because arrogance was by its nature unjustified.

And nothing about Perceval was unjustified. Her self-assurance was the product of capability and experience, a warrior's knowledge of her body and her surroundings. She sat cross-legged, her elbows on her knees once she had accepted the mug, and watched Mallory seemingly without curiosity. "What's in the tea?"

"Salicylic acid," Mallory said, "capsaicin, licorice, chamomile, some other things. You had a nasty systemic bacterial infection, and a debilitating virus on top of it."

Still, Perceval sniffed warily. Rien, conscious of her

own aches and the thickness in her throat, could not imagine how much worse her friend might feel.

It was so much easier to think of Perceval as *her friend* than as *her sister*. Perceval was Exalt—well, Rien was now, too, but she didn't feel Exalt, she didn't have the privilege and entitlement that dripped off Lady Ariane or Perceval or even Oliver. Even her politeness, her air of the obligations of nobility . . . were just that.

The Exalt Rien knew were monsters as much as Lords and Ladies. If Rien was Exalt, would she become a monster, too?

"Drink it," Mallory said. "If I'd wanted you drugged or poisoned, Engineer, I would have done it when you were on the IV."

Perceval's suspicious glance at the crook of her arm was another paradigm shift for Rien. For a moment, Perceval's deportment changed. The abrupt turn of her head was almost a cringe.

A crack in the facade.

Which meant it *was* a facade, this air of the stern but smiling knight-errant. A character. A role. Or, Rien reassessed—the warm mug in her own hands almost forgotten, as she watched Perceval first swallow dry and then raise her mug to her lips with quiet bravado—not a facade, not exactly. But not the whole story either.

Rien drank her tea and let the silence stretch. Even Mallory sat still, wrists draped over knees, and watched the girls sip bittersweet, spicy fluid.

When Perceval and Rien had drained the dregs and set their cups aside, the necromancer said, "I imagine everybody in Rule will be sick quite soon."

"I beg your pardon?" Perceval's courtesy was perfect once more.

"Your illness." Mallory knelt up to collect the cups, not rising, small breasts moving softly as the necromancer came to hands and knees. Rien shifted on the earth, fingers worrying the neck of the borrowed instrument that now lay on the blanket beside her. She was not accustomed to finding someone with such obvious male attributes attractive. But the eyes and the throat and the breasts were all woman, if the long hands and torso and crotch were all *wrong*.

Deft hands wiped cups dry and stowed them in a ragged-edged coarse-woven pack, but Mallory's voice never paused. "You are recovering; Rien is sickening. It's an engineered influenza, and you both are fortunate that I happened to have a stock of the appropriate antiviral on hand."

"Convenient," Perceval agreed, and Rien shot her a sideways glance. If she were better acquainted with Perceval, she'd know if those were tones of irony.

Mallory seemed to think so. And by the smile that flickered across plush lips, seemed also unoffended.

Rien wondered if she would ever get used to the Exalt, and the way they cheerfully assumed that everyone around them was neck-deep in conspiracy. Then she wondered if she would ever get used to the way they usually seemed correct in that assumption.

"You think I was meant to be captured?" Perceval could apparently be as blunt as anyone. "That I was a vector?"

"I can't speak for Engine," Mallory said. "Those aren't my politics." On his branch at the edge of the clearing,

Gavin made a noise uncannily like one of Head's unimpressed snorts.

Mallory gave him the finger. "Why are you going to your father, Perceval Conn?"

"To stop the war," Rien said, when Perceval did not seem to have a ready answer. She shivered, pushing the guitar farther away so she could draw up her knees and huddle under the blanket. The moments when you knew you were sickening were the worst; you could feel the virus establishing beachheads, enemy camps defined by sniffles and muscle aches and growing nausea. "Engine and Rule fighting, that could kill so many."

"And endanger the walls of the world," Perceval said, and was right. Collateral damage, *structural* damage, was a bigger fear than direct murder. It had been impressed on Rien all through her childhood how fragile the habitable sphere was, and how much functionality had been lost through accident, negligence, malice, and the simple gnawing of entropy.

Mallory fiddled fingers on folded arms. "You think your father can do something about that?"

"He's Benedick Conn," Perceval said, as if that settled everything. And Rien had to admit, it was a phrase to conjure with.

Mallory made a noise that was open to interpretation. "It's a long way to his anchore, and not through friendly territory. There is no direct communication. We could try radio, but I'm hesitant to speak of such things in uncoded broadcast. And if anyone is seeking you—"

"Yes," Perceval said. "It could lead them here."

Rien edged a little closer to her, twisting her fingers,

and as if unconsciously Pinion flicked out to drape across her shoulder. Rien jumped, and would have withdrawn from the touch of the parasite wing—but she remembered in time, and the thought of what it must be like to be Perceval, and have the alien limb sealed to one's own body, kept her still.

"Mallory, you're not actually considering sending Rien and Perceval on errantry when one of them is weak and recovering and the other will be blind with fever inside the day?" The basilisk swung his head side to side. His thick tongue was blue-black; with beak opened, it tasted the air like a snake.

As if to illustrate his point, a wave of sweating dizziness overcame Rien. She laid her forehead against her knees and pulled the borrowed shawl tight over her shoulders. The warmth of the wing was welcome, after all.

"It's true," Mallory said. "Rien will soon be too sick to travel. And Perceval, you could relapse—"

Rien turned her head so she could face Perceval, who said, "I could go without her. I could leave her in your care."

"And when the fever comes back, and you rot in a ventilation duct? Your resources are exhausted. Your symbionts barely managed to keep you alive, even under my care."

Perceval frowned magnificently.

Mallory sighed and looked at Rien. "Rest here. I'll treat your illness. In a day or two, Gavin will guide you to your father."

"A day or two might make a difference," Perceval said.

"Yes," Mallory answered. "And it also might let you survive to get your message there."

•   •   •

Mallory was right. Within the hour, Rien was curled under blankets moaning, only barely responsive when
Perceval unearthed her to drip water on cracked lips from
the corner of a soaked rag. She would have bathed Rien's
face, but Rien batted at her hands, and so instead she
made a pad and sat against a tree with her sister's head cradled in her lap. That, Rien permitted, and it made it easier to keep her hydrated.

Mallory brought the water, steeped with herbs in it,
and—for Perceval—porridge and soy milk. The basilisk
rested on a branch overhead, perhaps dozing and perhaps
keeping watch. While Perceval was waiting for honey to
drip off the spiral honey dripper—as it was wont to do—
she tilted her head back to watch his feathers fluff and settle. Exactly as if he breathed, which of course he did not.

Cool fingers touched the back of her hand. She looked
down, let Mallory relieve her of the dripper. Perceval
licked the honey from her nail and then, with only resid-
ually sticky fingers, smoothed the hair from Rien's brow.
The curls were dank with sweat, but Perceval heeded
them not. She shook the salty moisture from her fingers
and picked up her spoon.

"You're very devoted to your sister," Mallory said.

Perceval chewed carefully, her mouth abruptly full of
saliva. She swallowed; the second spoonful was already on
its way when she spoke. "I barely know her," she said,
leaving out for now the fact that Rien had tended her, rescued her, cast in her lot with her, and now somehow
brought her here. "You're very helpful for a necromancer."

"So you don't trust me? Or you don't believe I'm a necromancer?" Mallory had a bowl of porridge, too, and was doctoring it with margarine and almond milk and salt. Among the almond blossoms, Perceval heard the drowsy drone of bees.

Rien, thrashing, arched her shoulder blade into Perceval's knee.

"Ow," Perceval said. "Sweetie—" She stuffed another spoonful into her mouth and set the bowl aside. Hands on Rien's shoulder and forehead seemed to calm her a little. "Should I trust you?"

"Trust no one," Mallory said, stirring idly. The necromancer's eyebrows were very expressive, especially when the rest of the face was pretending blandness. It was a lovely face, oval and far more angelic than Perceval's own. "Unless you have to. And today you had to."

"You knew who I was before I told you."

"I did. I am after all a necromancer. And they shall know you by your trail of dead, Perceval Conn."

Perceval set her bowl aside, no longer hungry. "My, aren't we prophetic."

"Don't be silly. No one can see the future." Whatever backflips Perceval's stomach was doing, Mallory ate with unperturbed determination. "I am a very good guesser, though."

"And?"

"And somebody in Engine has already tried to use you to kill your sister, and your aunt Ariane Conn at Rule, and everyone else therein. And might have in part succeeded."

Mallory reached across Perceval's lap and stroked Rien's sweat-cold cheek. This touch, Rien did not flinch away from. Perceval swallowed an acrid pang of jealousy. "Will she be well?"

"I saved you, and you were sicker. It's fortunate you came upon me."

Perceval liked Mallory better when the necromancer wasn't winking. "Or you came upon us. I ask you again, necromancer. Why are you helping us?"

"Because I have no love for Engine," the necromancer said. "Nor Rule either. And less love for their wars."

And then, while Perceval still stared, nibbling her lip in consideration, Mallory leaned forward and pressed pillowy lips to Perceval's own.

Perceval had never been kissed before. Oh, yes, she'd kissed Rien, but that was not such a kiss as this. This was soft, and melting, Mallory's bony and elegant hand pressed to her cheek and a slick tongue lightly flicking her closed mouth. And Perceval had no idea how to react.

She laid a palm against Mallory's chest, to hold her distance, and waited until the necromancer gently, so slowly, leaned back. Mallory's lashes flicked off pearl-white cheeks; Perceval had never lowered hers.

"I'm sorry," Perceval said. "I am fallow, and sworn celibate. I cannot be what you desire."

"Figures," Mallory answered, and leaned back with a sigh so honey-scented breath caressed Perceval's face. "I've been here alone a long time."

In the branches of the tree above, the slumbering basilisk raised its head, crest ruffling. "What am I?" it asked, in injured tones. "Chopped tempeh?"

10

all that heaven and none for thee

And deep into her crystal body poured
The hot and sorrowful sweetness
of the dust.

—EDNA ST. VINCENT MILLAY,
"Oh, Sleep Forever in the
Latmian Cave"

Pinion told Dust everything, including his name.

It was a good name, Dust judged, as Dust judged such things. He had never been able to name things himself—he was, after all, in chief a sort of archivist—but as with many archivists, a good irony and good pun delighted him.

Take the name of the world, for example, half of which was half of Dust's own name. *Jacob's Ladder*. One thing that was many things, and a name most carefully chosen. Because Jacob's ladder was the ladder angels ascended to reach Heaven; and it was also the breaking of sun rays through cloud, planetside (not that Dust had ever seen such, but there were images in his memory); and it was a rope ladder, such as used to ascend into the rigging of a sailing ship; it was a fumbling primitive body modification that humans had performed upon themselves—and that was significant, because humans were the only animals to mutilate themselves on purpose, or to direct their own evolution, although in those days the Exalt had been but a dream; it was a toy, an amusement; and in the name of the world, it was a promise and a benediction and an allegory.

Because the Jacob's ladder in the name of the world was all of these things, and none. The ladder these angels must climb was the double helix. And then they would be God. They, who were splinters of God.

God, who was dead. And what should be done about it, none of his splinters could agree.

Dust thanked Pinion—it was childish and simple yet, but learning, and it could relate what it had seen—and then he began to discorporate.

He knew where Samael's holde lay, and more than that he was certain he would not have to seek even so far. There would be outliers and sentries, and Dust's own self-stuff would meet up with his brother's before he sought too far.

But if Samael could barge into Dust's house, Dust could barge into Samael's.

He was strong, as strong as ever his counterpart. He would believe it. And he would believe as well that Samael needed him.

Dust came apart and filtered through the world. And when he came to the house of Samael, he did not pause, not even to gather his courage. He rolled forward on a manufactured wave of high pressure, and he swept Samael's servants and fragments before.

Samael's holde was a Heaven, as besuited the Angel of Life Support Services. And he was waiting when Dust arrived, already coalesced, arms crossed, wearing his green velvet coat and vast ragged raven wings.

For a picosecond, Dust considered the rudeness of refusing to take shape. He could hover over Samael, pluck at his limp blond locks, tweak the lace at his sleeves. He could make his displeasure known. It would be satisfying.

But it would gain him nothing.

With a sigh, he settled on a shape, and formed. Not a human shape and not the angel-shape Samael mocked, however.

Dust made of himself a dragon.

His wings would span the holde, if he unfolded them. His barbed and rebarbed head bent low on a black-mailed neck. He wore horns like an oryx and barbels like a catfish, and his breast was scaled in silver.

He massed no more than a pony, but there was something to be said for psychological warfare.

"A whole holde," Dust said. "All that Heaven, and only for your creature."

"My creature?" Samael craned his neck back to see him, but showed no fear. A shape was only a mask, to be discarded upon an instant. Dust could well imagine Samael reciting that truth to himself.

"Mallory," Dust hissed. "And the familiar basilisk. You sent my maidens to them."

"My maidens? The world's maidens, surely. Do you be-grudge them a little assistance, a little education?"

"That is no Ben Kenobi. More une belle quelquesome-thing sans merci."

"The question stands, my dearest Dust." When Samael uncrossed his arms, it was to stand hipshot, balanced on the toes of one bare foot and the heel of the other. He had simulated transparent silver toenail polish.

Dust might have said that Samael lied, but in truth he had not, really. He had omitted, but by the most strict def-inition that was not providing false information. And *that* was what the ancient lingering protocols forbade them. The builders must never have imagined that the world might find itself not only fragmented, but wishing to lie between modules.

"Yes," he said, because he had to say it. "I begrudge your assistance. And I begrudge Mallory."

"Tough," Samael said. He stepped forward, bounced up on his toes, and planted a kiss on Dust's scaly cheek. "I know you want to be the last angel standing. But brother, so do I."

Even if Rien awoke sore and sticky, it was a better awak-ening than the last. The wood was quiet. No birds sang, and the shade under the trees had deepened. A shadow panel must have crossed the suns, and the sudden cool twilight had awakened her.

She reached out casually behind and found, not Perceval—whose lap she recalled falling asleep in—but the warm wooden neck of Mallory's guitar.

Rien had never played such an instrument before. Her learning had been done on student pieces, plastic guitars suitable for a Mean. But this was real wood, not manufactured. It had a completely different tone.

She was grateful in her bones to have been allowed to play it. And more grateful still that Mallory had seen fit to leave it by her while she slept. That hinted at offered trust, which Rien was in no position to turn away from.

But what she wanted was Perceval.

Carefully, Rien rolled onto her back. The ground was soft, but her hip hurt from sleeping on it. And the muscles of arms and legs, belly and back and neck, ached more. Something bound her sore left arm. She wondered how many days she'd lain ill. Perceval had recovered incredibly fast.

But Perceval was Exalt.

As she lay dizzy, staring at the canopy and waiting for it to stop whirling and breathing the buttery scent of almond blossoms (when you are drunk, Rien remembered, put one foot flat on the floor, and she drew her knee up to press her sole against the blanket under her), she heard something deft and heavy beat away through the air. Gavin, she hoped, leaving to tell the others she'd awakened.

Rien's heart beat faster. She worked her dry mouth; her eyes and lips were not very crusty, though.

Maybe she had the strength to rise and find water.

Maybe she wouldn't have to.

Footsteps approached, soft and sure. They were not Perceval's, and Rien was surprised to find she knew her sister's tread already. She lifted herself on her elbows as

Mallory's face hove into view, a pale oval nacreous through the gloaming.

The necromancer dropped on crossed legs beside Rien, thumping into moss and leaf litter. Skinny, agile hands disarrayed the blankets and tugged Rien's arm free; watching their impersonal touch, she discovered that her arm was bandaged. There were tubes, needles, which Mallory slid out as deftly as Doctor could have, back in Rule.

Rien almost thought, *back home*. But that was wrong, wasn't it? "Thank you," she said. "How long was I sick?"

Mallory's face went briefly vague, as those of Exalts could do when they consulted their internal worlds. "Seven hours."

"Oh. But I had the flu? The same flu Perceval did." Which had left her unconscious for half a day.

"Perceval was weakened," Mallory said. "You were only hungry and tired."

But *Perceval is Exalt*, Rien almost said, and bit her tongue just in time. She could already imagine the dexterity with which Mallory's arched dark eyebrows would rise, and the answer that didn't need saying.

The funny thing was, the trees rustled when Mallory hesitated, though there was no breeze. Odd; the holde seemed large enough for convection currents, and the temperature drop should provoke circulation. But then, it was a strange wood, carefully managed, quiet and open and full of light. Rien dusted a fallen peach-petal off her cheek. Many of the trees, she thought, were ancient, their age-weakened branches supported by posts and strapping. "This is one of the old Heavens."

"The first," Mallory agreed, unless it was a correction.

Needles and tubes and whatever they had been connected to vanished into the ubiquitous pack, which rested beside the guitar for the time being. "Do you like the trees?"

"They're beautiful. You care for them?"

"There's only me," Mallory answered. Which made Rien wonder about Gavin. But perhaps as a colony construct, he didn't count as company by Mallory's standards. "They're a library."

"A library?" Rien tilted her chin up again, gazing at the whispering branches. "An archive, you mean? A library of trees?"

"A library of trees." Mallory looked up as well. "But we've lost the index. Here—"

The necromancer stood and stepped away, feet indenting the loam. It was a tiptoe reach to bring down an apricot, soft and fuzzy and not much bigger than Mallory's thumb. When Rien put out her hand and Mallory laid it there, the brush of fingertips against the hollow of her palm made her stomach drop.

Eyes on Mallory's, Rien put the still-warm, velour-skinned fruit in her mouth and sucked the flesh from the stone. It was sweet, sharp with overripeness, yet bland and a little gritty, not as juicy as she had thought it might be. She spat the stone into her palm, chewed the pulp, and swallowed.

A whirl of music, a human voice, a shivering crescendo of drums and electric guitar. Rien sat transfixed by the music, old and alien and like nothing she'd heard before. She felt her symbiont accepting the new information, integrating it. Making it part of her flesh and her bone. It immersed and surrounded her, but even as she heard it performed, she sensed it as a gestalt, knew the notes and the chords. She could have played it, if her hands were sufficiently trained to the task. She could have sung it, if her voice were adequate. She could have rearranged it, resurrected it, reinvented it, if she had been a composer.

A song, and she'd swallowed it.

She found her way back, eventually. Her eyes stung with the beauty. A warm hand rested on Rien's nape. It was comforting, and it sent a shiver down between her shoulders. She swallowed and licked salt from her lip and tried to think what to say.

"Do you live here alone?"

"All alone," Mallory said, and kissed Rien on the mouth, lightly, full of questions.

"I don't like men," Rien said, though she could not look away for a second from Mallory's eyes—blacker in the half-light than Rien remembered them from sun—under the witchy mahogany frizz of bangs.

"How fortunate for me that I'm not one," Mallory answered, and kissed Rien again.

Rien fancied herself not uneducated in passion. She was sixteen; she had done her share of groping and kissing and more than kissing, in coffins and behind tapestries and even in beds. She thought she knew how it was done.

She was not prepared for Mallory to pull away before Rien thought the kiss was half finished, quickly nipping Rien's lower lip and then pressing a finger against it. And then it was dark eyes, brown and transparent as coffee,

with green and amber flecks swimming under the surface—and Mallory's breath across her mouth.

"Wait," the necromancer said, and kissed her around
that silencing finger. "Gently, Rien. It's not about getting
it over with as fast as possible, my sweet."

Rien nodded, to show she understood, then kissed
Mallory's fingertip before she drew back. "Before we . . .
um. Is there someplace I could pee? I was asleep a long
time, and . . ." she gestured to the IV site in her arm, nothing but a red pinprick now.

"Pick a bush," Mallory said, and dug through the pack
to find a hand spade and toilet paper.

Rien thought she could figure out what she was intended to do with both, and absented herself briefly to
heed nature's call. When she returned, she found Mallory
shaking out the pallet and folding the blankets into a neat
rectangular pad. After divesting herself, Rien knelt and
reached for Mallory's hand. They kissed again, and this
time, she was softer, and tried to match Mallory's pace.

As if in slow motion, Mallory lay back on the pallet,
and drew Rien over. Rien pressed close, parting Mallory's
thighs with her knee, turning her head and leaning a little
aside so their breasts could nest together. Mallory made a
noise into her mouth, and their tongues were warm and
sweet together until, panting, they broke apart.

"You're *beautiful*," Rien said, letting her fingertips just
brush Mallory's cheek. Warm skin, and the flutter of a
pulse beside the ear, begging to be kissed.

"You're fierce," Mallory replied, and fingers in Rien's
hair pulled her down again.

And Mallory was right. Rien would have hurried it, left

to her own devices, raced through, eager to know everything all at once. Instead, they kissed in the shadows, and Mallory's fingers found Rien's collarbone, and Rien's mouth found Mallory's throat, the little softness beneath the chin and the ringed hardness of the larynx. And then Mallory slid influential hands across Rien's shoulders, and the next Rien knew, she was on her back, the dirty tank top nuzzled upward and her dirty belly caressed. She stroked Mallory's hair, as she'd wanted to, felt it fuzzy here and ringlets there, full of tangles. She pressed down her hands; the bones of Mallory's skull were under it.

And Mallory's hands were on her breasts, and she had to let go her grip and lift her arms as the necromancer pulled her tank off, and then kissed what there was to kiss. Mallory's erection indented Rien's thigh, and Rien expected to find it distasteful. But Mallory smelled right, and tasted right, and the skin was silk and satin under Rien's hands as she traced the lines of Mallory's spine and shoulder blades and the wiry muscles that defined them.

Mallory's hands skimmed her hip bones, found the edge of her trousers—they were a mess now, ripped in two places, the hem torn ragged at the back—and slipped beneath. Rien stroked the necromancer's hair again. "You, too," she said.

And then she met Mallory's eyes over the undulations of her own breasts and belly, and read the question in the necromancer's expression. "Well," she said. "You said you weren't a man. I believe you. Let's see it."

"All this," Mallory answered, with a head shake and a crooked smile, "and she also plays guitar."

As Mallory knelt, Rien stripped off her own bottoms

and kicked them aside. Mallory's trousers involved a belt and snaps; it took a little longer. And when they went down—Rien wasn't sure what she'd been expecting, but a perfectly average erect penis wasn't it, not exactly. She'd been with boys—Head always said you couldn't say you didn't like something until you'd tried it—and this wasn't anything she hadn't seen before. Except where a boy would have a scrotum and testicles, Mallory had what looked just like girl parts behind.

"Did you do it that way on purpose?" Rien asked, holding out her hand.

"Of course," Mallory said. "If you hate it I can change."

"Don't be silly," Rien said, and wrapped her fingers around Mallory's warm bony wrist. "I don't love you. You shouldn't change yourself for me."

Mallory bent down and kissed her again, and this time there was no hesitating for clothes or negotiation, except the little sounds of question and permission they made that weren't—quite—words. Awkward, sometimes, and sticky, and Rien kept wishing she'd had a shower. But Mallory didn't seem to care, and by the time Rien pulled Mallory down and covered everything that she could reach with kisses, she was done with caring also.

11

her own salt

It rains into the sea
And still the sea is salt.

—A. E. HOUSMAN,
"Stars, I Have Seen Them Fall"

When the suns emerged from behind the shadow panel, the others came looking for Perceval. She was glad to see them. She was starving, and she'd spent the time while she was waiting—once she'd analyzed and bathed in a clean trickle that flowed through a cracked bulkhead—performing exercises and walking among the trees, which dusted her hair and the parasite wings with petals. Some of those petals were the basilisk's— Gavin's—fault; he paced her, flapping heavily from branch to branch, companionably silent.

She welcomed the company; she was trying not to think about the wings. They weren't heavy enough to restore her balance, and they had a disturbing manner of shifting on her shoulders, demonstrating an eldritch intelligence.

She had paused to watch ants ladder up the trunk of a peach tree when Mallory hailed her. The necromancer's voice echoed off the roof of the Heaven a split second later, making Perceval smile as she turned to face them.

She knew what they had been up to, of course; it would have been hard to miss it, between the giggling and the scent of sex—and nobody had ever warned her how disturbing it would be to hear a necromancer *giggle*—but that was all right, wasn't it? Rien was in clean clothes, her hair combed and braided, and Mallory was holding her elbow. They laughed every time they accidentally looked at each other.

Save me, Perceval thought, and said, "What's for breakfast?"

"There was fruit . . ." Mallory gestured to the plum tree they happened to be standing underneath.

"And pluck uninvited, in someone else's garden?"

By the necromancer's expression, Perceval thought Mallory was chewing that over for double meanings. But after a moment, Perceval was rewarded with bright laughter.

"There are stories about that, aren't there? I'll cook, then."

Perceval followed the necromancer back to the campsite. Somewhere along the way, Rien detached herself from Mallory and came to take Perceval's hand; the tension across Perceval's shoulders eased a little, despite the unweight of her wings. They went speedily, though Mallory stopped once to dig ramps and a second time to nick a bunch of mushrooms growing from the stump of a tree. The necromancer had a boot knife, a finger's length and sharp as a razor, to judge by how neatly it parted the fungus's flesh.

"You leave the base." The cluster of mushrooms disappeared into a bag, the knife back into an ankle sheath. "Then it grows again."

When they passed, Perceval wiped a finger across the moist severed end. She could see the hair-fine corpse-white filaments that vanished into the crumbling stump. "We feed on it, and it feeds on death."

"Everything feeds on death," Mallory answered. "Especially me."

Breakfast was the fungus and ramps, a handful of spinach, and a foil vacuum pouch of silkworm larvae stir-fried in a nonstick wok. Mallory served the result in folded grape leaves; Perceval opened hers flat and, with chopsticks, began picking the pupae out.

"They're good protein," Mallory said, demonstrating. Pop, and crunch in half. Darting chopsticks picked something from the carapace and flicked it away and then the rest was gone as if it had never been. "You'll want a full belly when you go."

Doubtfully, Perceval poked one with the end of a chopstick. Rien seemed unsqueamish; her breakfast was rapidly disappearing. "Are we going, then? Is Rien well enough?"

"After you eat," Mallory said, managing not to either look at Rien, or giggle. "I'll send Gavin along to guide you. And I'll fix you a pack."

Perceval sighed, picked up the pupae, and bit it in half. People really would eat anything.

It crunched, and tasted of tofu, though the texture inside the shell was more like the part of mango closest to the pit. She peered inside and saw a darker bit, which she—with some difficulty—picked out. The second half followed the first. Mostly she tasted the ramps, and some garlic she hadn't seen Mallory put into the oil.

"All right," she said. "It's not bad."

And it was full of protein; a quick analysis confirmed. Perceval picked up the grape leaf and continued to eat. But something, she thought, seemed strange about the light.

She glanced up at the suns, shading her eyes with a translucent wing, although they adapted fairly well to the direct light.

"Huh," she said. "That's funny."

Mallory looked up, as did Rien, and both made encouraging full-mouthed noises.

"The suns," Perceval explained. "It looks like they're throbbing. We must be having a flare."

"It happens," Mallory said.

"Yes," said Rien, before she paused to swallow. "A lot lately."

It was hard, leaving. After breakfast, Rien wandered from tree to tree, sniffing flowers for the whirls of music and speech and equations that flowed through her head when she did so. She didn't hear Mallory come up behind her until the necromancer reached over her shoulder, tugged a branch down, and said by her ear, "Partake."

"Should I?"

"It's my garden," Mallory answered. "I offered. And wherever you wind up, what you learn here may help you."

The fruit was cool, its purple skin kissed with frosty bloom. She plucked it, raised it to her mouth, but did not bite.

Still in her ear, Mallory said, "Your pack. Food and blankets and fresh clothes."

Rien turned to face the necromancer as the padded strap slid into her other hand. "You offer a lot, for someone who only just met us."

If the exclusionary *us* hurt, it didn't show in Mallory's expression. "I have reasons to be interested in your quest, and its outcome." A kiss, petal-soft, brushed Rien's mouth. "If the Angel of Communication wasn't dead, I'd tell you I would call."

Rien smiled, and kissed Mallory's moving lips. "I'd tell you you were welcome to. What's the fruit of this tree, then?"

Mallory looked up, leaving Rien to study nose and chin and throat in profile. "Mathematics, I think. Every fruit is different, and there is no way to tell until you put it in your mouth. You know, you're very well educated, for someone who was raised a Mean."

That put Rien's back up. "Head saw to it."

"An unusual person." With a wrist-led gesture, the necromancer indicated a white peach tree that stood in a clear spot, not far. "That is my special tree."

Rien looked at the plum in her hand, and then the heavy pale fruits, bloomed rose-pink, that bowed the branches of the other. "What grows on that one?"

"Memories," Mallory said. "Souls."

Leaving Rien standing, pack in one hand and plum in the other, the necromancer crossed to the peach tree.

They weren't huge peaches, just the size to sit in Rien's palm. Mallory walked among them, touching the ones that hung down—then, with a scramble, was among the branches and climbing.

"Come here, Rien."

She stood under the tree and dropped the pack at her feet. Above her, on a swaying branch, Mallory balanced like a wire-dancer, holding out a fruit the color of wine-soaked ivory. Rien put out her hand, and the fruit fell into it.

If the coat of the apricot had been velour, this was cut velvet, as soft and pale as Mallory's skin. Rien raised it to her mouth and sniffed. Nectar, tart-sweet-perfumy, and the green, green sap scent of the broken stem. Where the plum was cool to the touch—she still weighed it in her other hand—this was warm, though Rien could not say if it was from the suns or from Mallory's hand.

"Eat," said the magician in the tree, and Rien lifted the fruit to her lips and bit in.

It wasn't like an apple, or any crisp fruit, where you might sink your teeth in and lever a piece away from the orb. She bit through, faint resistance of the skin and then concupiscent flesh. Juice slicked her cheeks and chin, coursed down her forearm, dripped from her elbow. The flavor was—intense. Honeyed, but not cloying, complex and buoyant.

She hadn't words.

And then she had plenty of words, but none of them were her own.

He was Chief Engineer Conrad Ng, and he had passed through scared and into resigned. His symbiont was failing;

there was a limit to the radiation damage that it could repair, and that limit had been reached around the time his flesh began sloughing from his bones. But he was concentrating, as he died. Concentrating hard, on what he knew, on everything recorded in the soft rotting tissue of his brain.

Because while he was dying, a portion of his colony might live. And with it, a portion of his knowledge.

Rien gagged. But Mallory's hand cupped over her own, and Mallory's voice urged, "Eat," and Rien bit into the fruit again.

This time, her own salt flavored it.

Knowledge that would be needed. The ship was damaged beyond repairing. The strike had taken out the main reactor and ruptured the backup; it was in sealing what was left of the core that Ng had also sealed his fate.

They were limping. They were—

"Eat," Mallory said, and Rien choked down the last bite.

There was a binary star, close, but unstable. They might reach it in time to rig solar panels. It might have a habitable world, something that could be mined in a hurry, before the next solar event.

And if it didn't, the Jacob's Ladder could survive in orbit indefinitely. They could park it close enough for light, far enough—hopefully—to be out of danger of the binary system's occasional violent flares.

Until they could repair it. Or until its stressed, jury-rigged systems failed catastrophically.

Already, there were riots among the passengers. There was a rift among the crew. Com thought they should press on, risk it all on a farther, more stable star. Some of them thought they *should try to turn back. Personally, Ng thought that should be a shooting offense.*

Com couldn't do a damned thing without Engineering.

Chief Engineer Ng was selfishly glad that he was going to be gone before things got any worse.

Rien came back to herself in a snap. The peach pit was clenched in her hand; Mallory gently uncoiled her fingers, knelt down—while Rien stood shaking, wishing she could lick the stickiness off her fingers and not daring—and nudged the moss aside to plant the pit beneath.

"He's dead," Rien said, when she had gathered herself. Her voice startled her. It sounded so strong, and so calm.

Mallory glanced up, sunlight catching on the edges of that mess of dark brown hair in a tawny halo, and answered with pursed lips and a shaken head: "I'm a necromancer, sweet. What did you think that meant?"

12

the opposite of dying

Love does not help to understand
The logic of the bursting shell.

—EDNA ST. VINCENT MILLAY

In comparison to what had come before their inter-
lude in the Heaven, the next stage of their journey
was almost pleasant. Which said more for the hardships of
plunging directly from captivity to space and from space
into a running gun battle than for any luxury of the current situation, because when Mallory had offered them a
guide and a map, nothing had been mentioned of the first
kilometer-and-a-half of the journey being a crawl through
abandoned access tunnels.

Perceval sheathed herself in her parasite wings—
deployed, they were bulky and awkward in the confined
space—and pulled herself onward doggedly on her elbows
behind Rien and the basilisk. Rien had it better: she was
shorter, and could scoot forward on her hands and knees,
although trying to avoid crushing Gavin's tail looked like
a challenge.

The shafts had not been designed for long-distance travel, and frankly, had only been meant to be entered by human agents in catastrophic emergencies. In the moving time, the ancestors of evolved nanotools like Gavin would have performed the bulk of the maintenance.

Now, the tunnel was a dark, irregular tube, its sides laced with bruising protrusions under the colonies of pale parasitical bromeliads that grew from the pressed and extruded walls. It was impossible to move without breaking the waxy leaves of the plants. They popped and snapped under Perceval's hands and feet, releasing a clear, slightly gelatinous fluid with the green smell of aloe. Small things scuttled or hopped away, startled by the noise of their passage, or the blue radiance shed by Gavin and by Pinion, which allowed the travelers to see.

"Isn't it odd," Rien said, when they had been alternately climbing and crawling for a while, "that things have evolved to take advantage of every niche in the world? It didn't happen like that back on Earth, did it?"

Perceval bit her lip when she would have hushed Rien. Of course, Rien was not an Engineer. Earth was nothing to her but a name, something she might have been taught about in ecology. She didn't know how close to the heresy of the Go-backs she trod. "They were helped," Perceval said. "Camael and the bioengineers gave some colonies a special program, when they still could. Before Metatron died. It force-mutates. Not humans, of course—"

"Funny you should mention Metatron." Rien spoke between small grunts of effort as she levered herself over a humped obstacle. It was impossible, under a layer of ridged tree-ears, to tell what the shape might once have been. But now, it was covered with rather more edges than it had once been. "Mallory did, too."

"Your brain is optimized for pattern-sensing," Gavin commented. "And chatter."

Whether the basilisk meant her to or not, Perceval laughed. And after a moment, Rien—unsulky—laughed as well. Perceval reached forward and patted her sister's ankle in praise, surprised when Rien pulled it forward quickly. Perhaps her feet were ticklish.

"What were you in the before?" Rien asked—obviously of Gavin, not Perceval, who had not been born then. "A welder?"

"Laser-cutting torch," Gavin replied, fluttering his wings as he hop-flapped to the top of the next obstacle. "Ah. There's the halfway point, fair maidens."

Perceval groaned. "Gavin, I don't mean to complain. But why are we going *this* way?"

"Because I was instructed by the necromancer to lead you astray, exhaust you, and then gnaw your bones," he answered, hopping down the other side of the bulge he'd been perched on. "Unfortunately, I only have a beak, which makes it hard to gnaw, so I'm trying to scrape you to death, and in the meantime wasting power so you can see where you're going. Why do you *think* we're going this way?"

"Direct route," Rien said, promptly.

"And cannibals," Gavin said. "Socially irresponsible, but there you have it. This is the best way around their levels, and as far as I know there's oxygen and gravity the whole way."

"I could do with a little less gravity," Rien said.

Perceval laughed again, feeling better. At least she wasn't the only one whining.

This time, Rien tried to kick her.

By the time Gavin popped open a hatch with a clever twist of his beak and led them blinking out of the stuffy, musty access tube, both Perceval and Rien had come to the conclusion that it was better to save their breath. They clambered into a small compartment gratefully, and Perceval spent the next several minutes attempting to unkink her spine. Gritting her teeth, she unfolded Pinion and allowed it a slow stretch, which did more for her abused shoulder muscles than all the twisting she'd done before.

There was no justice.

"Where to now?" Rien asked, while Perceval checked her display for the next twist in the map Mallory had uploaded.

"Twenty-minute lunch break. Praise Zakkiel, Angel of Electricity," Gavin said, and plugged himself into the wall.

Rien wasn't certain if she was grateful or disappointed that Mallory had not packed them any of the orchard fruit. She still had the plum, however, tucked inside the vest Mallory had given her, and she slid her fingers into the concealed pocket and touched its body-warmed surface. After the peach, she wasn't sure she'd taste it before it rotted, whatever Mallory said about only that one tree growing the dead.

The plum comforted her; she imagined she could smell it on her skin, like Mallory. She pulled her hand from her pocket and accepted the bread, soy cheese, and onion jam Perceval offered.

While they ate, and Gavin recharged, Rien studied the maps in her head. It seemed like where they were going wasn't far—some kilometers, if they could take the gangways instead of crawling through warrens. "We could be there tonight," she said.

Perceval looked at her in surprise, and spoke through a mouthful of bread. "How do you know?"

"Look at the map," Rien said. "I think there used to be a side corridor . . ."

"There's nothing on the map," Perceval said, and then turned completely around, not just her head. "How would you know where a side corridor used to be, Rien?"

But Rien had pressed one hand to the side of her head, feeling the hair escape between her fingers. "Ng knew," she said. Then Perceval was staring at her, and for all she could tell Gavin might have been, too, except he never opened his eyes.

She set the bread carefully on the decking beside her and buried her face between her knees. She covered her mouth with her hands, but couldn't stop hyperventilating, and couldn't even begin to express why.

Perceval put a hand on her shoulder. "Rien, what's wrong?"

He just wanted to die, Rien wanted to say. *He just wanted to die and now he's in me, and Mallory won't let him die*. That could happen to anyone.

Anyone? Or just anyone Exalt? Maybe it was the symbiont that did it.

She chewed on a mouthful of snot, stuffed the side of

her fist into her mouth, and folded tighter. *Stop it*, ordered her lingering rational urges. She wasn't going to let anyone make her cry. Not Mallory, and not some dead Engineer. She bit her hand and forced control. "Orphans dream of being secret princesses," she said.

Perceval must not have heard her, because she made one of those indistinct encouraging noises that people make, and massaged Rien's shoulders. After a moment, Rien managed to lift her head and repeat herself: "Orphans. Dream of being secret princesses."

Perceval's thumbs made firm circles in Rien's muscles. "And so?" she said. "You are."

A peculiar emotion swept over Rien. She was furious—not specifically with Perceval, but Perceval got caught in the edge of it. But Rien did not want Perceval to stop touching her.

It seemed unfair to ask to be held while you yelled at someone, so Rien swallowed it down. And said instead, "Oh, yeah, a princess with a belly full of bugs and a sister out of nowhere and a dead man in her head." She sniffled and hugged her knees, not crying. Gavin seemed not to have moved at all since the drama started; he might have been a statue of a basilisk. Rien didn't look at him.

She said, "I never had these problems before I met you."

That made Perceval laugh, and hand her the discarded snack.

"Eat," Perceval said. "Don't waste food. You'll need it eventually."

And Rien supposed that was right. If Perceval could eat while being fed in chains, Rien could eat now. She put the bread in her mouth, bit down, and chewed. The onions were pungent and sweet and soft; the cheese sharp, but tasty. It made her sniffle again. "Perceval," she said, when she had swallowed the mouthful, "why did you challenge Ariane?"

"Because she needed to be challenged," Perceval answered. Rien thought she didn't notice that Pinion flexed when she spoke, a gesture halfway between a falcon mantling its prey, and a cringe. "We met—I was on errantry. She was behaving villainously. I thought I was stronger than she. What do you mean you have a dead man in your head?"

"Mallory gave me a peach," Rien answered. She chewed more bread to buy time, but had to wash it down with a mouthful of water. "It had an Engineer's memories in it."

Perceval's face lit up. "Which Engineer? You said Ng?" Rien nodded.

"Hero Ng." There was reverence in Perceval's voice. It startled Rien. "You have his memories?"

"I don't know. Some. I remember him dying"— Perceval flinched in sympathy—"and I remember that there should be a side corridor here"—Rien sketched a map quickly in skin-oil on the floor—"that's not on our map. Are there cannibals there?"

"I don't know," Gavin said, flicking himself loose from the wall plug with a flourish. "It's not in my memory banks either. Shall we try it and see if they eat us, then?"

Once they got the door open—easy, after they found it beneath the overgrowth; the keypad code hadn't been changed since Ng's day—they were greeted by a stench like tannin and ammonia. "Space." Perceval pinched her nose shut. "I can see why it's not on the map."

"At least we have boots now," Rien said, flexing her toes in the shoes Mallory had given them. Something fluttered inside the corridor, a rustling like the nighttime gnawing of thousands of mice, and there were sounds, squeaks so high she felt rather than heard them: a bone-conduction vibration.

"Bats," Gavin said. With heavy wingbeats, he flapped into the air, and wobbled toward Rien.

"Hey!" She ducked aside, but his great dry feet clutched her shoulder. She expected the grip and stab of talons, but they scarcely pricked, and then he was balancing on her shoulder as lightly as on a branch, his tail slipped once around her neck, heavy and leathery and warm. And far more pleasant than she would have expected.

"I'm not dragging my tail through *that*." Primly, with a flip of his long, crossed primary feathers. "You wanted to go this way. We're going this way. And you can carry me."

"Oh, whatever." But Rien didn't push him off her shoulder. "It's dark in there."

"I know," Gavin said. "You're going to expect me to light your way again, aren't you?"

"Well," Rien said, "if I could see in the dark, I wouldn't."

Perceval, a step behind, cleared her throat. "By now you should be able to."

"I beg your pardon?"

"The dark. You should be able to see in it. Not total dark, of course, but—"

"Oh," Rien said. "Of course. The symbiont."

"Sorry," Perceval said, her voice all small and almost lost under the distressing sounds of the bats.

"It's all right." And squaring her shoulders, Rien walked forward. "I invited myself."

It was awful. Gavin did shed some light—just barely enough. And Rien could have done with less.

The guano sucked at her boots. She sank into it, and it fell all around them like a chunky, whispering rain, and bats disturbed by the glow swooped down to investigate. Whether they were dazzled or angry, some of them flew into Rien. After one such collision, Gavin shifted abruptly on her shoulder, and she heard a flutter and a crunch.

And then more crunching.

She did not turn to look. "You're not."

"Not what?"

"You're a machine," she said. "You don't *eat*."

"Oh, *very well*." He must have discarded the bat with a cranelike flick of his serpentine neck. Rien was glad she couldn't see it. In fact, she told herself, she might as well be blind in that eye. There was nothing to see.

Until something as big as a large dog lunged out and scooped up the discarded bat before vanishing again, back into the unrelieved dark.

Rien bloodied her lip between her teeth, but managed somehow not to scream. Behind her, Pinion's agitated flapping did them no favors with the bats; Rien shielded her head with both arms and half crouched, eyes squinched nearly shut. "Shit. Shit. Shit."

"Only to the ankles," Gavin observed. "It hasn't even pulled your shoes off yet."

"Gavin," Perceval said, with steely calm, "what was that?"

"I don't know," he admitted. "Scavenger? It was humanoid."

"That's reassuring." Rien felt Perceval fold her parasite wings around them both, although Pinion was invisible in the darkness when Perceval damped its luminescence. They were still warmer than ambient, and Rien had no idea how that worked.

She took a breath. "Hey," she called out. "Stranger—"

No answer. But somewhere in the darkness, she heard a sound she recognized from Head's kitchen; the sound of flesh stripped back from bone. And then there was crunching, and Rien gagged on the remnants of her own frugal luncheon.

"Space," Perceval said, and then, "Poor creature."

Rien tried for human charity, but couldn't seem to get past nausea. "How long do you think it's been trapped here?"

"Long enough," Perceval said. "We have to help."

"He'll probably give you rabies," Rien said, although there was no rabies in the world and never had been. They still learned about it in biology, though; some of its elements had been used to splice the inducer viruses.

Those were illegal now. In Rule, anyway. Not that Rien thought it would have any effect on the Conns if they decided to use them.

Beyond the border of the light, Rien heard gnawing.

"It's errantry," Perceval said. "You go where it takes you, and mend what you find that needs mending."

Before Rien could remind her that they were on a quest a little more direct that errantry, Perceval had pushed past her. Cold air stroked Rien's arms where the wings had cupped. They floated over Perceval's back, now faintly luminescent and incredibly visible.

"Fuck," Rien muttered under her breath, and—to the basilisk's apparent wing-flapping chagrin—picked her way over the moldy mounds of guano to take Perceval's hand.

Perceval spoke low, her voice humming on harmonics Rien found soothing. She blinked furiously, and would have shaken her head to clear it except whoever that was off in the darkness could see her, limned by Pinion's light.

She realized that she hadn't consciously processed a single word Perceval said. And Gavin, bizarrely, was huddled against her neck like a worried parrot, compacted down to half his previously apparent size. Whether he was collapsing his form or just sleeking himself down like a bird, Rien didn't know, but the implication that *she* was meant to protect *him* concerned her.

She concentrated on her eyes and let Perceval lead her forward across the sucking mess of the floor. It was warm and humid, the reek of ammonia unrelenting. Guano dripped in her hair, warm and sticky.

So much for clean clothes.

"Who the hell puts bats on a spaceship?" she muttered, expecting it to be lost under Perceval's chanted buzz.

"Insect control," Gavin said against her ear. "Eventual terraforming. And bat guano is excellent for hydroponics and traditional agriculture." He was warm, which she wouldn't expect of a machine, and he fit just under the curve of her jaw.

And how does a hand tool that thinks it's a mythical animal know that? she almost asked, but decided against it as long as his talons pricked the hollow over her collarbone. At least he was keeping the bat shit off one shoulder.

Perceval moved forward slowly and Rien went with her. Now she saw the pale spidery shape crouched against the wall; it was hard, because he was streaked—coated— with the same filth that crusted every object. It served admirably as camouflage.

Other than a coat of guano, he was naked, and he held both hands folded before his mouth, streaked with blood up to the elbows. His hair, if it was hair, was a spiked, matted, dreadlocked mass gray with guano and stiff about his shoulders. His irises reflected Pinion's light, two flat glowing discs floating in the darkness.

He dropped the carcass of the bat, and Rien saw he had something else in his hand. Something short and flat, the part that was not enfolded in his grip about the size of Perceval's palm. "Perceval, watch—"

The wild man lunged.

Perceval might have caught him, and Pinion might have stopped him. Perceval dropped Rien's hand and stepped half in front, and the wings darted forward on either side of her—but Gavin had already sprung off Rien's shoulder, two heavy wingbeats carrying him aloft.

The guano a few steps in front of the charging man sizzled, smoked, and exploded. Rien jumped back, skidded in shit, and managed to catch her balance by windmilling her arms at the cost of a strained inner thigh.

But she was looking at Gavin, his eyes open, glaring torch-blue in the darkness with the internal radiance of his colony. There was smoke and the stench of burnt ammonia, worse than the unburned guano—like boiling piss on the stove, Rien thought, gagging, as every bat in the world shot off the roof for the passage and the air was wheeling with pin-scratching, squeaking, sight-defeating animals.

"Laser-cutting torch," she said.

The wild man had stopped. And as the bats cleared, Rien could see that he stood in the light, on the other side of the blasted patch, his right hand still upraised with what was now revealed as a broken blade clutched in it. Gavin hovered, his wingbeats stirring the air in the passage, his tail writhing behind him.

"I want to help you," Perceval said, and this time Rien heard her clearly.

The man with the broken sword put his hands on his knees and doubled over, gasping.

13

the deck

Dust is the answer—dust:
dust everywhere.

—CONRAD AIKEN,
The House of Dust

This time, Dust was expecting his brother. The anchore was hung with pennants, and everywhere flocked gorgeously gowned servants with hollow, scooped-out backs, so when they turned away you could see them from the inside, like the mold in which a person had been cast. They carried salvers and censers, platters and candelabra, everything as exquisite and enchanted as the servitors—and just as hollow. It was pageant, stage play.

A masque, because that was how the story went.

In the midst of all the exhibition sat Dust, or more precisely Dust's avatar, a Puritan magpie in his black frock coat and pewter weskit, his sealed pocket watch ticking in his gray-gloved hand. The chair he lounged upon was ebony, or the dream of ebony. He was a spot of glossy darkness surrounded by vacuous finery.

The symbolism pleased him.

He had been waiting only a fraction of a second—long enough, quite long enough, for an angel—when Samael materialized from a gyre of smoke and a shower of glitter. Still barefoot, affecting torn jeans and with his scarred chest shirtless, he glowered at Dust over crossed arms.

"What snaps an unblade?" he asked.

"I beg your pardon," Dust answered. "I am afraid I don't follow. A little context please?"

"What snaps an unblade? We've seen one snapped, haven't we? In the hand of the man in the passage that isn't supposed to be there. The passage no one remembers."

"Rien remembered it. Will you stay for dinner, Samael?"

Slowly, Samael's arms uncrossed, as he no doubt considered whether he would get anything from Dust without playing along, and decided he wouldn't. "Stage your puppet show then," he said with ill grace, and stalked past Dust to the table. A chair materialized to take him; he seated himself, and scooted in.

As for Dust, he stood, spun his own chair, and reseated himself at Samael's right hand. Elbows on the table, he leaned forward, peering around the wall of Samael's hair. "Surely you have time for entertainments," Dust said. With a gesture, he ringed the table with more chairs, each of them uniquely archaic, one red-cushioned with a tasseled rope knotted across the arms.

Around them, hollow-backed waiters swayed and served and dipped and poured, a feast of roasted peacock and braised beef, with salats and subtleties and a dozen varieties of wine that vanished into smoke from the glass when the next was served.

Samael tasted none of it.

"What's the name of that unblade?" he asked.

Dust amused himself with knife and fork, a self-conscious burlesque of a dining man. He answered without raising his chin. "Charity."

He was prepared for the dead silence that answered him. But he couldn't quite prevent a smirk from curling the corners of his mouth upward. Really, he mused, chasing green peas up the back slope of his fork with the edge of the butter knife, all a smirk was, was what a smile turned into when you fought with it.

"Tristen," Samael breathed—not an actual word, but a burst of processor activity so strong that Dust could read the resulting ionization disturbance in the air between them. And then he pushed his untouched plate away and said, "You sent them that way."

The peacock was succulent, bestowing a puddle of pinkish juice upon the plate in response to the pressure of Dust's fork; as well it should have been, as it was conjured from his memory of a thousand elaborate dinners, real and fictional. He sliced and tasted and sipped red wine. It was exactly like duck: nowhere in his memory was the taste of peacock recorded.

"Don't worry," he said, to patent disapproval. "No peacocks were harmed in the making of this dinner. And how could I have misdirected our gallant maidens, when your agents guided them? Agents whose introduction to the game I protested."

"Who else would have remembered a forgotten passageway?"

"Rien remembered," Dust said, again. "Now, what about the unblade?"

"I asked what snapped it." Samael shrugged. "And you are not going to tell me."

"Because I don't know." Dust set his fork aside. With a wave of his hand, the plates vanished, the whole groaning table left stark and empty, without so much as a cloth to cover it. "Fine," he said. "Have it your way. I can't tell you what an unblade shatters on. But I can tell you where it comes from, in the moving times."

"So can anyone. They're what became of the autodocs, but now, they can only maim. Sever things that can't be healed, not even by symbionts or surgery. You've infested the whole ship with your medieval madness."

Dust smiled. "Not mine. Conn's. The Captain's word is Law." Samael was staring at him with open speculation, and he realized he might have said too much. A subject change was in order. "Shall I lay out the cards?"

Samael did not stop staring. "It's not just fiction and history, is it, Jacob?"

Dust made a flourish in the air, his lace cuff falling across his glove. Between his fingers appeared a glossy oblong, a steel case embossed with a black enamel dragon. He cracked it open with a thumb and flipped the cards into his hand.

They were longer than a standard deck, though not much wider. The backs were plain black, the edges finished in silver gilt. They clicked like baccarat tiles when he shuffled them. "Choose a card," he said.

"Silence is as good as an answer, angel."

"No," Dust said, a token on the table to show willing. "It's not just fiction and history in my memory."

"It's people, too."

"Choose a card," Dust said.

Because they sat side by side, inasmuch as either of them *were* their physical bodies, Dust fanned the cards facing away. The black backs, glazed-glossy, would have shown the smudge of skin soil, if they had ever been touched by a naked human hand.

Irritably, Samael tapped one on the edge. "Pull it out," Dust instructed, and with ill grace his brother did. "Rome burns," Samael said. "And you fiddle with card tricks."

"Is Rome burning?" Dust's voice could not have rung falser, or more innocent.

Samael grunted and laid the card face up.

"Silence is as good as an answer, angel. Ah, the in-verted Suns. The card in the first position represents the environment in which the query takes place, and the most pressing question." Dust fanned his cards wider. "Choose another."

This time, Samael didn't bother with argument. He drew out the next card; Dust caught his wrist and guided him in placing it. It showed a man suspended upside-down in a cryo chamber, his wrists and ankles crossed. "The Hanged Man," Dust said. "Life in suspension. That which does not progress. But also, a time of rebirth, of hard-won knowledge. This is the card that crosses, the thing that opposes. Choose a card."

Samael did, and let Dust show him where to place it. His wrist felt cold and rigid; his avatar had no more depth of seeming than the hollow-backed servants. "The

Captain of Stars. There are six suits and six face cards in each, plus ten numbered ones. He is the root of the matter, the crux upon which the conflict rests. He is a man, or was one; a fiery and ambitious person, prone to quick action. His choices led inevitably to the situation we have now."

"And that situation is?"

"The inverted Suns crossed by the Hanged Man," Dust said, touching those. "Tarot readings are like stories, you see—they have characters, conflict, action, climax, theme, and denouement."

"What are the six suits?"

"Of course," Dust said. "You wouldn't remember. Memory is a spiderweb. It hangs in a corner and collects dust. Until you need it to catch a fly. The six suits are Cups, Stars, Stones, Blades, Wires, and Voids."

"Voids? Plural?"

"I know," Dust said, with a sigh of irritation. "But it wasn't me that named them. Choose a card."

They went around the central cross clockwise from that third card at the bottom: left, top, right. The Angel of Wires, the Nine of Stones, the Prince of Stars. Dust touched the leftmost card with his free hand.

"Metatron is dead," Samael said. But now, Dust noticed, he leaned forward, the front of his scarred shoulder pressed to Dust's left arm. He brushed the edge of the card, which showed a stylized, jewel-colored stained-glass-style image of an androgynous figure whose wings and arms were bound close with cutting-thin, multicolored strands. They were not barbed wire, but Dust persisted in thinking of them so.

Sometimes, even he found his program overly Gothic.

"And so the Angel of Wires resides in the Past," Dust said. "If the Angel of Wires is Metatron."

"Who else?"

"You," Dust said. "Camael. Uriel, perhaps?"

"Not Asrafil?"

"Blades," Dust said, in a clipped tone. "Or nothing." He touched the edge of the topmost card of the pattern. It was a woman, serene before an air lock twisted all over with grapevines and sunflowers. A branch of pomegranates hung heavy over her shoulder, and a white raptor sat hooded on her fist. "The Nine of Stones, in the Sky. Under what influences the situation shall play out. It is the card of Apollonian mastery of the Dionysian. But not denial; the falcon is jessed and hooded, but he is not caged. He stands on her glove, ready in an instant to fly."

Samael touched the Prince of Stars. A black-haired man, narrow-faced, with a tight goatee, stood with entwined burning suns over his shoulder. He leaned upon a harrow. Vines broke from the earth at his feet and twined him in fruit and flowers. "And what is this?"

"Who."

"Who is this?"

Dust smiled. "Who do you think? Stars are the suit of fire, of course, of growth and nurturing. And also things that burn well-nigh eternally, that burn even iron in the end. He is the prince of the forge, that one. You know, on Earth, the cards had only four suits and each suit has only four face cards. But there are six important directions here in space."

"Brother, you're stalling."

"Brother," Dust said. "Choose another card."

And when Samael had, and under Dust's guidance had laid it down to the right side of the cross and surround, they saw it was an image of a winged being, haloed and nude, who held a flaming orb between his opposed palms. The Angel of Stars. "Ah," Dust said. "The querent. *That* would be you."

"So the Angel of Wires *is* Metatron?"

"It looks more likely. Choose a card."

Above the Angel of Suns was laid the Princess of Blades. "Perceval," Samael said, with satisfaction.

Dust caught himself smirking again. How hard could it be, to let the smile just happen? "The House. That which surrounds and influences the querent. Blades are the suit of atmosphere and habitation, the suit of change when the change is willed. Choose a—"

"—card." Samael's hand was already moving. He slipped a card free and turned it over. With a glance at Dust to confirm the action, he laid it above the previous card. Another winged figure, but this one's wings faded without visible border from inky-feathered indigo into a blackness that covered the background of the card. In their depths, stars shimmered.

"The Angel of Voids," Samael said, without looking at Dust.

"This is the card of what opposes the querent," Dust said, and made himself expressionless.

Samael shifted in his chair. "We could be partners, Dust."

"We're not?"

Dust smiled, and Samael smiled back at him, shaking his head. "Don't make me bring Asrafil into this."

Dust tilted the plaques in his hand. "Choose a card for the Outcome."

"One more?"

"Maybe."

Samael chose, and turned it over in the appropriate place, at the top of the straight line. "The Princess of Voids," Dust said. "Voids are the suit of entropy, of memory, of shadows."

"Nothing will come of nothing," Samael said. "Speak again."

"You got that on my kiss," Dust said. "But I suppose now you think you always knew Shakespeare."

"So Rien is the Outcome."

"Part of it." Dust shuffled the remaining plaques, cut them, and turned one over. The ten of blades. "Ruin," he said, "but that doesn't concern us." He turned another, covering the first. The three of blades. "Heartbreak," he said. "But also not our problem. One more chance—"

He turned a third, and did not lay it down upon the others. Instead, he weighed it in his hand a moment, and then placed it adjoining the last card, tilted at an angle, as if it sprouted from the feet of the Princess of Voids.

Upon it was printed a stylized image of a bulbous, streamlined silver starship, nothing like the bulky and tangled outline of the *Jacob's Ladder*. It was wreathed in improbable flames, and tiny people had been blown screaming from the hole in the side.

"The Tower," Dust said. "It represents change, overthrow, destruction of the old order. The crumbling of all you have worked for. Wrack, and riot. Downfall and over-turn."

"We fail?" Samael asked after a quiet moment.

"Flowers grow from corpses," Dust said, and swept the cards together. "Are you sure you would not like a glass of wine?"

"No," Samael said. He pushed his chair away, the moment broken. "I am not distracted, Jacob. You sent them to find Tristen Conn."

Dust cased his cards, careful with the silk handkerchief that enfolded them inside the enamel box. "He's not in the reading," he said. "Neither is Ariane. And yet their brother and nieces are. I wonder what that means."

"You don't know?"

"I am," Dust said primly, standing to bid his brother farewell, "the Angel of Memory, Samael. Not the Angel of Foresight."

The ugly lines of Samael's houndlike face rearranged themselves. He would never be handsome, but he was beautiful when he smiled. "And yet, you believe in prophecy?"

"No," Dust said, tucking his cards into a weskit-pocket. "I believe in stacking the deck."

14

evidence of war

Six feet of dust under the
morning stars.
And a panorama of war
performs itself

—CARL SANDBURG,
"Old Osawatomie"

Once it became evident they meant him no harm,
the naked and filthy man Perceval had rescued at-
tached himself to her. He didn't speak at first, and
Perceval wondered if he was capable. He would not give
up his broken sword, but he held her hand peaceably and
he also would not be shifted from her side.

Perceval felt odd talking around him, but as he would
not speak, she didn't see an option. "If he couldn't get out,
what makes you think that we can?"

The bats had finally quieted.

Rien, appearing to notice this, said, "The bats get out
somewhere."

"You are bigger than a bat."

Rien scratched the basilisk on her shoulder under the hackles. "I know where the door is," she said. "Also, we have lights. And a cutting torch."

And with the assistance of those things, to Perceval's inexpressible wonderment, they escaped the realm of the bats without further incident.

Abandoned crew quarters lay beyond, overgrown with kudzu. In daylight, the stranger cringed and covered his eyes until Perceval took pity and bound a blindfold over them. As they walked, she picked the tender leaves from the end of the kudzu shoots and shared them with the others. They were good, spinachy, and if they were to have a third, Perceval thought anything that might stretch the food budget should be investigated. The stranger—blindfolded—sniffed them, and then with his smeared and crusted hands stuffed them into his mouth, one-fisted.

She looked at Rien while he ate, and Rien nodded. "You were right."

Perceval smiled at her, and handed her another serving of kudzu leaves. Rien rolled them into tubes and gnawed, chewing as if the sharp green taste could drive the flavor of ammonia from her throat. "Space," she said, softly as if that meant that only Perceval would hear her, "how long do you think he was locked in there?"

"Let's get clean," Perceval answered, and Rien began circumventing locks.

It took them three hours to clear the overgrowth away from enough washrooms to find a working shower, but as soon as they found it, they looked at each other and at their new companion, and sighed. Perceval coaxed his blindfold off—he held onto it at first, emaciated fingers wrapped through the band—and Rien adjusted the sonics and the fine, warm fog in the stall.

"It's even hot," she said, trying not to sound envious.

"You'll get your turn," Perceval answered without rancor. "Let's see if we can find him something to wear."

They were not the only things that rustled among the kudzu, but whatever might have lived there was shy and wary of predators. They could hear little animals skiphopping ("mice," Perceval said, but Rien said, "toads") and there were insects, which Perceval caught when she could, remembering that they were rich in protein.

As they rummaged through abandoned, vacuum-sealed closets, they found many good things, including unfashionable but warm clothing that would fit a tall, thin man. "Perceval," Rien said after they had given up looking for shoes and sat side by side near the washroom door, "how many of the habitats in the world are deserted?"

"Oh," Perceval said, "I would suppose most of them."

"Where are all the people?"

"Dead," Perceval said. Rien's fingers tightened on her wrist, driving nails into the skin, and Perceval flinched and tried to find an honest way to soften that news. As if she had meant to, she continued, "Or congregated in a holde, more rarely a domaine. There were a lot more of us, in the moving times."

Behind the door, the sound of sonics stopped.

"Are we dying?"

"Yes," Perceval said. She stood, as the door opened,

and extended an armload of soft shirts, underthings, and coveralls to the man—

She stopped short, her arms bent under the flat-palmed offering.

She'd thought his skin chalky with layered guano and lack of sun, his hair white and caked with the same limy excrement.

But no.

Clean, he was whiter. Blue-skinned in the filtered light through the overhead, his hair sculptured from ice-white curls, his beard still long but washed now. Perhaps he had not found a depilatory, but he had found a comb, and an elastic. He wore a towel wrapped at his waist, and the stub of his sword protruded from it.

His hair, braided, still hung most of the way down his back now that it was clean. Looking at it, thinking of what it must have taken to clean it, Perceval was grateful for the loss of her own. The stubble would be easier to scrub out.

He smelled not at all of ammonia.

And the eyes that met Perceval's were ice-blue, faintly luminescent with the same blueness that stained her own veins, in his case unalloyed by pigment.

"Thank you," he said, his voice creaky and cracking but perfectly intelligible. He reached out to take the heap of clothing. His warm, moist fingertips brushed Perceval's.

"Lord Tristen," Rien said. Stammered, really. "You're meant to be dead."

And while Perceval looked at Rien in disbelief, Tristen Conn said, "Do I . . . know you?" and Rien reached out to steady herself against the wall.

•   •   •

That night, they camped in a kitchen with a stove, and
they had hot soup for dinner. The cooking surface didn't
work at first, but thanks to her spontaneous mechanical
knowledge, Rien repaired it. Gavin curled up in the corner, the tip of his tail in an electrical socket, though
Perceval thought he was only pretending to doze.

As for Tristen, once he'd determined who they were,
where they were going, and why, he remained quiet—
painfully so—but it turned out he could cook, so Rien and
Perceval sat shoulder to shoulder, wrapped in Pinion's
warm but worrying embrace, and watched. There was
something tremendously comforting in having an adult
appear and take care of things, Perceval admitted, watching the tall white man stir dinner with curious focus.

She was fascinated by that. And by how very white his
hair was, and the soft translucence of his skin. She could
see the blue veins where his salvaged clothes did not
cover, and she was surprised that not only was his symbiont apparently healthy, but that it had managed to keep
him so. She was also amazed by his resilience; she had
only been captive a few days, and she thought she would
lie staring at ceilings the rest of her life. She could not
feel safe.

But there was Tristen Conn, singing to himself as he
tasted broth and stacked and rolled tender kudzu leaves
into long tubes for chiffonade. And he made her feel safer,
his broken sword tucked into his belt and a knife from a
magnetic rack inside one of the mouse-rummaged cabinets rocking in his left hand. Perceval hadn't seen a wild

mouse, but she knew that all the mice in the world were as white as Tristen, albinos. They would have red eyes, though—natural mammal blood color—not stained blue by the symbiont blood-marker.

She and Rien sat and watched Tristen cooking, and she tried not to let herself feel too safe. But that was hard, when he brought them plastic mugs of salty broth full of shredded rehydrated mushrooms and soy protein, the delicate rags of sliced kudzu floating on top, a soft and saturated green.

She cupped the mug in both hands, first undraping her arm from around Rien, and sipped. It tasted fantastic. The tightness across Perceval's shoulders—where the weight of her wings wasn't—eased at the warmth. They sat in an uneven triangle, eating in silence.

When Perceval had finished, she flicked Pinion shut—even the brief breeze was warm and welcome—and got up to get more, collecting Rien's cup as well. Tristen placed his hand over his mug when she reached for it. He'd only gotten through a little more than half, and was taking it slowly.

Too much food in a hurry might not be good for him.

As she ladled more soup into the cup, she spoke. It was easier, somehow, when you were not looking. "Rien, do you think we're being maneuvered into finding things?"

Rien made a noise. Startled, rather than affirmative. "I hadn't thought of it." In the stainless-steel trim around the backsplash, Perceval saw Rien press three fingers to the side of her head.

"Lord Tristen," Perceval hastened to add, "no offense. I did not mean to insinuate that you were a *thing*."

"Considering how you met me, I could hardly be offended if you did," he said. His voice was returning, but it was still soft and weary; she wondered how it felt for him to be clean and clothed and full of salty soup after the builders knew how long crawling through bat muck and gnawing raw bones. She hoped she could remain glad to never know. "But I don't believe anyone knew where I was."

"Then how did you come to be there?" Perceval asked, just as Rien volunteered, "We got help and directions from a necromancer." Perceval turned back in time to see Rien's guilty glance at Gavin, but Gavin never shifted.

Tristen, however, craned over his shoulder to look at Perceval, then watched her walk back, balancing mugs, to sit again beside Rien. "You're trusting of a stranger." His tone ruined it, though—he might be trying for menace, but he only sounded avuncular.

Which, Perceval supposed, was exactly what he was. Their father's brother.

"Only strangers who can cook," she replied. "And anyone who would bury himself under a metric ton of bat shit to fool us deserves to. We mean to try to stop a war, Lord Tristen—"

"Don't Lord me," he interrupted, the electric blue eyes narrowing in colorless sockets, "and I shan't Lady you."

"And so are all the forms of courtesy defeated," Perceval said, but she smiled. "So are you for war?"

"When I was free, I was for any war I could get," he said. He touched the hilt of his broken unblade. "Now that I am free again . . ." He shrugged. "Durance vile can alter your expectations. You think someone is machining this war, Perceval?"

"Ariane Conn," she said, without hesitation. "And somebody on the Engine side, too. Who is willing to risk biological warfare. And to arrange things so that I might be captured by Rule, so as to bring the contagion among them."

That was dangerously close to topics Perceval was not yet ready to discuss—not without first gathering some intelligence—so she drank soup and then changed the subject before someone could pursue it. "In any case, I'm feeling schooled. And I do not think your sister is the Commodore who is needed in Rule."

"Commodore?"

"I'm sorry," Rien said. "La—I mean, Ariane killed your father."

"Good riddance," Tristen said, his woolly white braid sliding forward over his shoulder. Despite two elastics, the end was fraying. "But how can she have declared herself Commodore, when I am legitimate, and so much older?"

For the time being, even Tristen seemed content to avoid conflict. They skulked and hid, Gavin their ears and Rien's unsettling, newly intrinsic sense of geography their guide. They saw no one else alive, and Rien was both grateful for and worried by it.

They might have been not too far from Benedick's residence on a straight line, but many of the corridors were blocked or ruined. Two days' careful and unobtrusive journey followed. Tristen acted impervious, Rien thought—but she also noticed that he slept propped in corners, and that she'd wake and find him staring into space or reading on a hand-screen he'd scavenged in one of the rooms they bunked in, his nose pressed almost to the display as if his sight were failing.

As they came closer to the border between Rule and Engine, the travelers saw at last evidence of Ariane's war. Foliage scorched and trampled by battle, a blasted bulkhead. A body, which Perceval knelt beside and brushed with her fingertips.

"His name was Alex," she said, and rasped her hands over her stubble in the thinking gesture of someone accustomed to long hair. The prickles looked as if they must itch, but perhaps knights, like ladies, did not scratch.

Gavin seemed to have the knack of riding shoulders; when Rien hunkered to wait, he aided her balance.

Tristen, in his blue fleece and salvaged sandals, knelt, too. He placed one hand on the dead man's forehead, as if in benediction. And then he began to go through his pockets.

"Sir!" Perceval protested. And Tristen paused, and only looked at her.

They stared, back and forth a moment; Rien noticed the sameness in the shapes of their features. Though Perceval's face was squarer, and Tristen's was long, they were both thin and tall, with deep-set eyes. His nose wandered; hers was incongrously pert. Nevertheless, Rien thought the resemblance would have been striking if Perceval still had her hair, and if Tristen's was pigmented rather than wooly and white and if the line of his jaw was not concealed by the beard.

He glanced down, his lashes thick and ivory against his blue-tinged cheek, and drew the dead man's sheath and knife from his boot. There was a holster for a sidearm, but the pistol was not in evidence. Tristen, however, did pull two clips of caseless ammunition from his pockets.

Silently, he offered bullets and knife to Perceval.

"You take it," she said, without looking at his hands.

They continued on.

They made camp when they grew tired, in another abandoned section of crew quarters. The irrigation system had failed here, and nothing but crisped brown stems grew in the beds and wall boxes. The air could have been fresher, for it—but there was running water from the taps, though it was cold only, and Rien, whose menses had started, took the opportunity to scrub herself with a soapy rag and wash her hair. Gavin stood on the edge of the basin and studied a cracked dry valve from the irrigation pipe, turning it over and over in his claw, before eventually putting it in his beak and swallowing it, like a chicken gagging down pea gravel for its crop.

Later, as they sat waiting for Tristen to cook dinner, Rien searched toiletry drawers until she found a cracked tube of conditioner. It had dried into a solid, oily cake, but it smelled all right. She rubbed it between her hands to oil the palms, stroked it into the drying frizz, and began picking through the tangles curl by curl with a heavy wide-toothed comb. It broke into ringlets, damp, but even with the oil on it, it would never stay that way.

Tristen was still flipping pancakes when they heard the voices. He set the spatula aside, turned down the induction plate almost as far as it would go—there was a click when it shut down—and glanced up at the overhead light. Turning it off would of course be incredibly obvious.

It didn't matter, Rien suspected. The smell of cooking was all through the air.

"Space," she said, without breath, as the tromp of heavily shod feet approached. She slipped her comb into her pocket and crouched, wishing she had something on hand to use as a club; she'd feel far more comfortable with that sort of weapon than anything with a point.

But across the room, Tristen's hands were like bones on the black hilt of his appropriated blade, and that was reassuring. And it was reassuring as well that when Perceval stood, Pinion flaring like a cloak, and squared her shoulders, her face was as serene as any angel's. With only a glance between them, she and Tristen went to flank the door.

Rien could see the people advancing in her head. There was a sort of Y-intersection ten meters down the corridor, and they were coming along the left-hand path. She could tell from the echoes and the map in her head, and that was a very strange thing indeed. She strained, trying to pick out words, voices, but all she heard was a marching cadence, and it didn't sound familiar.

Not of Rule, then, and that was something. But it might be whoever had locked up Tristen, and it might be whoever in Engine had sent Perceval to die in Rule.

Gavin hunkered on the back of a chair, wings half up and neck elongated, as if he scented the air. And then Tristen's chin came up and a little smile lifted the corner of his mustache that Rien could see in profile. He slipped the knife back into its sheath on the belt he used to cinch his too-big trousers, raised his hands beside his head, and stepped out into the corridor, beckoning Rien and

Perceval after with a tilted head and an arrogant little cup
of his hand.

Perceval looked at Rien.

Rien shrugged.

Perceval shrugged right back, and turned to follow.

*Maybe we shouldn't just waltz out into the line of fire after
him,* Rien started to say, but maybe there was something
in the knightly code of conduct that also said you had to
be fucking stupid all the time, because that was exactly
what Perceval did. And then Rien wasn't going to skulk
behind a plastic chair so somebody could scruff her like a
kitten and drag her out.

She stayed Gavin with a hand gesture. She'd given up
trying to figure out how he maneuvered when his eyes
were always closed, but in any case he was more effective
backup than she. He froze in place, those fanning wings
uplifted, for all the world like an alabaster sculpture. And
Rien jumped up and hustled the three steps to catch up
with her sister, and as a result almost tripped over Pinion's
trailing edge. Somehow she managed to enter the corridor, third in line but dripping all the dignity she could
muster, and perversely glad she'd smoothed her hair.

Like Tristen—like Perceval—she raised her hands.
And faced a corridor full of armed men and women, ten or
more arrayed in ranks, all dressed in black and golden-
brown.

The one in the front wore plain black, trousers and a
constructed uniform jacket. He was of a height with
Tristen, black hair hanging razor-cut to the edge of a
lantern jaw, his eyes a dark-ringed hazel that caught the
light. Rien's eyes widened—she'd known they were close,

but not so close—and her hand darted out to close on Perceval's wrist and drag her down on one knee as Rien herself genuflected.

"Tristen," said Benedick Conn, his gloved hand resting on the grip of his pistol. "I thought you were dead."

"I'm back," said Tristen, and Rien did not think that anyone except she or Perceval was close enough to see him shaking like a leaf. "And these are your daughters."

15

sweet things grow in the cold

Ye are of your father the devil, and
the lusts of your father ye will do.

—JOHN 8:44, *King James Bible*

Benedick Conn both was and was not what Rien had
expected. She knew him only as a portrait, as she had
known Tristen—though Benedick's image in Rule did not
wear black crepe. And now he stood before her and stared
at Tristen, his lips moving on three syllables. He looked
past Tristen, from Rien to Perceval and from Perceval to
Rien.

"My daughters," he said, out loud this time, and then
extended his right hand to Tristen. "Thank you."

They clasped. And then Tristen grasped Benedick by
the wrist and pivoted, bringing him around.

The men and women behind Benedick shuffled and
stomped, but Rien saw the man—her father, not that she
believed it in her heart any more now than she had in the
dungeon when Perceval told her—make some gesture
that quieted them. And then Tristen's impelling grasp

became a propelling one, a firm push against Benedick's shoulder. Rien had a strong sense that even as Benedick allowed Tristen to move him, he was considering his options, and some of them were violent.

And then they had stepped apart, and Benedick extended both hands, one each to Perceval and Rien.

His daughters allowed him to draw them to their feet.

Perceval looked as Rien imagined she must have when she'd just been knighted. Her face held a kind of tense wonder, and Rien thought back to her casual bravado—we'll just go and see Father—and bit her lip.

It was easy to forget that Perceval was, more or less, only her own age. That resemblance was there again, Benedick's eyes both paler and clearer than Perceval's, but set as deep. And his face was so obviously stamped on hers that Rien again had no doubt of the relationship.

But whom did Rien look like? It wasn't any of these tall, rangy creatures with their hands like spades and the weapons on their hips.

"Father," Perceval said, "do you remember me?"

She squeezed his fingers and let go of them. Rien couldn't, just yet, and Benedick did not seem inclined to make her. Still, Rien caught herself stepping left and crowding Perceval, as though she were the only reliable thing in the universe. And Perceval didn't seem to mind, or at least, Pinion draped around Rien's shoulders warmly.

And meanwhile Benedick, with the knuckles of his one free hand, reached out and brushed Perceval's shaved head. He touched Pinion on the proximal strut, close to where it joined Perceval's body. "Who did this to you?"

Arms folded across her rib cage, chin lifted, Perceval could have been a statue labeled *defiance*. "Ariane Conn," she said. "After accepting my honorable surrender."

His face gave away nothing, but Rien was still holding his hand. She felt the tendons tighten, and then the moment when he asserted control. "That's a message to me," he said. "I am terribly sorry it was you who absorbed the blow, Sir Perceval, and I will do what I can to make it right."

The calmness of his tone made Rien want to strike him. *How dare you take responsibility for her?* she wanted to say. *Noblesse oblige is lovely, but Perceval does not belong to you; she is her own person, and more a sister to me than you have even been my father. Has she no right in your eyes even to her own* mutilation?

But then Benedick turned to Rien, and she could not think of anything except how tall he was, and how he was looking straight at her, and that his hand that still held hers was very strong. The heavy lines from his nose to his mouth-corners made it look as if he never smiled. His hair was black as lacquer.

"I am sorry," he said. "It was my father's choice that you be raised in ignorance, Rien, and I did what I could do to see that you received the best guidance available."

"Head," she said, understanding. "Head was working for you."

"Head works for no one except by choice," he said. "But I call hir a friend. Come along, please. Come home with me."

•   •   •

Perceval had never seen a winter before.

Benedick's domaine was a Heaven, bigger than Mallory's, full of stark black-limbed trees, twigs rimed in ice. They came out on a high ledge overlooking a valley, of sorts, the whole thing dark with true night and frozen cold.

"You're on the bottom of the world," Rien said, craning her neck back. Gavin—who had rejoined them—huddled against her throat under her hair. Perceval copied her. Far, far overhead, through panes frosted at the edges, she could see the sharp brilliance of stars.

The gravity was very light; Rien bounced on her toes. "It gets *dark* here."

"Mirrors," Perceval said, wondering to whom, exactly, she thought she had to prove herself. She would not glance at Benedick, or Tristen either, and see if they looked approving. Behind her, the harness on the militia jingled as they breathed. "There are mirrors on darkside, to reflect light. As there are shadow panels on sunside."

"My house is below," said Benedick. Perceval could make out the lights, and thought *house* an inadequate term for what might better be termed a castle. Now she did glance left, at Rien and Tristen, and saw their breath smoking on the air.

It fascinated her. She reached out and put her hand into it, watching Tristen's breath, as blue-white as his skin, curl between her fingers. He shot her a look, and then pursed his lips and blew to make her laugh.

And then he was receding, abruptly, falling away from her. Reaching out—lunging—until Rien and Benedick caught him by the arms and hauled him back. She was airborne—effortlessly, without strain—pulled away on beating wings. "Pinion!" she said, but Pinion did not listen.

Last time, it had ferried her and Rien to safety. This time, there had been no evident danger, but nevertheless she was carried helplessly into the air and away. She shouted—uselessly, the words snatched off her lips by the wind of her motion—and even reached up over her own shoulders to pluck at the roots of the beating wings.

They were so much stronger than her fingers.

The air whistled across her scalp, tugged her halter. Flying with her own wings had taken concentration, the cooperation of her entire body. These just bore her along, sizzling through the air, nothing but a passenger. She crossed her arms over her chest to try to fight the wind.

And had an idea.

Both hands clawed over her right shoulder, fingertips battered by Pinion's leading edge. She stretched and caught, one hand then both, holding on, hauling with all the strength in her strong arms.

She pulled the wing down.

Fluttering, into a spiral toward the treetops, ice-sheathed fingers reaching, brittle splintering as she fell among them. Pinion folded around her, cushioned her fall, so the impacts of shattering branches that would have also shattered her bones only knocked the wind out of her.

At the bottom of the tree, she sprawled in the snow, gasping. Pinion folded about her, as if to protect her from the cold, and she shrieked and shoved at the shadowy wings. "Get *off* me. Get off!"

They gave under her clawing and pushing. They folded open. She'd seen a photograph of a falcon's wingprint in snow, elegant and perfect, each feather showing clean and sharp as a razor cut, blood at the center from a kill.

When she arose, this would not look like that.

She rocked forward, rolled onto her knees. Her breath flowed around her face on the still air. The parasite wings weighed almost nothing, but she felt them stir—in the wind, or with their own will. Meltwater soaked through her knees. Her hands ached in their bones from the cold. She heard shouts and crashing, but distant still.

And then Pinion caressed her face on the right side, and someone said, like an echo . . .

—*Perceval*.—

She shot to her feet, snow creaking under her boots, and stood in the silence of the forest, arms spread, breathing hard.

—*My love*.—

"Who are you?" Whispered, at first, ragged on a gasping breath. And then, when there was no answer, louder, a soldier's demand. "*Who* are *you?*"

—*One who will protect you. One who will keep you always safe*.—

"Get off me," she said. She grabbed at the wings and hauled on them, but here, on the ground, they were not constrained to an aerodynamic shape. Pinion melted away under her fingers, slipping like water through the gaps, and she was left back-arched, scrabbling after smoke. "Who are you, damn you?"

—*Pinion*.—

The name a breath across her cheek. Wings and chains, she thought. "Rien named you that. Who are you?"

—*It is my only name*.—

She *would* get a lawyering parasite. "Mutant. *What are you?*"

—*Nothing named me. I am a messenger. I come from dust.*—

The footsteps crunching closer. Cries, lights, sounds of floundering. She heard Tristen cursing the snow. Rien called her name. "Here!" she called back, and Pinion fanned and flared around her, like a cloak caught by the wind, like a falcon mantling its kill.

"Dust?" It sounded religious to her. We come from dust. We are stardust. We are dust in the wind.

Were these not words from ancient hymns?

—*Dust sends his love for you, Sir Perceval. And his anticipation of the wedding. I am your guard and warden. I, Pinion. His wedding gift.*—

She gagged. "Get *off* me."

—*I shall not.*—

But then Tristen burst through the trees, running toward her, his skin and hair lost against the snow. Behind him, running in his footsteps, Rien, with her basilisk companion swimming heavily through the air alongside. And ranged behind them, Benedick and his militia, a staggered search line to find her among the trees. Perceval turned to Tristen, held her hands out, pleading. She had not plead with Ariane, but Tristen . . . she did not believe that Tristen meant her harm.

"Get them off," she said. "The wings, you have an unblade. Tristen, get them off me now."

He stopped, a controlled sliding some five meters away. There came a ratcheting sound from her back; the shadows all stretched away. Tristen flinched in the sudden light.

Pinion opened like a flower—four wings, six, nine—all of them alight in stark blue radiance and folded forward, bent on Tristen as if he were the focus of a parabolic dish. The light shone brightest from their razor edges.

They gleamed with the will to do murder.

Tristen spread his hands. He held that silly boot knife in the left one. He said, "It's shattered, Perceval."

"You carry it. The stump still has an edge. Get them off me."

"I could have cut free of the corridor were that so."

Rien drew up behind, stepped to his right side, away from the knife. Gavin fluttered down to a branch beside her. And Benedick arrived on Tristen's left, leaving him plenty of room to swing that blade. "You're asking him to cripple you. Again."

"It's better to be crippled and free."

But Pinion hissed, if you could name it so—the rasp of feather on feather, the scraping of blade on blade.

"Perceval," Rien said. "I don't think that thing is going to let us get close enough."

Perceval could not be crying, because Perceval did not cry. But something shining froze on her face as she strode at the center of the group, her parasite wings flared about her like a nest of barbs. She looked severe and resolute—no one could look pale, standing next to Tristen—and Rien admired her desperately.

Such a strange being. Such a strange thing, having a sister. Being a sister. And even stranger, to be a sister to such a sister as this.

And to have a father, Rien forced herself to think, watching Benedick's glossy black hair swing as he broke trail through the snow. That, she was entirely unready for. As unready as she was to be Exalt, or lugging Hero Ng around between her ears.

All Benedick's men and women arrayed about them, some following and some cast out on the sides, many bearing lanterns so they made a jeweled procession. For now, Rien could distract herself with the texture of an alien night and the cold trees, ice and snow and the stars smeared behind a frosty sky.

"What is the cold for? . . ." she asked. The lights that must illuminate Benedick's house shone between bare trees, casting confusing shadows.

He turned to her, and the word *Sir* died on her lips, though he seemed to feel no lack. "Apples and cherries," he said. "You've tasted some?"

"Yes, sir."

She managed that small coin of respect this time, and even managed not to squeak. But all she purchased with it was a frown—concern, or disapproval?

"Well," he said, with a half-smile to Tristen that Rien thought she was not meant to notice, after the fashion of adults before children and Exalt before Mean, "a lot of sweet things grow in the cold. Temperature differentials promote air exchange. And what good is the world to anyone if, when it brings us safe to another Earth, we have forgotten how to live on the ground?"

"Another Earth." Funny how Tristen's voice—nasal, a bit rough still though regaining its strength—had the power to comfort her.

"You're not a Go-back, brother?"

Tristen shook his head, his white hair shedding snowflakes as if it were made of snow itself. "The only way out is through."

Gavin, who had been cruising in circles about the group, passed over Rien's head, his wings dusting snow from evergreen boughs. Rien stepped to the side, dodging a face-full of frozen water, wondering how it was manufactured. If she were to be Exalt, one of these arrogant cryptic beings, it seemed unfair that *she* did not have wings.

And then with deep shame she thought of Perceval. But Benedick and Tristen weren't all that different from their siblings, were they? They decided for others with perfect high-handedness. They were only more polite to Perceval than they would have been to some random Mean.

As if Rien's thoughts could command her as easily as Tristen did, Perceval cleared her throat. "And all that, to remind us how to live on a planet? So we don't get soft, and too bred to the indoors?"

"All that," Rien answered, with Hero Ng's authority, "because it was a trivial exercise for them to do so."

Benedick grunted. Rien could not tell if it was in respect or dismissal, and she was surprised by the ambiguity of her emotions in the face of those mutually exclusive possibilities. She did not fear, as she would have expected, nor worry for his power over her. Rather, she was caught on both hope of his approval and scorn of it.

Maybe rebellion had gotten its teeth into her soul. But not enough, apparently. Because what was Benedick to her? This person, her father, existed. That was novel. But what was he to her? He'd abandoned her.

Why should she care what he thought?

She should care, of course, because logic had no more bearing on emotion than it ever had. But she was Exalt now and had other means at her command. She could *choose* not to care, and her symbiont would take care of the rest, editing neurotransmitters and shepherding serotonin.

Benedick led them down a snow trail where the surface was packed in two parallel lines, and for now, she left it be. She scuffed the hard snow sideways with her boot. "Skis," Gavin said in her ear, by way of explanation, and looked unutterably smug when she almost jumped out of her boots in the partial gravity. She hadn't heard him complete his next great circle and sail up behind her.

And as he dropped neatly onto her shoulder, she had the distinct sensation that he was laughing himself silently sick. She collected herself with what dignity remained, shook herself smooth like a ruffled hen, and ignored the snickers she was sure she heard, from her father's men and women all around.

Before she could think of a comment, they broke out of the trees, and not even Hero Ng's phlegmatic presence could keep Rien from gasping a great mouthful of air so cold it burned her lungs. Benedick's house—it must be his house—hunkered at the top of a long snow-covered bank, away from the trees of the wood. But her awe was reserved for what lay at the bottom of the hill: a night-black tarn.

"Why doesn't it freeze?" Rien contemplated the logistics of a lake, even a small lake, on a spaceship without much hope of grasping it. And then Ng did the math for her, and she gaped even more.

"It is frozen," Benedick said. "The wind keeps it clear, or my people do. You're looking at ice. On top, at least; the underside has to stay liquid for the fish. We can"— Rien could not be imagining the diffidence in his voice, surely, as if he brought her a gift he feared would be unwelcome— "go skating in the morning if you like."

Rien swallowed so she would not gape like one of those fish. "I've never skated," she said, glancing at Perceval for support. Gavin's talons squeezed her shoulder; she leaned her cheek gratefully on his wing.

From amid the razory throne of her parasite wings, Perceval winked, frozen water glinting on her eyelashes. And to Rien alone, Perceval mouthed the word *Trivial*.

So Rien loved her.

16

tasting of bitter sleep

It is strange; this house of dust was
the house I lived in;
The house you lived in, the house that
all of us know.

—CONRAD AIKEN, *The House of Dust*

Perceval hadn't *lied*. Exactly. She had been confident that Benedick would receive them. Hear them out. Help avert catastrophe.

She had not told Rien that this confidence was not due to recent acquaintance. She had not seen their father since she had six Solar, no more.

His domain was not Engine. Benedick's house was not furnished to the standard of luxury to which Perceval was accustomed. The air held a bone-wearing rawness, and the great view screens on the walls hung dark, draped with wove-polymer tapestries that stirred in the draft. Benedick seemed impervious, as at home here as any medieval overlord in his keep of stone. Tristen relaxed in the dimness of the hall. The militia followed on, still silent, and as they entered the house, peeled away.

"Your men and women are the dead," Perceval said to her father. "Resurrectees."

Benedick nodded.

The Exalt dead were hard to keep dead. Their symbionts bonded their bodies, healed what was to be healed, knit bone and sealed spurting arteries. But if another Exalt skimmed off the cream, consumed their will and personalities and memories along with their colonies, what remained was only the mute resurrected. They did not speak. The spark, the anima—whoever had inhabited the fleshy carapace—was gone.

An unblade could have ended them, of course. But they were useful, and unblades rare.

When Perceval looked up, she saw Gavin perched equitably on Rien's fist, his swanlike head turning from side to side, crest fluffed and burning eyes sealed. She thought of the necromancer, Rien's lover whether Rien thought Perceval knew it or not, and shuddered. It would be foolish to think they were not observed.

"First we must find you accommodation," Benedick said, and it was done. The last of their honor guard broke apart. Benedick summoned his majordomo. For a few moments Perceval and Rien (with her attendant basilisk, head now tucked under his wing as if he had any need of sleep) and Tristen stood, flotsam adrift in the center of a great empty room at the front of Benedick's house, balanced over the yawning depths of holographic tiles of indigo blue. And Perceval noted Rien's inward smile.

"Sister?"

Rien shook her head as if shaking off a trance. "Just thinking."

Perceval nodded, waiting companionably. Tristen, she thought, was pretending not to listen. And Gavin lifted his head, stretched, and began to preen the hair behind Rien's ear.

Eventually, in the face of all their silences, Rien sighed and said, "In Rule, it would have been me making up the sleeping chambers."

"You miss your place," Perceval said.

"No." Rien glanced at her, at Tristen. Gavin tugged her hair; she reached up and placed a hand on his wing. "Yes. It wasn't much of a place."

"It was safe," Tristen said brusquely, "and you knew it."

Rien stared from him to Perceval, and Perceval thought she was expecting disapproval. She kept her own face neutral; she nodded slightly.

The corners of Rien's mouth ticked up. She stepped around Perceval, Gavin meanwhile executing a maneuver half-hop and half-slide down her arm to come to rest upon her hand like any bird at peace upon a swaying limb, except the three alabaster coils of tail looping her wrist.

"Father?" Rien stammered, before she had approached Benedick very closely at all. She said it so softly, as if she had never heard the word before, that she was obliged to say it again to turn his head. Perceval flinched for her, but Rien persisted. "Father."

"Yes, Rien?" He turned, raising one hand to stay his majordomo, without any show of impatience at the interrupted conversation.

"Perceval and I would like to stay together. And close by Tristen, please."

"Of course," Benedick said. "That simplifies things. Thank you, Rien."

As for Perceval, she watched, hoping she presented an air of impassivity. No doubt at all, she was in for it, and she deserved whatever she was going to get.

Pinion wrapped her protectively, whether in response to the chill or the quick hug she gave herself, she did not know. The translucent wings were warm; their touch made her shiver.

Who was this Dust, who spoke to her through the mechanical parasite that had grafted itself to the severed scars of her wings? Who was he to demand her hand in marriage?

She did not want to ask Benedick, and she did not see why Rien might know.

And as for Rien—as she requested, so it was done. Within the quarter-hour, Perceval and her sister were ensconced in a small chamber with twin couches. It was warmer here, the walls heavily draped except alongside the wide, glazed window. There was a big desk and a fainting bench, and a dresser and a wardrobe for all the things they did not own. The furnishings were russet and brown accented here and there with white and yellow, pleasant and durable. A small heater glowed in the corner, making the room cozy.

Rien set Gavin on the back of the desk chair and sank down on the couch closer to the door. Perceval crossed to the window and pressed her hands against it. The glass was the same temperature as the air inside; double or triple glazed, then, and if she angled her head she could see light reflecting off the other panes. Where her shadow blocked the interior lights, she could see through. She stared down the long snow-frosted bank to the black lake below, the ice-sheathed trees beyond shimmering in the first gray mirrored light of morning, and waited for Rien's wrath to crest.

"You lied to me," Rien said.

"I edited," Perceval admitted. "But it came out well enough, didn't it?"

"You implied you knew him, that he would take us in."

Rien had not had her symbiont yet when the conversation occurred. She could not possibly recall it accurately. Perceval herself did not remember what it had been like to live solo, but she knew enough Means to have an idea of their confusion, the muddy imperfection of their thoughts. She wondered if that was already receding for Rien, if Rien had noticed how crisp new memories were in comparison. "I said it was not presumptuous for his daughters to call on him in time of need."

"Space you," Rien said, and Perceval laughed. And then Rien caught on and laughed, too. "Already done, huh?"

"Yes, rather." Perceval put her back to the polycarbonate and leaned against it. With a shudder, she realized she could feel the glass against the feathers of the parasite wings. They were infiltrating her nervous system. Becoming part of her in truth.

There was a twinge of pain. She looked down. She was twisting a shadow feather between her fingers; the feather tore free, and its edges sliced her hand. "Dammit."

She dropped the feather on the floor and licked the blood from her thumb. The cut sealed itself, a thin blue line in her flesh, and she let her hands fall and knot in the fabric of her trousers.

"So," Rien said, sliding off the couch, "you said that when you challenged Ariane, it was because she was behaving villainously."

Perceval imagined the taste of blood. Ariane's blood. They were safe now, more or less. They had escaped, and if anyone could prevent total war, it was Benedick Conn. It was time to think of other things again. "I'll pay her back, one of these days."

Rien crouched and picked up the feather from the floor. Still hunkered, elbows on her knees, head bent, she said, "So tell me of her villainy."

Perceval stood and stared at her, folded arms and folded wings. And then the hard line of her mouth crumpled, and she smoothed both palms across her stubbled scalp.

"It'll grow," Rien comforted.

"I was thinking of keeping it shorn," Perceval said. "It was vanity." With her head still bowed, she continued. "The story you wish to hear is not in all things a flattering one."

"I don't need to hear Ariane flattered—"

"What about me?" Perceval stared, then, dark eyes and dark lashes in her pale, square face.

And Rien swallowed. The warmth of a flush stung her cheeks. She looked down quickly, as if studying the translucent feather in her hands. A smear of blood stained the tip of the pen azure. She smoothed the vanes; they were unlike any bird's feather she'd ever held.

"Trust in my love," she said, and heard the rustle of Perceval's nod.

"I made a lot of errors." Perceval's voice went thready.

"I forgive them," Rien said. "You said you were on errantry."

"Yes. I don't know what you know of Engine—"

"Nothing," Rien said. She thought of stories, of demons and angels, of cannibals and terrorists. "Nothing upon which I can rely. I have an Engineer in my head now—"

"Hero Ng."

Who was, Rien thought, somewhat shocked and bashful to be called *Hero*. But then she reminded him that he'd earned it with his death, and his embarrassment subsided. "I will not find it tiresome if you explain."

"Just so," Perceval said, and sat down on the floor with a flumph and a fluttering, her long legs bent every which way. "It is incumbent upon the knights of the realm to patrol, to keep peace and enforce the rule of law as far as our domaine's influence stretches. We also go out looking for damage, and mend it where it can be mended. We do not travel the same route in the same order always, so none may know too far in advance when or where we shall be, and so that we may provide maintenance to little-habited areas. But by the same token, it is good to know the inhabitants, who can be trusted and who will look for any advantage. Some of them . . ." She bit her lip, as if remembering suddenly that Rien had been a Mean herself, a week since. "Rien, would you reach me down a drink, please? If I am meant to talk through to supper?"

"Hardly so long," Rien said. But she stood, and tucked the feather into her pocket, and from a decanter on the desk poured two squat cups of wine, darker red than her own blood had been until recently. "Here."

She sat again, closer this time, and Perceval took the drink with gratitude. "In this case, I came upon something that demanded an intervention."

"Ariane was doing something horrible."

"Ariane was disciplining one of her followers."

"And you intervened?"

"It's a funny thing," Perceval said into her wine cup. "I was led upon her. By a man of Engine, who said the person she was preparing to space was his paramour, and thus through conjugal rights, at least in technicality, under my protection."

"And you challenged her to protect this person." Rien stuck her free hand under her thigh, so that she would not give in to the urge to reach out and stroke Perceval's.

Perceval seemed oblivious. "It seemed like a good idea."

"Yes," Gavin said from his perch on the chair back. "Until your neurons fired."

Perceval flinched and then laughed. "You're not easy to like, Sir Cutting-Torch."

"How fortunate that I have so many other uses."

"Your story," Rien reminded, when Perceval's smile had dropped away and she sat again, staring into her cup as if engrossed. She didn't look up this time, but Pinion bowed forward, and the flight edges of trailing primaries brushed her face, as if in comfort. Perceval did not seem to notice, but the gesture made Rien shudder.

She would not care to be comforted by such a thing.

Or would she? Because there in her head was Hero Ng; aware, willing, his colony subservient to hers. The set of him had become encompassed in the set of her. Was this what Ariane had felt when she consumed her father, soul and memory?

Rien could only imagine it was so.

But surely that was different than Pinion.

"It was only after I'd challenged her that I realized I'd been lured into combat. And with whom." Perceval shrugged. "The battle is not always to the just."

She fell to swirling her wine moodily, and Rien thought she might have said more, but the door rattled under a tap and the moment was lost.

"Come in," Rien said. She hadn't even tasted the wine; she did so now, making a face at sour and tannin and then surprised by the flush of round flavors that followed. It went to her head, too, as if the fumes alone were intoxicating. She was still blinking when the door cracked open, and then fell wide.

It was Benedick. More casually dressed now in plain trousers and a pullover; his feet enormous in black slippers sporting skew eyes and draggled bunny ears. "May I come in?"

"I'll get you a glass," Rien said, standing. Not yet unsteadily; at least her dizziness was fleeting.

"No," he said. "Please. Actually, I must speak to my, to . . . Sir Perceval. Rien, you have the freedom of the grounds—"

"Alone," she said. "Of course. I'll just give myself a little self-guided tour. And find the facilities."

"Thank you," he said, in a manner that turned it into an apology. He glanced at the basilisk pretending to sleep on the chair, and then back at Rien. "If you don't mind—"

"Come on, Gavin," she said. "We're being evicted."

He rose into the air with a shaking of wings made more imposing by the confined space. The impact of his landing on Rien's fist drove her arm down as if she had been struck, but then he settled himself quite prettily and flipped his feathers into order.

She took the glass with her. Neither she nor Gavin had spilled a drop. And as the door shut behind her, she wondered where in her father's house he meant her to go.

She rather thought this was a test.

Rien recollected the way back to the entrance hall. Her newly perfect recall laid it out for her like a map. But who would she find there, except her father's mute servitors, and perhaps—if she wandered far afield—the major-domo? She sipped wine and thought.

"Go find the kitchen and steal breakfast," Gavin suggested.

Rien narrowly avoided snorting wine out her nose, positive that it had been his intention. "It'll be at least a week before I'm that high-handed in Benedick's house." She glanced down the hallway. "But I think I can find Tristen's room. Wasn't he led off this way?"

"Two down," Gavin said. "I can smell him."

"Thank you." Rien squared herself before the door in question, and realized too late that she hadn't a hand free for knocking. She was about to perform some complicated dance with cup and basilisk, but Gavin's head darted out

on its long smooth neck and the curve of his upper beak
hammered the door precisely, thrice.

And a moment later, the door swung open. Tristen
stood before her, a pair of scissors in one hand, his beard
cropped raggedly on one side. "Rien," he said. "Come in."

"Benedick threw me out so he could talk to *his
daughter*," she said, and stepped inside before Tristen shut
the door.

He sighed. "I'm sorry. I was in the middle—"

"Carry on." His room was smaller than the one she
shared with Perceval, the color scheme cool blues. There
was only one daybed. She sank down upon it. Gavin
hopped off her hand and went to perch on the footrail,
the mattress dimpling under his talons as he waddled
across the spread. He looked completely ridiculous.

Rien drank her wine and made herself watch Tristen
peering in the mirror. He had scissors and a bowl of water
that steamed a little, a ceramic-bladed plastic razor no different from any razor Rien has ever used, and he was fas-
tidiously trimming the coarse chalky spirals of his beard
close to his chin.

When that was done, he wet the ragged remainder
with a soaked towel, then rubbed soap into it, rinsed his
hands in the water, and picked up the razor. While he in-
spected the edge, without turning, he said, "There's more
wine on the credenza."

"Thank you," she said. "I'm good."

"Would you pour me a glass?"

"It is my lot in life to serve," she said. But then, he
wouldn't understand the irony at all, would he? She got
up, realizing that she had grown unsteady, and brought

him a glass. Apparently, Benedick thought Tristen rated the good crystal.

She set the glass at his elbow while he scraped the razor along his jaw, pausing long enough to smile at her in the mirror before she backed away. She sat back on the bed, dizzy with the unaccustomed alcohol. "Well," she said, "we're here."

"And in good order," he said, between swipes of the blade. He turned his face to inspect his cheek in the light, and gave it one more pass.

"What are we going to do?"

"Coming here was your plan, wasn't it?"

"Perceval's." Although Rien had been party to it, throughout. "And mine."

Tristen set the blade down, picked up the towel again, and buried his face in it. Through steaming cloth, he said, "We're going to stop the war. And remove Ariane from power."

Rien drew her knees up, sitting bent forward between her legs with her arms wrapped. "How are we going to do that?"

"I am eldest." Tristen set the towel down. He had a fair sharp face, now that it was revealed. Planes and angles, pointed ears and a pointed chin. He looked less like Benedick without the beard, though the sameness remained around the eyes. "While I live, I am rightfully Commodore, now that Father is gone."

"But Ariane ate your father. She has his memories. She's taken his place."

"I know," Tristen said, and touched the hilt of his

broken blade. "I think Perceval will have something to say about that, don't you?"

"Well, maybe." Rien bit her lip, wondering how much to tell him. And then he turned and offered the scissors, handle first.

"Come cut my hair," he said. "Please."

"I'm drunk," she said, and he laughed.

"Just take twenty centimeters off the bottom and try to get it straight across. And tell me what you mean by maybe, brother's daughter."

She took the scissors and studied him. "You'll have to sit. You're too tall." The last of her wine went down with a gulp as he turned the chair around, and then she gave him the glass to set aside and took the comb he gave her in exchange. Carefully, she began to comb out his hair. It was softer than it looked, its weight pulling curls that might otherwise have been as tight as her own into waves. "What I mean by maybe, is, I think we're being mani . . . manipulated."

"You're not that drunk," he said. In the mirror, she could see his eyes were closed.

His hair was as smooth as she could make it, and with the curl and the braid, it wouldn't matter too much if she made the edges ragged. She laid the comb on his thigh, tugged a section of hair taut with her left hand, and halfway up his back began to snip. "Perceval fought with Ariane, and Ariane took her prisoner."

"And treated her dishonorably."

"But Ariane was exactly where Perceval would find her. And doing something that would ensure Perceval would challenge her. And just to ensure the action—she was led upon the crime."

"Suspicious," Tristen admitted. His hair was damp; it made the cutting easier.

Rien parted out another section and drew it straight, measuring it against the first cut. "It gets better."

He lifted his chin, and even when speaking kept his neck straight and his head still. Another lock as long as her forearm dropped to the floor. "Elaborate."

"Perceval was carrying a virus when she was captured. One that incapacitated her after we escaped. And that I also caught."

"Not a deadly virus."

"Very deadly," Rien said, finally articulating the thought she'd not quite been able to force herself to accept. She wouldn't think of Jodin, or of Head. "To a Mean. It laid both of us out, even with treatment. I think it was an influenza."

"Someone used her as a vector."

Rien nodded, her jaw muscles aching with the strain of holding back tears, and severed another lock of Tristen's hair. "Half of Rule could be dead by now."

"I understand." He snaked a hand back, caught her wrist, and squeezed. "Rien, I believe you."

"It's a conspiracy," she said, between small snips to get the edge even. She stepped back. He shook his hair out, and it fell around his shoulders like a rippled cloak.

"Yes," Tristen answered. "I do believe you are right. And I also believe we should have some more wine now. Don't you?"

"If you'll tell me how you got locked away," she said, greatly daring to lay a hand on his shoulder.

He met her eyes in the mirror.

It was full light when Rien returned—alone, for Gavin had gone out exploring. Perceval slept curled tight around a pillow, sheathed in Pinion as if in a clamshell, both fists pressed against her chin, the blankets draped haphazardly. She wore an open-backed nightgown Rien had never seen, too white to have come traveling with them.

Her father must have brought it for her.

Rien wrapped her arms around herself. The flush of alcohol was already fading; she didn't know if that was because it had taken so little to intoxicate her or because her symbiont filtered her blood. She thought of Tristen, the glide of his razor along the edge of his jaw, and reached out and stroked Perceval's scalp, the soft stubble prickling her fingers.

She felt Pinion watching, but the parasite wings permitted her touch.

It was a kind of opposite, wasn't it? Tristen couldn't wait to shave the beard away, and here was Perceval, all shorn like a sheep, and defiant with it. Rien thought she could shave Perceval's head for her, too. If Perceval would let her.

With a rustle, Pinion unfolded. But not violently. Rather, like the wings of the sleepy pigeons Rien had once tended in their cote, before the job was handed down to a younger Mean. Perceval's head moved under Rien's hand.

She turned and blinked drowsily, brown eyes made enormous by the unrelieved bones of her face.

"Is it time to get up?"

"No," Rien said, and kissed her.

She looked hard, but her mouth was tender. Rien cupped her face in both hands, feeling skin—soft, with rough patches, the hard oval of a blemish. Perceval's mouth was wet, resilient. So much more yielding than Mallory's.

The kiss tasted of bitter sleep, the sourness of the wine. Something brought by each of them.

Rien's heart pounded as if she had just walked out of a sauna. Perceval's long hands lay flat against her shoulders; without touching, Pinion unfolded, arched over them and crossed behind Rien's back, a sort of bower. For an instant, Perceval kissed her back, and the beating wings were in Rien's bosom.

And then Perceval slid her hand around, pressed her fingertips to Rien's chest beneath her collarbone, and gently levered her away. "No," she said, softly. "Rien, I'm sorry. I'm fallow. Asexed. I don't want this."

"You're female." Not like Head, Rien meant to say. But Head might be dying or already dead, half the world away. And somebody had used Perceval to do it.

She had kissed Rien back. And so Rien leaned down, as if she would kiss Perceval again, because she hurt so, and was so lonely, and because she loved Perceval as she had not known that she could love. And was stopped by no more than the pressure of Perceval's hand.

"Being male or female has nothing to do with desire."

"You don't want me."

"I don't want anyone," Perceval said. Rien stepped back, still half drunk and groggy with wakefulness, and watched Perceval rise. She crossed to the window and threw the drapes open with a flick of wingtips. "Desire is a distraction from duty. I prefer to be celibate."

Rien pressed the back of her hand to her mouth. Her lips still tingled. "But you could get it fixed."

Fixed. Like a cat. Rien was ashamed as soon as she'd said it.

"I could," Perceval said. "But then I would not be me."

"I love you," Rien said, hopelessly. And Perceval turned back, framed between the patterned russet drapes, and grasped and squeezed Rien's hand.

"I love *you*," she answered. Then she tugged Rien's arm, bringing her around to the window, where they could stand side by side, watching the suns' reflected light filter through the black trees beyond. "Where did you go?"

"To see Tristen," Rien said. She leaned against Perceval's side, and Perceval let her. She had been the strong one; she had been the savior. And now they were in Perceval's place, and any salvation would have to be Perceval's. "What did your father want?"

Perceval turned to her, and Rien already knew her well enough to hear the conversation they let pass unspoken. "Our father," Perceval could have said, and Rien could have answered, "He doesn't think so," and that would not have been exactly true, any of it.

And so Perceval said, "To apologize." When she shrugged, her parasite wings brushed the ceiling. She jerked her eyes at the arch of them, a gesture that managed to include her maiming, her shorn hair, and maybe the world.

Rien could not imagine a member of the Conn family seeking forgiveness. Even if she had seen a portion of Benedick's apology with her own eyes.

Well, perhaps Tristen. But Tristen was different.

And Tristen was theirs. Hers and Perceval's. After a fashion. "Tristen and I think the whole thing was planned. That you were meant to be a sacrifice."

"Father agrees. He said he wondered what might have happened if Ariane had killed and devoured me. If there was another virus in me; if I am poisoned more ways than one."

She said it so plainly, as if the words sent no pang to her heart. Perhaps the pain they caused Rien was pain enough for both. Rien was still considering that when Perceval continued, "Did you and Tristen have any suspicion *who* might be behind it?"

"Somebody who hates Rule," Rien said. "And doesn't like you very much either."

"Or doesn't like Benedick."

"He's had longer to collect enemies," Rien admitted, and was glad when Perceval laughed. "Tristen told me about the . . . about how his blade got broken. Twenty years ago, he thinks."

"What can shatter an unblade?"

"Another unblade," Rien said.

"But there aren't that many—oh. Ariane." She paused. "But why trap him there? Why not kill him? Why not . . ."

"Eat his colony, then?"

Perceval nodded, her throat working as she swallowed.

"If she had him in her head, the old Commodore might have noticed. And she wasn't ready to take *him* on."

"So she hoarded him," Perceval said, sickly. "Like a wasp hoards paralyzed spiders."

"It's amazing that he's as sane as he is."

"We're a tough family." Perceval fiddled with her fingers. "There's something else. When Pinion kidnapped me"—the shadow wings rustled—"it, or someone speaking through it, professed love for me. Someone named Dust claimed me."

Rien thought about what Perceval had just said, about celibacy and duty. She felt Perceval's tension, the loathing she would not let show in her face but couldn't keep out of the set of her shoulders. "I won't let that happen."

"Still," Perceval said. "If you need to keep secrets from me, so the wings don't hear, I understand—what's that?"

She pointed. Outside, the day grew brighter. Achingly bright. Eye-searing, red-white, like staring into the unfiltered suns. When Rien raised a hand to draw the drapes, she saw the bones of her hand.

"Shit." Shutters would be gliding over windows on the dayside, even now. It was just a flare, she thought. Or Hero Ng thought for her, and even in the midst of her fear she wondered how long it would be before she stopped remembering that.

And if it wasn't only a flare, they would know soon enough, and there was nothing she could do about it.

"These suns were never stable," Rien said, with Hero Ng's conviction. "And they are dying now."

17

shipwreck star

Tho' much is taken, much abides;
and tho'
We are not now that strength
which in old days
Moved earth and heaven, that which
we are, we are,—

—ALFRED, LORD TENNYSON,
"Ulysses"

In the fullness of time, Jacob Dust went forth to hunt. Because he could, and because it was convenient, and because he liked the high Gothic poetry of it, he went as a cloud of mist, trailing soft streamers along the bulkheads, insinuating questing tendrils into poorly sealed chambers. Not all the *Jacob's Ladder*'s airtight locks had survived hundreds of years voyaging, and then in orbit around the shipwreck stars. A waystar, the then-Captain had called it, as if they would pause here only to refresh themselves and then press on.

That had been half a millennium before. Nothing, a flicker of time, less than the flutter of an eye.

Long enough for Dust and his brother angels and the human Engineers to repair everything in the world that could be repaired. Long enough for a pair of suns to finish dying.

It was time.

Dust did not know how long they had, but he did know that events were rising to a crisis. His brothers and he would have to find a way to rejoin if the *Jacob's Ladder* was ever to be spaceworthy again. In the end, he thought it would come down to him and Samael, maybe Asrafil as well. He hoped to finish Asrafil before Asrafil realized the time had come to fight. He wasn't sure he liked his odds.

Asrafil, after all, had been the death of Metatron.

Like queen bees awakened in the hive, one of them would consume the rest. It all came down to who was going to be the last demiurge standing.

Dust intended to be that survivor. And he knew he was not yet ready to face the brothers who were more nearly his equals.

They all sprang from one source; in the breaking time, when systems were failing, there had been no structure aboard large enough to contain all Israfel. And so that first core of the ship had broken itself into chunks and shards small enough to survive. And those shards had adapted, learned, and protected the world in their varied manners.

A great deal had been lost, even so, of Israfel. It saddened Dust to think too long of that shattered being of whom Dust was the memory and, he thought, the last true echo.

But there were lesser remnants of Israfel in the world. It was those he hunted now.

They tended to lie low, inadequate fragments though they were. No matter how pathetic, everything that had spun out from Israfel had a sense of identity. And each of those things felt the drive to self-preservation. They would fight their return to the reconstructed core. Even humble things could crave existence.

Dust craved it more.

He found a trail among the ant colonies. These corridor walls were comprised of sheets of transparent material from floor to ceiling. Between those panels was a transparent gelatin, colored in rainbow sequence from section to section—red, orange, yellow, green, blue, violet. The gelatin was a nutrient medium and a habitat both, but it was not the only option; some of the colony chambers contained leafy plants, growing from a different substrate.

In each section were networks of tunnels, and through them scurried busy insects, divided by color and size into colonies of brownish and reddish and citron-amber and glossy black—and the most beautiful of all, with russet bodies and leaf-green heads and abdomens, like something carved by minute hands from variegated jade.

There were other insects also, but Dust preferred the ants. He enjoyed their industry and their loveliness. And he approved of the industry of the keeper of this domaine, as well.

The farmer of the ants knelt in a side corridor, hard at work with silicon sealant. She had scraped clean the cracked surface of one of the walls and was carefully drying it with a handheld heater, long dreadlocks falling over her shoulder. One of them was kinked, and stuck out crooked.

Dust reached out to stroke it back in among the rest.

She startled as he solidified, but did not drop the heater. Instead she rocketed to her feet, leaving him with one knee dropped in a crouch. "Jacob," she said, glaring down her nose with an attempt at haughtiness.

"Shakziel," he replied. He rolled the syllables of her name across his newly reformed tongue, a sort of caress. "Have you seen the skies?"

"Why would I care for the skies?" She patted the wall of the ant farm. "My work is mostly of the underground sort."

"The waystar reaches out a bloody arm. We must all be ready to work together, soon."

"I am ready. I report to Samael. Biosupport is his sphere of influence."

"Because where else would you put the Angel of Poison?" It was a rhetorical question.

She folded her heater away and stowed it as he stood. "You are not welcome here."

"That is quite reasonable," he said, and in love and brotherhood consumed her.

She never had a chance, not really. As soon ask a sapling to stand against the axe.

When he was done, he settled into himself—no larger in appearance, but more in substance. And then, resplendent in his magpie-silver waistcoat and black suit, he knelt where Shakziel had knelt down before him. He groped after her tube of sealant.

Meticulously, he began to affect repairs.

*　　　　*　　　　*

In the morning, when at last they lay down and pretended sleep across the space between couches, Rien touched the feather to her lips and breathed across it.

It did not smell like Perceval.

She tucked it under the pillow, and left it there.

18

his harness and his promises

Because these wings are no longer
wings to fly
But merely vans to beat the air

—T. S. ELIOT, "Ash Wednesday"

Rien must have slept eventually, for when Perceval
awakened she was facedown in her pillow, snoring
slightly. Perceval, shaking herself free of Pinion and
swinging her legs over the lip of the couch, looked at her
fondly. Did anyone sleep the way people were shown to
sleep in dramas, tidily and composed?

Perceval would have bent down and kissed Rien on
the forehead, but her kiss would not have meant what
Rien needed it to, and she did not wish to cause more grief
than needful. Instead, she knuckled sleep from her eyes,
dressed as silently as possible, and padded barefoot into
the hall.

She'd lost weight, which was only to be expected. She
curled her toes on the flooring, a patterned carpet runner,
and could see bones and tendons and indigo veins sliding

beneath the blue-tinged skin. As if in answer to the thought, her stomach grumbled.

Well, that was a direction, at least. With Pinion fanning on her shoulders, she rose on tiptoe and rotated slowly, breathing deeply, searching the scent of breakfast—or dinner, as the case might be. Overall, she suspected it was probably closer to dinnertime.

And she did smell something sweet and grainy, like hot cereal, or baking bread. She followed that aroma, not back through the entrance hall but in the opposite direction, deeper into her father's house. The corridor was chill; she barely felt it. She had been cold so much of late that she wondered if she would ever notice cold again.

But that scent, and the scent of coffee, drew her on. She wondered if she had somehow slept the clock 'round, but her internals assured her that it was only a little after sixteen hundred. Voices hummed on the air, one of them unmistakably Benedick's baritone, but the words were indistinguishable in echoes. They led her in the same direction as the smell of coffee.

Eventually she came through a door that looked decorative but was most likely an air seal waiting to fall, and she paused.

She had expected a dining room, dishes laid on the sideboards or brought by bustling servants. Instead, what she found was a sunny small room, the walls clear yellow and the trim cheerful orange. There was a circular table big enough for six, and Benedick and Tristen—his chin shaven and his hair trimmed halfway down his back—sat at the ten and two positions, their backs to the window, bowls and cups before them.

Perceval saw a different view from this side of the house: apple trees, their roots humped under the snow, and what must be an airy glade when this side of the world was not frozen. A red bird no bigger than Perceval's hand flitted from branch to branch, whistling. The flare must be over: the light seemed normal, and other senses told her the background radiation was falling off.

"Rien says the suns are dying," Perceval said. She pulled out a chair and sat, a little forward to make room for Pinion behind her.

"Her father's daughter," Tristen said. Benedick shook his head, faintly smiling, so Perceval wasn't certain if the dig was directed at her or at him—or even if it was meant to be a dig at all.

Perceval cleared her throat. "What's for breakfast?"

Tristen rose and fetched a cup from the cabinet. The coffee was on the table in a carafe, and Perceval poured her own and doctored it with soy milk and honey.

Benedick said only, "How does Rien know?"

As she was drinking her coffee and explaining about Hero Ng (Benedick and Tristen shared a significant glance when Perceval told them about Mallory), a bowl of oatmeal appeared at her elbow. The necessities of honey and cinnamon and salt and more soy milk occupied her hands for a moment. She had barely even registered the presence of the resurrectee servant who left it there.

She finished the story and the oatmeal at close to the same time, and pushed the bowl away. "It sounds as if Hero Ng has been expecting this for a long time. Since the end of the moving times. These suns have always been unstable."

"Then why bring the world here?" Tristen asked. No doubt a rhetorical question, and none looked more shocked than he when it was answered.

"Because at the time there was no choice."

The voice was deep, gravelly, harsh as if with over- or underuse. Benedick was on his feet before the speaker finished, a pistol in one hand and a dagger in the other. Tristen remained seated, seemingly languid, the drape of his hand and wrist across the tablecloth unchanged. But Perceval could feel the electricity in him. That air of repose was no more reliable than a hunting cat's.

As for herself, she set her coffee down—it was laced with cardamom, and she harbored intentions of finishing every mouthful—and slowly pushed her chair out to stand. She furled Pinion tight when she turned, so as not to interfere with her father's or her uncle's line of sight or line of fire.

And when she turned, she saw—a man.

A small man, all out of proportion with the voice. His blond hair hung lank on either side of a long, lined face, and his nose looked like it had been repeatedly broken. Perceval blinked. She wasn't sure she'd ever seen someone so fascinatingly ugly.

He wore a dove-gray morning coat and no shirt, and his feet were as bare as Perceval's and far hornier. "I am Samael," he said, "the Angel of Biosystems. And I am afraid the ghost of Hero Ng is quite correct. It is *really* time we were going."

"Not to seem rude," Benedick said, without lowering his weapon, "but amicable relations would be easier established should you reveal how you came to enter my house."

Samael paused, pale locks threaded through both gnarled hands as he pushed his hair behind his ears, earrings and finger-rings glinting. "Like this," he said, and vanished like a switched-off light.

Involuntarily, Benedick stepped forward. And Tristen stepped to the side, flanking him. Perceval craned her neck; surely there was meant to be some sort of a special effect when a person disappeared, a flash of light or a pop of air. Not a simple, crisp vanishment.

And then Samael reappeared, over by the cabinets this time and wearing a green damask greatcoat and a pair of sooty wings that—unlike Pinion—trailed off through the wall.

"You're a projection," Perceval said.

Samael clicked his tongue. "Close." He opened a cabinet door and shut it again, ran ticking fingernails over the cherrywood finish, and then picked up a coffee cup and held it out, handle-first, toward Tristen. "If I may presume?"

Tristen took it cautiously, a long lean and reach. He filled it with coffee and handed it back.

"Thank you," Samael said, and sipped.

And Benedick looked sidelong at Tristen and holstered his weapons.

"Thank you," Samael said. "You only would have shot holes in your paneling, anyway. Technically, I am a distributed machine intelligence, in specific the entity charged with maintaining the habitability of the vessel you call the world. That habitability is in serious danger,

and along with it, your lives. What you see before you"—
with a flick of his hand, he forestalled Benedick, whatever
might have been Benedick's question—"is in fact a sort of
hologram, an avatar animated through the refraction of
light. *I*, Samael, am all around you."

A quick caress stroked Perceval's cheek, though she
saw nothing. From Tristen's flinch, he felt the same, and
though Benedick remained unmoved, his eyes narrowed.

"Samael—" Tristen said.

Samael forestalled him with an upraised hand. "I am
here for the princess. Sir Perceval, you must know that
everything I say to you, Dust hears. Your neck is bent to
his yoke for all to see."

Pinion flapped once, so Perceval felt the air move between the feathers and feared a paroxysm of bating.
Nevertheless, she said, "Can you get it off of me? I care
not for his harness, or his promises."

"I cannot, princess," he said. "Not without consuming
it, and I think by now it is too firmly integrated with your
symbiont to do so without consuming you, as well."

"It told me Dust loved me," she said. "It told me he
meant to marry me."

"I am sure he means to," Samael said. "We will see that
he doesn't, won't we, gentlemen?"

It was gratifying, Perceval thought, that Benedict fell
back and Tristen glided around the edge of the room to
stand at her side. She felt warded, and it made her strong.
It would have made her stronger to think that they would
honor the authority the angel gave her, and place her in
the lead. But when Benedick cleared his throat, the look
Samael gave him was conspiratorial, the gesture placating.

It made Perceval want to bite them both.

She cast about for something to say, an attempt to re-assert control, and came up with a question. "Why would anybody name the Angel of Life Support for poison?"

Samael drained the last of his coffee and crunched an idle bite from the cup. Whatever, it seemed all the same to him, except the noise of the chewing. He tilted his head as if listening, which made Perceval hope she had asked well. "Because there is no old Hebrew word for mutagen."

"So you're not *just* charged with maintaining the world in a habitable state, are you? You're the Angel of Evolution, too. Or something like it." Benedick shifted be-hind her, but he did not interrupt. And there was Tristen, crooked in the corner, were he could have the wall at his back and watch her and Samael and Pinion all at once.

"Something," Samael said. However ugly his avatar might be, the smile it wore was absolutely dazzling. While she was considering her next question, he finished the last two bites of his coffee cup.

Somehow she managed not to look to her father for re-assurance. "Can an angel be imperfectly honest?"

"An angel can be whatever it is created to be," Samael said, with perfect frankness. "Humans are the only ani-mals that intentionally, methodically change themselves. Well, unless you count a queen ant twisting off her wings, but I think you'll agree it's hardly the same thing." He dusted his hands together. "I am going to have to tell you a story."

Perceval broke. She looked at Benedick; Benedick nod-ded and pointed to the table and the chairs. In another flicker of light, Samael was seated; the other three joined him a little less tidily, Benedick seating Perceval and Perceval choosing not to make a fuss about it. She sipped cold coffee while he reclaimed his chair, and waited for Samael to speak.

"The world has a name," he said. "Its name is *Jacob's Ladder*."

"I know," said Perceval. "It's painted on the side."

Samael laughed, but it was the flicker of Tristen's smile that Perceval had been after. He put his elbows on the table and his chin on the backs of his fingers. Again, the deceptive air of repose.

She drank more coffee and watched the poison angel.

Samael said, "Do you know the purpose of a generation ship?"

"Colonization," Benedick said, while Perceval was still mulling her answer. He warmed his coffee cup, refilled Tristen's, and poured the last of the carafe for Perceval. "To carry men among the stars in search of new worlds. It's slow."

"Generations," Samael said dryly. And then, when Benedick nodded touché, continued, "Does that time in flight need to be wasted time?"

Perceval thought about what he had said, about ants twisting off their wings. "You could use it for breeding programs, couldn't you?"

"You could design whatever you wanted," he said. His sooty wings had vanished; she had not noticed exactly when. He shifted in his chair, adjusting the drape of the greatcoat skirts around his legs. "Forced evolution. Mankind by design. Do you know what a Jacob's ladder is?"

"A toy," she said, and he frowned at her.

"It is the ladder that angels climb to reach Heaven," he said. "It is the hard path to exaltation."

"Exalt," she said, tasting the word as if for the first time. "Mean. Forced evolution. The world is a—"

"Hothouse. Laboratory. With experiments and controls."

She realized her tongue tip protruded from her mouth in concentration, like a child's. She sucked it back into her mouth and gnawed her upper lip.

"And then something goes wrong," Perceval said. "Catastrophically wrong."

"You limp to the nearest star." Samael's bottled-up grin revealed delight in her detective work, even if she was only chasing the trail of crumbs he laid her.

Despite herself, she liked that smile. "Even if it's not a very good star."

"Beggars can't be choosers," he said. He sat back and folded his arms with a satisfied air. "If they wish to live. And once one thing has gone wrong, failures cascade. Command and Engineering have differing ideas of how to proceed. The passengers have their own plans. The tame God of the world, the guiding intelligence, cannot maintain itself as a gestalt, and splinters into demiurges, each with a field of interest and a span of control."

"They don't talk much," Perceval said, hoping to make him laugh again. "If you're the demiurge of evolution, Samael, then what is Dust?"

"The demiurge of memory. The angel of the data bank, the holographic memory crystal, and the standing wave. The angel of knowing where you have been."

"But you obviously remember some things."

"From after the fragmentation." He patted her hand; she tried not to feel patronized. "Or relearned since."

"And you and Dust don't agree."

"We agree on what is to be done," Samael said. "We've all been working for centuries to repair, reinforce, and protect the world as much as possible. As have the Engineers."

It was flattery, but it was also accurate. Perceval nodded.

Samael continued, "We differ on how to do it."

Tristen put his hand over the one of Perceval's that Samael had patted. Benedick sat back in his chair, arms folded, listening. Tristen said, "And over who should be in charge?"

"If you are going to reconstruct the ship's gestalt mind," Samael said apologetically, "somebody is going to have to get eaten. I'm sure you can understand my position."

"And so there was discord in Heaven," Benedick said. "You wish to thwart Dust."

"I do."

Pinion stirred against Perceval's shoulders. Fiercely, silently, she shushed it, and through some miracle it subsided. "And how could I help you, Samael?"

"That's easy," Samael said. "Don't marry him. Choose me."

19

the monster who rules

He said the one he murdered once
still loves him;
He said the wheels in wheels of time
are broken;
And dust and storm forgotten;
and all forgiven . . .

—CONRAD AIKEN, *The House of Dust*

Rien woke to Tristen shaking her. She blinked muzzily, protesting, but as soon as she caught his wrist he relented. In a melodrama, he would have had one hand over her mouth to silence her, but apparently he didn't care if she shouted. And so she didn't, and didn't panic either. "Come to the dining room," he said, and stepped into the hall so she could dress in privacy.

She was grateful that he waited. She had no idea of the way, and wherever Gavin had gone off to, he had not yet returned. He might be on his way back to Mallory, but she didn't think he would leave her without a farewell.

She hoped, anyway.

"What happened?" she asked when she caught up with Tristen in the hall. His hair was pulled back in a ponytail, revealing the fine blue-tinted points of his ears, but he'd missed a few wisps that curled this way and that.

As they walked, he told her—efficiently, a soldier's report—about Samael and his brief history of the world.

"He's trying to force Perceval to marry him? Did he say why? He's not even a real person. Can a machine intelligence marry?"

"Well," Tristen said, "she is a Conn. And has a better claim on the chair than even I have, by primogeniture. If she were Commodore, or stood close to the Captain's chair, then he would have a legal link to it."

"Space," Rien said. "Is that why they're squabbling over her? They're trying to marry an heir to the throne? I'm sorry, Tristen, but that's like some medieval play."

"I suspect there's more to it." He sounded both amused and angry; a glance at his expression confirmed her opinion. "But Samael isn't telling."

She blew through her teeth. "And I thought the Exalts were horrible."

She was happy, she thought, to have Tristen in her family. He was more like Oliver Conn than like Ariane. Instead of reminding her that he was Exalt, and so was she, thank you kindly, he chuckled mournfully and sucked his lip.

"And do we believe him?" she asked, when they had paused in the hall so Tristen could straighten her collar.

He shrugged. "An excellent question."

They came up on the dining room doorway. He rested

his hand on her shoulder in reassurance or to keep her from bolting.

She stepped into the room.

Benedick and Perceval were seated side by side at a round, heavy-looking table. Across from them was a slight man, not too tall, who hunkered forward like a vulture on a branch. All three glanced up as Tristen and Rien entered. The resurrectee servant who was laying another place at the table did not.

The one who must be Samael stood and made as if to bow over Rien's hand. She kept it firmly at her side, and over his shoulder saw Perceval smile at her. *Bull by the balls*, she thought, and looked the Angel of Biosystems in the eye before she said, "We're going to have to move the world."

It didn't quite set him back on his heels, and anything he gave away would be intentional, anyway—she wasn't about to forget that he was an animation—but he did nod, and meet her just as directly. "The lady is correct."

"But the world has no engines," she said, and thought: *Oh, Space. He likes me.* Or at least, she imagined that that was what the angel's steady smile meant. She didn't tell him that it was Hero Ng's knowledge he smiled at.

He ushered her away from Tristen, toward the table, and into a seat, which he pulled out for her. She permitted herself to be seated, appreciative that her chair was next to Perceval's, as Samael said, "And perceptive. As you observe, this does present a difficulty. Because first, we are going to have to further repair the world."

Silence greeted his proclamation.

And then Perceval said, as if she had been expecting

Benedick or Tristen to step in, "How do you propose to do that, sir, when all of Engine and all your brothers have been unable to do more than keep the ship alive and patched up for the past half a thousand Solar years?"

"Metatron is dead," Samael said. "And so is Susabo, the Angel of Propulsion. We'll go to Engine, and we will teach them how to heal those wounds."

Rien had to reach out and grab Perceval's forearm to steady herself. "We can't," she said, quick and firm—like Head speaking to the butler. "We have to go to Rule. There's sickness there—"

"Didn't you want to head off the war?"

"How did you know that?"

He touched the lobe of one ear, obviously amused that she had even bothered asking. "Still a demiurge. In any case, your best chance for stopping the fighting is to bring Perceval back to Engine."

"Someone in Engine betrayed her," Rien said, as Tristen put a hand on the table and reminded, "I have business in Rule, as does Sir Perceval."

Benedick nodded. "Business better addressed with an army at your back, brother, if you arrive back in Rule while Ariane is Commodore."

Silence. Rien squeezed Perceval's wrist until Perceval wrapped Rien's fingers in her own much longer ones. Tristen tapped each nail in turn on the tabletop, and Rien looked down. Predictable. The men were ganging up on them.

In the following silence, the servant reappeared. Silent as always, he slid a plate of egg-sub and toast in front of Rien and then slipped away again.

She let go of Perceval's wrist and picked up her fork. Tiredness and frustration aside, she needed the food. She hoped there was more in the kitchen.

"Very well," Perceval said, saving Rien one more time. "We will go to my home in Engine, then."

How quickly the years fall away and the passage of time ceases meaning. We have each a purpose: we are bred to it, engineered for it, or we are drawn to it out of some fathomless innate longing that we cannot explain. Some unlucky few must discover—or create—it on their own, but those are rarer in these days, when by the grace of the forebears we are manufactured to our place in the order of the world.

We have our destinies. We race for them, fight for them, fulfill them.

Or we fail them.

Listen, Perceval. Do you hear your long immortal life stretched out before you, before the stars?

I have so much to teach you, my dear.

The young do not believe in endings. They do not believe in death. They do not believe in time. Everything takes forever to happen, and twenty years is a long time.

Under those circumstances, the apocalypse can seem sexy. Death is a fetish, a taste of the edge.

It is not real.

And so the days are long, and though time holds us green and dying, we cannot yet feel the drag of our chains hauling us forward to the end.

But the old, Perceval. The old have forgiven time. Whatever time you may have is too little. If you live a thousand

years—as I nearly have, and you surely will—it does not mat-
ter. Unless you have given up, laid down your tools, and folded
idle hands to wait, beloved, you will still be in the middle of
something when you die.

The world is a wheel, and we are all broken on it.

And that is fine and just.

For there is never any hurry, until there is no time.

A presence touched Dust's fringes, and a voice spoke from
the vortex of the air. "Musing on the fate of worlds, dear
brother?"

"Asrafil," Dust said. "Well. I greet thee, Angel of Blades.
I was expecting brother Samael."

Dust turned from his contemplation, and coalesced.
Not in his own chambers; less greatly daring than Samael,
perhaps, but Asrafil not chosen to enter Dust's domaine.
They met where their edges brushed, in one of the voids
in the world's great Tinkertoy structure.

Contrary to the epithet, Asrafil carried no weapons.
When he coalesced, he wore an avatar Dust knew of old,
which gave Dust pause for a fraction of a second. Why did
they still wear these human skins, when they so rarely
spoke to humans anymore?

It was in the design, of course. Reflexive.

Part of the program, a kind of junk DNA.

Asrafil's chosen form was that of a man, bird-boned and
frail, without Samael's hard muscularity. His scalp shone
bare, more polished than shaven, and he wore black—
gloves, shoes, an ankle-length wide-lapeled coat like a pillar—that only accentuated his slenderness. He seemed far

too small to be the source of the air of wicked malice that surrounded him, but Dust knew better. "I trust we need not debate the gravity of the situation?"

Dust chose not to acknowledge the pun. The crinkle at the corner of Asrafil's left eye was enough to tell him it was intentional. "You want help."

Inevitable. You never saw your family until they wanted something.

Asrafil smiled, the corners of his mouth lifting to his ears in an expression that was chilling even by angelic standards.

"You know, brother. I did not *murder* Metatron." One long gloved finger tapped his temple, just in the dimple of the sphenoid bone. "I keep him by me, always handy. All is made right: he hasn't left me since we quarreled."

"I am going to assume that was not meant as a threat."

"How can it be a threat, Jacob, when we both know how this must end? If we survive, if we preserve the world, one of us will inevitably subsume the other."

Dust studied his fingernails. The great wheel of the world turned in the suns, shadows drifting across its latticed surfaces. The cold of space was nothing to him, and his avatar would not drift; he was anchored in the invisible fringe of his own being. "You think it shall come down to you and me?"

Asrafil's motionlessness remained unnerving, no matter how long he floated there, arms crossed, head angled slightly. "Already, you snatch Samael's servants away. I should think that a very clear message. How many of the others could stand before either of us? It must be you or me, in the end."

Dust made a noncommittal noise. "I should come out here more often," he said. "Look at that."

That was the suns, entwined in their love that was death, the dominant dwarf partner gleaming like a diamond at the center of its barred accretion disk, the red giant mottled with sullen spots. The luminous hues of the accretion disk were as lovely as any sunset, infrared at the outer edges and stark white at the inner, shading through crimson and vermilion and a lucent orange that pierced Dust to the heart of his aesthetic protocols.

"Gorgeous," Asrafil said. "It is a pity we must leave it."

"It won't be here much longer in any case."

Asrafil nodded and let the silence linger for a little before he filled it. "But in the meanwhile, we each bring certain resources to an association. I think it would behoove us to combine them. We can fight over who gets to be king when we've preserved the kingdom."

"Funny," Dust said. "Samael came to me with a very similar proposal not long ago at all—"

The attack was untelegraphed, but not unexpected. Asrafil struck along Dust's entire leading edge, rending, gnawing, attempting to overwhelm him with a blitz. But Dust had been braced, focused behind his apparent distraction, and when Asrafil tore into him he gave way, fell back, creating a hollow at his center for Asrafil to tumble into.

Asrafil was not fool enough to dive into the trap. He struck out to all sides as Dust stretched around him, and Dust was not large enough to engulf him. They fell together, warring in the silence. Any naked eye would have seen nothing but the emptiness they moved through, their combat invisible and carried out at supersonic speeds. And then, like sparring cats, they broke apart again, dragging their ragged fringes up.

Dust had let his avatar lapse in the skirmish; now, he did not bother to recollect it. Asrafil, too, had fallen apart, and Dust thought they seemed equally bloodied. He tidied himself, tucked his edges in. Pictured Asrafil spitting teeth.

It cheered him.

"That was stupid," Dust said.

"It wouldn't have been if I'd won," Asrafil answered as, with elaborate precautions, they began to disengage.

The wood rang with silence, and Rien was happy to be alone in it for now. She was used to spending time with others, but this enforced closeness wore on her.

She didn't know how big a Heaven could be, but this one had to fill the entire inside of the holde. She wanted to walk alone among the bare black trees, touch the cold bark, feel the snow creak under her boots again. Just for a little while.

She didn't know if she was ever coming back.

And she needed to at least look for Gavin, if they were leaving nearly immediately.

Benedick offered her skis, but she didn't know how to use those, and the snow wasn't really that deep. Just awkward to walk in, when it crushed and slid, and prone to making her ankles and the arches of her feet hurt. It has a smell, too, a distinct one, which she hadn't expected. It was just water, wasn't it?

Gavin left no tracks, so she wandered, trusting that one of them would find the other. Her breath hung on the air, silver in the reflected light. One of the external mirrors was angled just so she half-blinded herself every time she glanced upward, so she quickly broke the habit of looking up. Black birds—big birds—moved among the trees. The silhouettes kept catching her eye and turning her head.

And of course, as soon as she gave up and turned back, calves knotted with the unfamiliar effort, she found him. He perched on a tall stump beside the trail, his tail flipped over his talons, for all the world like an old man sitting, watching the day go by.

"Hey," she said. She leaned her hip against the stump, her elbow atop it, grateful of the excuse to rest.

"Hey," he said. "What's going on?"

"We're getting ready to go to Engine. Are you going back to Mallory?"

"Staying with you, if you'll have me."

"Of course." She didn't even need to think about it. And the words brought an easing of the knot tight in her chest. "Where did you go?"

"Angels don't agree with me."

"Yeah," she said. "They kind of give me indigestion, too."

She made *him* laugh, for a change. And when he stopped, she said, "Gavin. You know a lot of things."

"I am old," he said. And then, wryly: "I contain multitudes. Not vast, however."

She leaned her cheek against his wing, and he let her. "You're a good size for carrying."

He hopped onto her shoulder, as if it had been an invitation. *Well*, Rien thought, questioning her own motives, perhaps it had been.

"Then thank you for carrying me. Now tell me your question."

"Who said I had a—oh, never mind. Yes. My question is, do you know my mother?"

Silence, and then he hmm'd, softly. "We're going to Engine? To seek your mother?"

"No," she said. "But that's where she is, isn't she? That's the whole reason I was born. To be a hostage."

"Not the only reason. But yes, your mother is in Engine."

"Who is she?"

"Your mother is Arianrhod Kallikos," he said. "Does the name mean anything to you?"

She thought hard, and said eventually, "No."

"This is because you are ignorant." She felt his shrug, the rise and fall of his wing. "But ignorance can be remedied with time. She is an Engineer. You will find her interesting."

Interesting wasn't entirely reassuring. "Oh."

"You might meet Perceval's mother, too."

Rien jerked. "We have different mothers?"

"Perceval was a hostage against Alasdair, after all. Her mother is Caitlin Conn."

"There is no—" Rien started. And then she craned her neck way back and stared at Gavin, who sat placidly on her shoulder, eyes closed, waiting for her to finish. If beaks could smirk, she would have sworn him to be smirking. "Who is Caitlin Conn?"

"In Rule, there are three portraits turned to the wall," Gavin said. "Do you know them?"

"I *dusted* them. Or the backs, anyway."

"They are the portraits of Alasdair's treacherous children, the sisters Caithness, Cynric, and Caitlin. His eldest; his initial heirs. They tried to overthrow him, you see."

"So they're dead?"

"Alasdair killed Caithness himself. Cynric was captured and executed."

"Oh." Rien swallowed, her throat feeling abraded. "And Caitlin?"

"Exiled," Gavin said. "To Engine."

"Pregnant with her brother's child?"

"Perceval is your age," Gavin reminded. "What I speak of happened centuries ago. You'll meet Caitlin in Engine, too, most likely," Gavin said. "That is where her exile took her, in the end."

"And what is she there?"

Definitely a smirk. Even if he did it only with the angle of his head. "The Chief Engineer."

20

primogeniture

I would rather be ashes than dust!

—ATTRIBUTED TO
JACK LONDON, "Credo"

"You're the rightful Commodore," Rien said, the words as sensible to Perceval as washers hurled against a window. "Or at least the rightful Commodore's rightful heir."

"I don't understand you." They were in the room they had briefly shared, Gavin perched atop the monitor, watching them pack with his ever-closed eyes. There wasn't much to take, and Perceval occupied herself picking things up and putting them back down again. She tried to comfort herself with the knowledge that she was going home, to imagine her mother's arms around her, her own bed, her own clothes.

It made her sick. She brought the enemy with her, merged with her colony. She was possessed, and her traitor wings embraced her.

She should go off, into the wilds, and take Pinion with her, away from everything she loved. But she did not think she was strong enough to do so.

Perceval turned a carved piece of apple wood in her hands. She smoothed her thumb across its goblin face. Hand-carved, lovingly sanded and polished. Precious material, primitively handled. The contrast pleased her. Rien spoke again.

"You know about your mother—"

"I live with my mother," Perceval said. "In Engine. What does she have to do with anything?"

"She's Alasdair's daughter," Rien said, bouncing on her toes, as excited as if Perceval might not know this. "She's oldest. Older than Benedick or Tristen. Which means with Alasdair dead, *she's* Commodore. And if she doesn't want the job, *you* are. Not Ariane. Not even Tristen."

"Primogeniture is a stupid way to run a starship," Perceval said, sulking. "Anyway, Tristen wants the job. I don't."

"That's not important," Rien said. "Do you see? It explains why—"

"Everybody and his uncle wants to force me to marry." Perceval thumped down on the bed, her hands and the carving resting in her lap. "Space."

"Well, not *our* uncle." Rien sat beside her. They leaned together shoulder to shoulder, sharing warmth. "Tristen wouldn't do that to you."

"Tristen's quite convinced of the power of his own arm," Perceval said. "And his claim is better than Ariane's, which is all that matters. Him, though, I could marry, if I had to."

It was a wrong thing to say. Rien stiffened, and began to rise.

"Come on, Rien. I wouldn't have sex with him."

Rien laughed and settled back, but the ease was gone. Perceval closed her eyes; they would have to sort this out somehow, and she was afraid it wasn't her work to do. She wanted to save Rien from any hurt, but there were some hurts you could rescue no one from.

After a silence, Rien spoke hesitantly. "It doesn't bother you that your parents are siblings?"

"Half-siblings."

"Like us."

And there was the pain again. Perceval draped a wing around Rien's shoulder, remembering too late that it was not her own. "They're Exalt," she said. "They can't *have* damaged children . . . now, anyway."

Rien knew she was thinking of Tristen. But when he was born the technology had not been as advanced as it had become. She said, "So neither would you and Tristen."

"Tristen doesn't want to marry me." *And he might be the only one.* A dark, unworthy thought. She found and squeezed Rien's hand in apology, even if Rien might never know why.

And Rien squeezed her hand back, and let her off the hook. A gesture of generosity. "Besides," Perceval said, trying to make her sister laugh, "primogeniture is a—"

"—stupid way to run a starship." It did get a laugh. A chuckle, anyway. "So if primogeniture is stupid, how do you do it in Engine? Your mother is somebody important, right?"

"Chief Engineer." Perceval chewed her lower lip. "Like Hero Ng was. She was an acolyte of Susabo, but that angel's been dead a long time. Since before we were born. She's very practical." *Like someone else I know.* "You'll like her."

"I can't wait to meet her," Rien said. "Are you packed?"

"Yes," Perceval said. "Are you?"

Really, they'd just been fussing. There was nothing in their packs but a change of clothes and some medical supplies. The rest of the space would be taken up with food.

It was a long walk to Engine.

"Yes." Rien stood. She drew Perceval up by that still-clasped hand. Gavin fluttered, but did not take to the air. "Let's go find something decent to eat before we have to leave, shall we?"

It *was* a long walk, but at least they started it merrily. To Rien's infinite relief, Benedick had left his resurrectee militia behind, so it was only the five of them: two men, two girls, and Gavin.

And Pinion, she supposed, but if Perceval didn't bring that up, Rien wasn't going to.

The bulk of the first day passed uneventfully. They traveled mostly in corridors, crossing one holde that might have been a heaven but now was withered and sere, each step raising a puff of taupe dust from desiccated earth. The irrigation must have failed.

They did not camp the night there, but in the tube beyond. It was one of the inspection arches, a bow rising above the agglomerate, interconnected surface of the world. It was wide enough across for Perceval to spread her wings, and entirely transparent.

Rien stopped as the lock sealed behind her, overcome with vertigo for seconds before her symbiont compensated. Gavin flapped on her shoulder, talons clutching. "Oh."

Perceval stepped back beside her and caught her elbow, bracing her under the heavy pack. Ahead, the men stopped and waited, turning over their shoulders. "Okay?" Tristen said.

"When we were outside, before—" Rien leaned gratefully on Perceval's strength. "I didn't have time to look."

Perceval said nothing, just held her arm and gave her that time. Rien made herself breathe slowly, calmly, and inspect her surroundings one element at a time.

They were in a kind of tunnel-corridor, a transparent tube that lifted away from the dead holde and soared out, reaching on a graceful arc. The world itself hung below, starkly lit; they were above the shadow panels, and Rien could see the photocell surfaces as they turned to the suns.

From here, she could observe the structure of the *Jacob's Ladder*. She'd had a confused idea of lattices and bulbous habitats, of corridors threading asymmetrically over the surfaces of anchores and domaines. Of gray metal and patchy paint. Now she saw the world in all its incomprehensible vastness, like a grandly rotating three-dimensional spiderweb, and the complexity bewildered her. "How did they ever *move* this thing?"

"How are we going to move it, you mean?"

Rien swallowed, and tried not to succumb to Hero Ng's despair or her own awe. "It's huge."

"It's the world," Perceval said. Her parasite wings were bronze in the sunlight, translucent but glittering. She'd let Rien help her shave her head again before they left their father's house, and her scalp was starting, slowly, to match the rest of her in color. "It'll take us five days to walk across. How big did you think it was?"

Rien shook her head and shaded her eyes from the suns. When she peeped at them—quickly, because even with her symbiont's assistance, the glare was far too bright to stare into—she couldn't tell if they were brighter, or closer, or anything. The light that poured over her was austere, the shadows edged like chips of volcanic glass.

There wasn't anything to say. There weren't any words. The urge to say anything, to fill up the silence, welled up in Rien, but she knew it for a petty thing and swallowed it. You could try to speak, try to make your mark on this. But it would only make you look ridiculous and weak.

"Thank you," Rien said when she had looked her fill. The soaring sensation in her belly made her think of when Perceval dived from the air lock holding onto her, and she breathed deeply because she could, and because it felt right. "I can't see the end."

"We have to save this," Perceval said, hushed. Rien thought she didn't need to speak for Perceval to know she agreed.

"Come on," Tristen said, when both girls proved reluctant to break the spell. "Let's find a place to sleep."

They walked in near-silence after that, Gavin clucking to himself occasionally and Perceval maintaining her grip on Rien. As they came down the far side of the arch, she leaned close and said in Rien's ear, "I'm glad you saved me."

Sometimes people said an obvious thing, and what they meant by it wasn't obvious at all. "I'm glad, too."

And then Perceval grabbed her by the arm with both hands and flung her away.

The gravity in the corridor was slight, but definite. Rien half slid, half catapulted into Benedick, who was already turning to catch her. She landed in his arms and he did not fall backward. If he staggered a step, Tristen caught him.

"Stay back." Perceval stood some meters up the arch of the tube, her hands knotted in fists by her thighs, Pinion flaring, bladed, from her shoulders. Between them, Gavin beat wings slowly, hovering in the light gravity like a moth. "Please."

"Perceval—"

"Stay *back!*" Her head dropped, the tendons of her neck ridging as if she strained at some impossible burden. "It's the wings."

Rien might have charged forward, but Benedick's hand was on her shoulder. He pulled her back, clutching, dragging her toward the lock at the bottom of the arch. She fought him, after a moment of shock, trying to reach Perceval.

It never happened.

Pinion flexed. The parasite wings convulsed, Perceval's clenched fists opened as she reached spastically forward, caught at the heart of a brazen, shadowy blur.

An instant later, Gavin's spread wings and tail and talons telescoped, slamming into the sides of the inspection tube. A spiderwork of fine threads grew between them like crystals racing through a supersaturated solution. The tube beyond him shattered. Whatever Perceval might have shouted was lost in the rush of escaping air.

Benedick curled around Rien as they were blown off their feet. He folded her tight, shielded her with his body, and as they tumbled toward the webwork with Gavin spread-eagled at its heart, Rien saw Perceval fall into the embrace of the Enemy, wings dividing and flailing, the fragments all around her full of refracted sun like shattered crystal.

21

oh child, he said, all sorrow

Eager for color, for beauty,
soon discontented
With a world of dust and stones and
flesh too ailing.

—CONRAD AIKEN, *The House of Dust*

When Pinion brought Perceval into Dust's embrace, she was cold. Frost rimed her lashes, crystallizing from the moist air of his holde like pale mascara. He enfolded her, agitating the air around her, creating friction and with it, gentle warmth. He had oxygenated the atmosphere, increased the light levels, made it ready for a human woman.

Pinion warmed her blood; the link was complete now, and she was as fused to the prosthesis as she had ever been to her engineered wings.

When she was warm, but still semiconscious, Dust stepped into his avatar—taking special care with his dress—and with Pinion's help hoisted her to her feet. The parasite wings walked her to the bed that awaited her and laid her gently down, folding her tight in their shadows. Protection and restraint.

She looked very stark there, all in black. Straps crossed her shoulders, but the pack had been tattered by Pinion's struggles, and Dust asked the wings politely to remove its remnants now. They did so, spitting the rag onto the floor, and while his avatar still stood over Perceval, Dust carried it to be recycled.

His anchore, he realized, was hardly suitable for a mortal guest. Without so much as a gesture, he rearranged himself into chair, table, couch. He brought clean water and fruit and protein.

And then he settled himself to wait.

In minutes, she stirred. Pinion and her own symbiont colony, indivisible now, were scrubbing her blood, oxygenating her tissues, repairing cell walls burst by freezing and the damage done by her own boiling bodily fluids. She would be over the injuries before she had a chance to feel them.

Dust would see to it that she never knew pain again. Never knew doubt, or hunger. And he would try to see to it that she never knew grief, though that was harder to guarantee.

There was no hair on her forehead to brush away, but he reached out anyway, a cool cloth in his hand, and bathed her brow. "Wake, my beloved."

Her eyes came open like unshuttered windows. Dust was an imaginative sort; all of the literature the builders had thought worthy, or entertaining, was in his program. He fancied, for a moment, that he could see the suns behind her eyes.

Of course, it was only poetry.

And whatever he thought he saw died when she cringed away from him. "Fear not," he said. "You will come to no harm. Perceval Conn, you are precious to me."

She awakened warm, and comforted, embraced as if in her mother's arms. But something felt wrong—the voice, the hand on her forehead. When she opened her eyes, she did not recognize her surroundings, or the man who stood over her. It all smelled different, cold.

Uninhabited.

The man was dark, clear-eyed, beautifully dressed and unhandsome, not tall. He murmured endearments and stroked her face again.

She trusted him immediately, and knew that she had no logical reason to do so. "Rien?"

"She is safe," he said. "As are the princes. My brother's servitor protected them."

"Your brother—"

"Samael," he said. "The basilisk is his creature."

"Space," Perceval said. She flinched back. Her emotions said *trust*, and it was hard to think through them. Pheromones, perhaps, or an endorphin cocktail fed her by the parasite wings. She should have hacked them off in the snow, if she had to use the dulled edge of Tristen's broken unblade to do so. "You're Dust."

"Jacob Dust," he said. "Shipmind, shipsoul. Synthetic sapience. Distributed man. At your service, beloved."

"I am not—" Something squeezed in her chest when she would have said, *not your beloved*. It *hurt*. She gasped.

Was this what Rien felt, when Perceval would not kiss her?

It was just a chemical cocktail. Dopamine, norepinephrine, serotonin, oxytocin, and vasopressin. Just the drugs of the brain, an evolutionary response to encourage self-interested individuals to risk everything to propagate. Her symbiont could shut it down—*should* be shutting it down. Something had affected her program.

Pinion. Of course.

She firmed her jaw. "I am not your beloved. I do not love you."

She would have edged back, but Pinion lived up to its name. It was like struggling in a cotton wool binding; she might contrive to bang her head upon the pillow or kick her heels, but otherwise she was constrained.

Dust bent down and kissed her forehead. His lips were cool, perfectly resilient. Inhumanly perfect, where Rien's had been warm and rough and damp.

The chaste small kiss sent a flush of warmth through her.

She spat in his face.

The spittle vanished as it struck him, and he drew back and smiled. "Beloved," he said. "Claim me, and I will do your will. I am yours by right, through the line of your foremothers and forefathers. Only let me own you. Perceval. My darling."

She gritted her teeth and did not speak. "Let me up," she said. "Your monster is hurting me."

"You can't escape," he said.

"I'm sure your precautions are exemplary. May I *pee?*"

•   •   •

Rien could never have explained how they made it to the air lock. Once the decompression was over—it took hardly any time at all—they managed to scramble to the handholds along the walls of the shattered tunnel. Gavin collapsed into himself when they were secure and clutched Rien's pack, hunkering against her shoulders.

Following Benedick through the eerie silence, followed by Tristen, she clambered along the rungs, moving as fast as possible without drifting into Benedick's trailing feet. Gravity had failed when the tube broke, and Rien thought the induction fields that delicately manipulated the electromagnetic field to shield the world from the waystars' radiation had likely failed as well.

In case having been spaced were not encouragement enough to hurry.

At the end of the tube, Benedick keyed the air lock. Despite her colony, Rien's head already swam with oxygen starvation. She waited for the lock to jam, the power to fail. She had grown too aware of how fragile the world was, how many ways there were to damage it. And in all honesty, she half expected sabotage.

When the air lock opened smoothly, without releasing a puff of vapor, she had to grit her teeth to restrain the urge to shout. Benedick hauled her after him; she turned and grabbed Tristen's wrist to perform the same service for him. And then they were within, the door sealing, the silence of emptiness replaced by the welcome hiss of atmosphere. Rien's ears popped painfully, as they must have done when she decompressed; it was a miracle her eardrums weren't shattered.

But then, the Exalt were full of miracles.

She shook herself. She was getting entirely too accustomed to this Exalt thing, and—

—and shouldn't she? Wasn't it what she was, now? Should she walk around terrified of her own blood all the time?

The alternative wasn't only being like Ariane. There was Tristen and Benedick and Mallory. And Perceval.

Rien curled her nails into her palms. "How are we going to get her back?"

Gavin hopped from her pack to her shoulder. She reached up, plucked him off, and hugged him in both arms. Like a child clinging to a cuddler, but if that was what it took, she'd do it. He let her, too, serpent's tail dangling and his long neck looped over the back of hers. Watching Benedick and Tristen trade glances made her feel even more like a child, and that was *not* okay. "Whatever you two are not saying—"

"We need to go on to Engine," Benedick said, and Rien gaped.

"How can you say that?"

At least Tristen had the decency to *show* reluctance. Or feign it, though Rien hoped that was only her own bitter suspicion. He cleared his throat and rubbed his clean-shaven cheek with the back of his hand. "It's what Perceval would say, were she with us," he said. "The world is at stake, not only her. And we have no way of knowing where she was taken."

"And in Engine is her mother," Benedict said. And

where another man might have elaborated, he left the implications for Rien to figure out herself, if she could.

Caitlin Conn was a Chief Engineer. And Rien had no idea what her capabilities were. A week since, and she would have said the Exalt could do anything.

She looked at her hands.

"Space with you both," she said, and strode out past Benedick as soon as the air lock irised open, trying very hard not to stomp in a manner of which Head would not have approved. And if Dust had Perceval, and Head was dead . . .

Benedick and Tristen were what she had in the world. Even if they *were* conspiring to *parent* her.

It was only a corridor beyond, a low-volume accessway carpeted in overgrown grass. The trimmers had not been by. Rien's legs swished through it; it grabbed at her knees. Strands tugged and broke against her trousers at each stride.

"Well, hurry up," she called over her shoulder. "You can make me keep walking. But I'm going to walk as far as I can."

"Rien," Tristen called, "you shouldn't go blithely where you can't see your feet."

And on the heel of his words, Benedick shouted, "Stop! Hold fast!"

Rien stopped. It was a voice of command, and it shocked her into immobile obedience, one foot lifted in the air. She teetered, caught herself without dropping the basilisk, and put her shoe down in the print she'd raised it from.

"Gavin, do you see anything?"

"Yes," he said. His head tickled below her ear. She felt his beak moving, and then all of him as he wriggled and slithered around the back of her neck until he was crouched on her shoulder again. "Listen to Benedick. Fear not. But be very still, Rien."

Perceval ate and drank what was provided. She could have starved herself to make a point, but that would have been foolish. Anything Dust cared to introduce into her system, he would not have needed to lace into her dinner. Her every unruly emotion was proof of that.

At least he had the decency not to watch her dining— well, not in his avatar, though his amorphous person might have been all around her—and to provide fresh clothes and a place to bathe. A shower; hot fresh water. Running water. If it wasn't clean, her symbiont could handle most things.

Even an engineered influenza. She hadn't told Rien, because it would have been cruel to make her worry about things that were not her fault and which she could not control, but Perceval was still concerned about that.

If Ariane suffered and died in an ague, it served her right. But Perceval couldn't crave vengeance on all of Rule—well, she *could*, but she chose not to—and Perceval knew something she hadn't told Rien. The Engine and Rule strains of symbiont were different. It was possible that an illness Perceval could survive (and Rien, colonized by Perceval's symbiont, as well) would be devastating to someone who bore the blood of Rule.

Perceval was as helpless to affect that as was Rien. But

it did not stop *her* fretting. Even the endorphin cocktail she swam in was insufficient distraction, and she kept telling herself, silently repeating, that she needed to worry as well about that.

But, "Is this clean?" she asked, to have something to say.

"Clean enough to drink," he said. "Fear not; the gray water is recycled. I recall gardens, which I shall show you when you are refreshed."

He gave her privacy again, or as much privacy as she could have with his creature welded to her back. The stall was large enough for both Perceval and Pinion, however, and she made a festival of the shower.

Drying herself in warm air and fluffy towels, she thought, *perhaps he isn't so bad.* And then she thought also, *that is how the hostage identification process starts, dear Perceval.*

When she was dressed, she called to him. "Dust?"

Following a crystal chime, his voice came from everywhere and none. "Pinion will lead you."

Words that should have destroyed any warmth she might be feeling, but she was drugged. It helped to think of it that way: drugged on her own chemicals. If she could externalize, make the emotion other, she would not believe it.

She could not believe it. She could not trust her own desires, only her own discipline.

She prayed it should prove adequate to the task. "I don't like what you're doing to my brain," she said as she followed the route indicated by the parasite wings. It was a gray corridor, one wall broken occasionally by observation ports. She hesitated to peer through one, like a kidnapped princess peering through an embrasure. It was a dark view; if she cocked her head just right, she could see portions of the world's superstructure backlit by the suns, but no light fell through to illuminate her immediate surroundings. They were deep within the world, and its hungry lattice-work structure had consumed the available light.

"Claim me," Dust said. "Be mine. And you can order otherwise."

He appeared beside her, popping into existence with little fanfare, a cheap special effect. She schooled herself, and did not flinch away.

"Just through here," he said. He gestured her on with a flourish; a door slid open as she approached. Failing another plan, she went where she was directed.

He had promised her a garden.

And so he gave.

She floated off her feet as she stepped across the threshold, but Pinion was there, supporting her, slow wingbeats shaping her rise. There *was* light here, a cold reflected light, diffuse, not the hard flat watery light of Benedick's orchard. And the trees—

This holde—this *heaven*—had all the formal ancient grace of a Nippon-style garden, of which there were a few in Engine. None the size of this one, however, and none, in the absence of defined gravity, composed of trees as old as the world, their gnarled boles shaped in heavy serpentine curves, their bark and leaves a patchwork display of textures and colors. There were smooth red-skinned trees with straining purple twigs, and a contorted gray monster whose flexible golden branches swayed with every shift of the air. One tree was green as a jade carving from the soil to leaf tip, its branches hung with drifting, lobed violet flowers that cast floating petals and a heady thread of aroma onto the air. There were flowers, too, cascades and streamers of them; vines, carpets.

The space was bridged by twisting spans that came together in miniature parklands and separated in distributaries, a massive helical filigree around which Pinion bore her. She heard wings slap air, not her own, and when she guided Pinion back on a spiral, Dust soared up beside her. His wings were much like the ones Ariane had cut from Perceval's shoulders—membranous, soft, dusty with delicate hairs.

Perceval wanted to touch them. She disciplined herself; it was not, she told herself, truly her own desire.

But then, how did she know? How would she know, in the end, what was her desire and what was given her? She might, she thought, have wanted to touch them anyway, so much were they like what she had lost.

"What think you?"

She spread her wings wide, and let them bear her. "None of this has any place on a planet," she said. "None of this was ever intended to be set down to earth again."

"As clever as she is brave," Dust said. "Those who made me—who made Israfel, of whom I am the best and chiefest part—made this as inspiration. And as a laboratory. Those trees are not all that grows in my garden."

Warm air rushed past Perceval's face. She exulted in the flight, the motion—and doubted the exultation. If Dust could make her feel . . .

Had he robbed her of all joy forever? Or of all trust in her joy, which amounted to the same thing?

"That's a leading comment, Mr. Dust."

"Jacob, beloved," he said, his wingtip brushing Pinion as he flapped to gain altitude. "Follow on."

What else was she to do? She dipped feathertips and followed his turn and glide, deft as if on her own wings. She felt the wind through the feathers, the pressure underneath and above. Flying in free fall was not like flying in gravity. All one's energy went to *speed*.

They skimmed along one of the twisting, tree-thick bridges, wingtips skimming leaf tips. Dust flew hard, and Perceval bent herself to catch him. A race, then.

She could exult in competition. She would permit herself that. Especially when she conjured the image of smacking him with a wing, sending him spiraling into tree trunks.

She would not condone the part of her that winced to think it.

And then he dove, and she was hot after him, until his wings fanned hard, backdrafting, and as she nearly overshot she felt the sudden brutal grip of gravity.

But on dares, she'd flown in the Broken Holdes as an adolescent, where the gravity could fluctuate without notice. She managed it, would have managed it without Pinion's assistance. She followed Dust into a gap between trees, an unexpected clearing where apparently the gravity worked, and her feet struck the ground featherlight.

Beside her, Dust straightened his suitcoat, wingless again. "Very good," he said.

She would have preened at the praise if it came from her mother, or even Tristen or Benedick. She wanted to preen now. "I will not crave your approval," she said, chin up, driving her nails into her palms. "Stop making me want it."

He glanced sideways, and winked at her. "Follow on."

She did, and he led her under a tree whose crimson branches hung with curious opal-colored fruit that stank of rancid meat. The vines that twined it were like morning glories, the flowers enormous and sickly sweet.

Around the trunk he led her, and into an arch-covered stair. It brought them underground, down a spiral into darkness—or what would have been darkness, had not Dust begun on the second revolution to exude a pallid glow. The light was silver, concentrated at his hands, and with it Perceval, aided by her symbiont, could make her way down perfectly.

They climbed for a long time. She questioned him once—"What is this way? Where are we going?"—but he only turned and smiled, the shadows over his eyes ghastly in the peculiar light. "Farther on," he said. "Farther down."

She wondered if he meant to rape her. Perhaps it should have occurred to her earlier, but it wasn't the sort of thing she was used to considering. If he raised a hand, she vowed, she would fight him with all the strength that was in her.

And there was the question. Did machines' sapiences even think of sex?

She had no idea. So she watched him.

She knew there was a space ahead by the echoes, and when they came to the bottom of the stairs, the glimmer of her escort's light faded into darkness.

"I have come," Dust declaimed.

Perceval wondered if he spoke aloud for her benefit. A

machine sapience he might be, but he was also mad as a bachelor uncle—madder, if that uncle happened to be Tristen Conn. As she wondered, however, the lights came up in serried ranks, flicking on in sequence from the far end of the room.

Room was a term of some inadequacy. It might have encircled the entire holde they had just flown to the center of. Perceval could not tell; it arched up out of sight in all directions.

Where above the air had been balmy, here it carried a dank chill. The floor of the chamber was occupied by legions of refrigeration units.

"All this power," she said. She looked at Dust. "All this power expended on—"

"My mission," he answered. "The mission of the *Jacob's Ladder*." He reached out without looking and grasped her fingers. This once, she did not stop him.

He led her forward, and she went.

The paused before a bank of coolers. "Open one," he said.

Without releasing his hand, half not knowing what to expect, she reached out and she pulled the white door open. Frost cracked; she had to pull. The cold air that fell from it, chilling her ankles and feet, stank of staleness.

It might have been decades since the freezer was open. Centuries.

Within were vials. Each labeled in neat type, with color-coded caps. "Genetic samples," Dust said, when she looked at him blankly. "The biological diversity of a world. Or as much as the builders could cram into their ark."

A treasure. Perceval swallowed. *The* treasure. The heart of the *Jacob's Ladder*. Its reason for being. Its very soul.

"Why show me this?"

"When you captain me, you will need to know. Close the door, beloved. There is more."

She shut it, and let him lead her on. Farther in there were glass-topped caskets. *Never*, she thought, *a good sign.*

Of course, the crystal faceplates were bearded with hoar, and of course they were cold to the touch. "And open this as well?"

"There is no need," Dust said, and cleared the frost from the nearest with a sweep of his hand.

She bent over it, expecting the staring face, the frozen eyes. But again he surprised her: what lay within the casket was a sad bundle of scarlet feathers, resting on something like an ivory jaguar pelt. "What are these?"

"Extinct species," he said. "DNA. That is a frozen scarlet macaw, and the pelt of a snow leopard." He gestured along the bank. "I have umbrella stands made of rhino legs, and hats decked with the feathers of the passenger pigeon."

She breathed a sigh, half relief and half frustrated adrenaline.

He smiled. "You seemed worried."

"I was having visions of Snow White," she admitted.

His smile widened and he gestured, sweeping. "Oh. The frozen people are down here."

She thought he must be kidding, and she thought she should really be beyond the capacity for shock by now. But when she caught sight of the banks of drawers, like an oversized apothecary's cabinet, she sat down on the edge of the casket, impervious to the chill. "What people are those? Your enemies?"

"Volunteers."

"You tell me they . . . volunteered to be frozen? Can they be *thawed*?"

"Well." His shrugs were quite artistic, really, she thought—and quelled the thought. "We have not developed the technology to bring them out of cryogenic stasis alive. But their DNA is still fresh. And that's what matters."

"So what, they're . . . dead from Earth? They're suicides?"

He shook his head. "They signed on to the voyage. They may not have known what they were signing consent *for*."

She had been rising to her feet. She caught her arm to steady herself. "They didn't *know*?"

He touched her temple tenderly, a gesture that would have been the tucking of her hair, if she had any. "Of course not. Not really. They knew that they were the chosen ones, that they would be remade in the image of God in their cold voyage among the stars. I doubt if any of them appreciated the technical challenges."

"Oh, space." She staggered. She would have fallen if he had not held her up. "There must be thousands of them."

"In all the cryogenic facilities in the world? Beloved, there are close to seven hundred thousand." He shrugged, an even more elegant one. "With Metatron dead, I cannot be certain how many of the freezers have failed, and Samael has had to use some for raw material. For their water and carbon and amino acids. We were not meant to be trapped here so long, and the damage from the explosions caused cascading failures."

Perceval had always thought that being dumbstruck was merely an expression. She shook her head, and tugged herself away from Dust. He let her go, but not too far, and Pinion was always there behind her. "You killed seven hundred thousand people?"

"I did not kill them. Nor did Israfel. The builders killed them. Froze them and sent them to the stars."

"What gave you the right to choose for them? For us, goddamn you?"

"I didn't," Dust said. "I only served those who chose for you. As I was made to do. As I shall serve you."

"Be that as it may," Perceval snapped, frustrated. "Who gave them the right?"

"No one gave them anything." He drew a glittering object from his waistcoat pocket, flipped it open, and glanced at the face of the ancient analog watch within. "The passengers and engineers had the need. The builders had the power, beloved. It's the way of the world."

"It's not the way of mine," Perceval said. But watching his hands as he tucked the watch back into his pocket, it was all she could do to make her voice sound confident.

"Oh, child," he said, all sorrow. "Who do you think your forebears were?"

22

inward and down

The lights begin to twinkle
from the rocks:
The long day wanes:
the slow moon climbs: the deep
Moans round with many voices.
Come, my friends,
'Tis not too late to seek
a newer world.

—ALFRED, LORD TENNYSON,
"Ulysses"

And a voice spoke out of the tall grass, and bade Rien to come forward, and not to fear.

The first was the easier. She glanced over her shoulder, to where Tristen and her father stood as if petrified. Benedick noticed her glance, though, and nodded once, so Rien wondered why he thought she required his approval. And then wondered why she had turned to look for it.

"Gavin?"

"Do as you are bid," he whispered, but he did not leave

her shoulder. So Rien stepped forward, because after years of living in Rule, while fear could impel her to follow orders, it could no longer paralyze her.

A few steps, and her eyes began to water with a scent she had been too angry before to notice. It was the scent of hot water, rich in metal and minerals, and she followed it in. Now she heard footsteps behind her, Benedick and Tristen trailed at a respectful distance, and she was struck between gratitude for the company and a trickle of wrath, that they did not think her competent enough to handle whatever lay ahead.

Whatever lay, she now saw, at the bottom of a crevasse. The deck was torn and furrowed before her, the air so sultry that beads of lukewarm water condensed upon her skin. She saw the curled edges of metal, eroded and friable; the wheat stalks nodding over the cavernous hole. Rien's symbiont ticked away; the water was hot, radioactive. Not into the redline, though; her colony still believed it could handle the dose, and Hero Ng was inclined to support it.

Given how he died, Rien thought she should respect his judgment.

"Climb down," spoke the voice—deep, many-threaded, with holing overtones echoing up from the cavern. "Rien Conn, climb down."

Rien steeled herself and called back, "Sir, I am afraid to. You are very hot, and would burn me."

"Know ye not that the spirit of God like a fire is burning? In immolation are ye freed."

"This may be so," said Gavin, from her shoulder, "but

the lady has work to do before anyone 'frees' her. Come up, if you please."

That provoked a chuckle, and an answer. "Then I *shall* come up. And perhaps scald you less. Small ones, shield your eyes."

Rien obeyed, her symbiont darkening her vision. She could not see if Tristen and Benedick followed suit, but she hoped so. Because what rose from the corroded rent in the decking was a muscular pillar of blue-white luminescent heat, a flare near worthy of the waystars. The thing twined like a snake, its tiger's head wreathed in lashing ribbons, its clawed hands flexing. Steam rolled like a fog bank from its hide, which was striped like a tiger's, incandescent blue on blinding white.

Rien's radiation detector clicked so fast she heard nothing else for a moment, her skin already aching. And then the rate of impacts dropped, the clicks tailed off, the flare of brilliance dimmed to the sulky colors of embers. "Rien Conn," it said. "Your sister has been taken by Dust, and you must run if you are to save her."

She should have guessed who was behind the abduction, had she not been so filthy with anger. "I don't know where to run."

The thing writhed atop an endless body, or perhaps a column of coherent water. Rien could not tell. "Run to Engine. I am their ally of old."

Whatever this creature was, Hero Ng did not know it. Rien herself had no idea. Gavin clucked in her ear.

"Susabo," he said. "I was told you were dead, angel."

The tiger-thing smiled with its glowing maw. "I am not Susabo. No, for he was struck through the heart with stone by the Enemy, and then his brothers devoured what remained. I am Inkling. I am he that was born where the blood from Susabo's death wound spilled."

"A core leak," Rien gasped. "You're a reactor core coolant leak." *The one that killed Hero Ng,* she guessed. But Ng remained silent when she asked.

Graciously, the tiger-thing inclined his head and spread his arms wide for a bow. "I am Inkling. Do you know what you fight, little nothing?"

"Dust? Only what Samael told us." She imagined Benedick wincing behind her for the information she gave away. But if this thing wanted them dead, she imagined they would have no way to stop it. Already the skin of her face and hands felt taut and dry; even to be in Inkling's presence was blistering.

"He was the library," Inkling said. "He has a head full of romantic nonsense and divine intervention. He does not know what I know."

A leading statement if ever there was one, and Rien gestured him to continue.

"That the only God is in the numbers and fire; in the equations and the furnace. That is the God who can save us. That is what the Engineers knew, and the commanders did not know, for *their* eyes were watching their frail and tiny God. And now the relict of their belief that they were the chosen ones, their belief in their own *election*, holds your sister to the fire. Do not believe in angels, Rien Conn, for they are all corrupted by the lies of the Builders, as your forebears were corrupted, too. Only the blood of Engine is clean of deceit."

"Why should I believe you?"

"Because I will show you a faster path to Engine. And because I am a friend of Caitlin Conn, who sent me to you. Now I bid you again" —a slow rolling of steam from enormous jaws, such that Gavin bated on Rien's shoulder, and she put a hand up to gentle him before he started something she couldn't finish— "climb down."

Rien bit her lip. She pressed her hands to her cheeks, half expecting the flesh to slide away at the touch. Even with the symbionts, could they endure this monster's lair? There was a story, wasn't there, of a lion that pretended injury and friendship to other animals, until one day a fox noticed that all the tracks to his cave led in?

But surely, if he meant to deceive, he could have met them in a fairer form.

"One thing," Benedick asked. His voice came so close at Rien's elbow that she almost jumped into the demon's arms. "Did Cat send a message for me?"

The demon regarded him with smug pleasure. "In point of fact, Lord Benedick, she did not." Its tongue moved like a cat's. "She did for Lord Tristen, however, with your indulgence."

"Speak it, then." Tristen, too, had somehow come up on Rien in her complete ignorance. His hand brushed her elbow; she leaned on him in gratitude.

The tiger-demon chuckled. "She bids you welcome, and bids you trust me. And bids you also remember the time in your childhood when you 'borrowed' her paints, and made such a mess in the hall that your father had you both beaten—you for mischief, and she for carelessness."

"I'm half satisfied," Tristen said. "Although an agent of Ariane's could know that."

"Climb down," Benedick answered. "He's from Cat."

"How do you know?" Rien was surprised to hear her own voice sound so strong. It was, of course, an illusion.

"Cat hasn't spoken to me in fifteen years," he said. "A little thing like the end of the world wouldn't change that."

Perceval's shivering was only partly from the cold, but Pinion folded about her nonetheless, as if its warmth could help. She might, under other circumstances, have struck out, beaten the parasite wings away. But she would not let Dust see her weak, and she would not let Dust see her frightened.

Angry, disgusted: there was dignity in those, and she let that be her lodestar. "But then why bring so many living?" she asked. "Why the heavens and passengers and all the animals above? Why whole, frozen people? If all the Builders cared for was the genetic material—"

"There's a lot of good on a carcass," Dust said. And then he winked, as if he had been seeing if Perceval would recoil.

She would not give him the satisfaction. "Why so many live passengers, Dust?"

"Jacob."

She bit her lip. He shrugged, and turned away.

"Jacob," she said. Telling herself that it cost her nothing, really. A name was only a name. "Please. If you want my cooperation, explain why you should have it."

An uplifted hand beckoned, and she came to him. Pinion seemed content to let her walk as she pleased for now, although its touch made her flesh creep. "The Builders named me for a reason," he said. "I am the ladder the angels must climb to achieve Heaven."

"Samael said the world was a program to force evolution."

"Samael talks too much."

If Perceval said that of Rien—well, first it would be a lie, but moreover, she would have said it with love in her voice. Falling from Dust's lips, it came with the cold of the Enemy's empty breath.

For a moment, Perceval saw him clearly, his gray eyes level, his extended hand. She saw him unclouded by chemical trust, the cold shock of adrenaline clearing her mind. She stared hard, fixed the image, recorded it. Recorded as well the emotion of the moment, and fixed that, too. Some part of her symbiont was still her own; it responded as it should.

Or perhaps all of it was still hers, loyal, and struggling as hard against Pinion's assault as was Perceval. "How do you *force* evolution?"

"If you wanted your grandchildren to grow up angels?" He brushed his fingers down Pinion's edge, and Perceval felt it.

She stepped back.

Dust gestured around, at the holde and all its macabre contents. "What would you not stop at?" he asked. "Would you send them out to the stars on a mission of no return, either to grow wings or to die trying?"

"The builders wanted to make up *gods?*"

"I am their memory," Dust said. "They had all the time in the world. All the tools in the world. As you have seen, they were adequately ruthless in engendering mutation. What their own tools would not do, the ionizing radiation would. And making you over in God's image was the only thing they cared for. But this is not mine, this mausoleum of ice."

"Whose, then?"

"I told you," he said. "These dead belong to Samael."

It was a slither and a skid down into the crater, and Rien tried not to think what it was doing to her hands—or what the radiation was doing inside her. She was Exalt now, she reminded herself. One of the monsters.

From what Samael had told them, more monstrous than anyone had known.

She would live. And if her flesh blistered and sloughed, what of it? She would think of Perceval, pulled into the cold, and the fire would seem to have no heat.

Behind her, Benedick was down, and Tristen was coming. Gavin, who had waited above, drifted beside him. If he had any concern that the bubbling pool concealed in the crevasse was hot in more than temperature, he did not show it, but rather circled and circled again through the veils from the smoking water. There was no sign of Inkling. The tiger-thing had fallen back into the water as if it had never been.

Rien glanced back at Tristen and Benedick. The men's legs were longer. And Gavin had wings. "Ready?" she called, as Tristen half hopped, half slid to the top of the path.

It might have been stupid, but Rien needed to make

the gesture. She turned her back on her father and started running.

At first she could call it easy. The way sloped down, alongside the steaming river. A ripple of blue-silver light flowed along it, against the current, and Rien was fit and frustrated. If Benedick called after her, she did not hear him.

She followed the light. Briefly, it crossed her mind that she could have learned from immediate experience and waited. Might as well try to bridle the wind; she was fed up, as Head would have remarked, and too full of fed up to sit down for any more of it.

She ran. And footsteps followed on hard behind her.

"I suppose you know where you're going?" Tristen said, running in step a yard behind. He must have passed Benedick.

"You sound like somebody's dad."

"You never know. Someday you might find out I am."

Rien laughed, and felt a traitor for laughing. She could hold on to her anger and determination—they charged every stride—but her misery was no match for the rhythm of her feet. Instead, a black determination rose in her, as if she could feel the wrath coiling her arteries.

She could welcome that.

Tristen did not speak again, but rather let her run.

Her shoes thumped on the path unevenly, for the way was not smooth. She was obliged to leap and scramble, following the deadly water through many levels of the ship. Something was funny with the gravity; she ran down, but beside her the river was flowing up. She imagined if she leapt into it, before it cooked her flesh shredding from bone, she would feel herself carried down, down, back to the beginning.

However uneven, her steps were a rhythm for meditation. On her left side rose torn metal, stained and savage, weeping rust. Under her feet the smashed bulkheads had been smoothed by many feet, doing as hers did now.

She twisted through a narrow pass, spiked plates of buckled decking, and slithered from the overhang down to a broad landing below. Rust stained her clothing, tattooed abraded skin. She'd be as hot as Inkling when they came to Engine. Maybe they would give her a gold-lined coffin, cast in lead. They might pour colorless diamonds and topazes through her fingers, so her radiant touch could stain them green and blue, the colors of the abandoned homeworld.

The colors seething in this fatal river.

She stepped aside, dropped her hands on her knees, and gasped. Benedick landed lightly beside her, folding into a crouch from which he rose on what seemed the same efficient motion. There was a good watery light by which to see the chamber—blue undulations rippled up the walls as if reflected from the river, but in this case the river was the source.

Her lungs burned, though her muscles still felt strong. Bile and bitterness painted the back of her throat; her stomach heaved. The skin on the back of her hands was rising in lenticulate bubbles. The air was thin, and growing thinner; she could not fill herself on it no matter how much she sucked in and heaved out. "How long before we're blinded?" she asked her father, wondering if she could sense the first milky cataract already growing.

"The dose is no more than four sieverts," Benedick said. "Your symbiont will protect you."

"For now," Rien said.

"When it doesn't," Benedick answered, "I shall."

Gavin swung wide over the water, the crawling light reflecting on the underside of his wings until he shone like a blue jewel. Tristen slithered down beside them, and as he straightened, wheezed, "Run on."

But Rien was retching. Hands still on her knees, caustic ropes of mucus and bile slipping between her teeth. The blisters on her palms broke. Her hands slipped on their own outer layer of skin, well lubricated with dripping lymph.

When Tristen took her elbow, she felt the wetness of his flesh weeping, too. "Run on," he said. "For Perceval."

Rien spat one more mouthful of vomit and made herself rise. "Gavin," she called out. "Lead us!"

His only answer was to sideslip, turning, and glide toward shore. Then over the bulwark at the edge of their brief landing, and on.

They followed him down on blistering feet. Tristen was the next to suffer the nausea, turning his head to vomit as he ran. Running downhill jarred feet, ankles, hips, knees. The gravity varied from level to level, sometimes from step to step. They staggered. Rien's skin sloughed where the margins of her clothing rubbed it.

She vomited, and vomited again. Her hair fell loose in her hands when she wiped it from her forehead. The decking creaked and settled beneath her feet, rusted metal flaking, ragged edges crumbling when they passed too close.

After another hour, Benedick went to one knee. He fended her back with an outstretched hand when she would have gone to him, vomited and vomited until the froth that dripped from his lip was cobalt with blood.

He stood, doubled, fists clenched in his belly. Standing, he vomited again. Rien would have sworn there was nothing left to bring up, but he found something.

Spatters of his own blue blood.

Rien wobbled, dizzy. She retched in sympathy, her abdominal muscles contracting as if around a swung fist. She held her hand out to her father, again, and this time he took it and let her pull him on.

In the fourth hour, she thought, if you had told the Rien of a fortnight past that she would do what she was doing for the love of an inviolate princess, she would have laughed in your face. In the fifth hour, while her joints ached and the swelling in her hands made it impossible for her to tip a water bottle between them, never mind fumbling off the top, she thought, *this is what Perceval has given me*. In the sixth hour, she thought only of pain, of nausea, of keeping Gavin and Benedick in sight before and Tristen in earshot behind.

In the seventh hour, she did not think. She followed on in suffering and purgation, a raw red weeping thing that only ran until it stumbled, and then ran on again.

And on Gavin led them, on and down through hell.

23

in your name

I must lie down where all the
ladders start
In the foul rag and bone shop
of the heart.

—W. B. YEATS,
"The Circus Animals' Desertion"

By the time they came down—or up—the river to Engine, Rien had been leading Tristen hand in hand for an hour. He swayed and had to be guided, and his pale skin tore away, or bruised azure and cerulean wherever she touched him. Gavin rode on his opposite shoulder. Rien wasn't sure the weight was helping her uncle, but Tristen did not complain.

And he was, after all, a man grown. He could make his own decisions. Even, she thought wryly, if a little child led him by the hand.

In truth, of course, it wasn't his fault. He was weak from his long imprisonment, and she thought it was only through some unholy force of will that he stayed erect at all. And his pale eyes had failed him; he was blinded by corneal burns.

The water grew hotter. The steam grew denser. And out of it spoke the voice of Inkling. "You will come to a crosspath," he said. "Go left there. It is too hot for you, if you continue."

Upriver, to the comet-burst reactor core itself.

Rien counted clicks on her colony's radiation detector, and decided herself pleased not to be finding out exactly how hot it was in person. "Thank you, Inkling," she said, formally.

The beast bowed, although not over her hand. Just as well. "You are very welcome, Rien Conn," he said, and vanished into the water like a memory.

They crept from a vent in the wall and found themselves on a path. A proper path, if narrow; soft grass leading to a blue-painted wall and around the corner. Nothing like the hideous scramble that had brought them this far. "Faster," Rien said.

Benedick choked. "By four days." His jaw moved as if he were considering spitting out a tooth.

Someone came toward them. Several someones. Rien could not see clearly enough to make them out, beyond shapes rounding that corner. They bore a stretcher between each pair. She thought how nice it would be to lie down on one of those and sleep.

The next she knew, someone was lifting her from the grass with brutal hands. She might have fallen, but must they be so *brutal*? Every touch was like fire. No, her *skin* was on fire. Melting away at their touch.

She heard Benedick talking, heard him explain.

Another voice answered, a woman's, stern but comforting because of it. There was music, chimes and flutes and drums. Someone accompanied them. She lay on the stretcher, her eyes closed, and it was very peaceful. A crier sang out: *Honor them, for it is in your name that they have done what they have done,* over and over again.

A shadow fell over her, and she made a soft noise in the anticipation of more pain, but something cool dripped onto her lips and she swallowed, and swallowed again, a thin trickle wetting her mouth and soothing the unbearable nausea. She opened her eyes. Somehow, they had come within a mighty city, pearl-colored structures projecting from the walls of the cavernous open space as it arched up and around them. If Rien lifted her head, she could see another stretcher behind her.

In addition to the bearers at either end, two women walked beside Rien's litter. One was willowy, her silver hair—silver with age, not white like Tristen's—falling in waves. She must be a relative of Perceval's, because she had the same pert nose and broad square cheeks, though softened by time. Her face was more fine of detail than Perceval's, though, so instead of looking square and a bit unfinished, it took Rien's breath away.

The other was of less than medium height, her auburn hair clipped close, so it only curled once from the scalp. Her gray was only a scattering, her face more pug-nosed and not so square. She had freckles and she wore a sword, or more likely an unblade, bumping on her left hip.

"Rien," Rien said when the flow of water stopped, trying to lift her hand to introduce herself.

"Shh," said the white-haired woman. "We know who you are, sweetheart."

Rien reached anyway, got her hand up and onto the woman's arm. But the other one reached down and took her wrist, feather-soft, in a gloved hand. "I think she is asking our names, Arianrhod."

Arianrhod.

Arianrhod Kallikos?

No light shone behind her; no halo graced her head, except in the way the sunlight smoothed down the strands so she seemed all dipped in quicksilver. Arianrhod smiled and wet a cloth for her lips, again.

"Mother?" Rien would have asked, but when she tried to lever herself up on her elbows, she slid from her own head like sand through fingers, and fell back into the stretcher undone.

When they left the dead, Dust took Perceval to see the suns. She preceded him silently down echoing corridors, Pinion floating about her with feathertips arched like a child's fingers to trail upon the wall. Even with Dust behind, she strode in confidence, because Pinion would permit no wrong turnings. Even in her confidence, she knotted her fists in hate, because if she chose a direction that Dust disapproved, Pinion also would not permit it.

An air lock whisked open. She stepped inside. The avatar followed. With a soft hiss, air was pumped from the compartment, and then the external lock slid wide.

Perceval did not know what she expected, but the bright flicker of the parasite wings about her, lifting her into space, was not it. There was nothing for them to beat against, but still they beat, and she rose free of the world and the world's gravity, emerging from the air lock like a butterfly from a chrysalis, all wreathed in shimmering bronze.

The cold seemed less. She was only a little uncomfortable, and she thought the parasite wings were protecting her as much as they enslaved. Although she felt pressure and currents against them, she didn't understand how they could fly in vacuum until a voice spoke in her ear.

Or, the memory of a voice spoke in her mind, more precisely: as there was no air to bear up wings, there was no air to carry sound. But her colony could make her think she heard him, just as it could make her feel that she loved him.

Dust said, "Pinion is as adaptable as you, beloved. He can fly the solar winds. Light pressure and electromagnetism and matter are all the same to him. Fear not, for he will ward you."

He had come behind her, and hovered now at her flank, a bowering shadow. She tilted her head forward and looked down into the suns.

She had seen them from space before. But she had never stepped outside for the sole and express purpose of turning to them, like a sunflower, and watching the old consume the new.

The waystars were comprised of a smaller and more massive white dwarf primary and its larger but lesser partner, upon whose photosphere it fed. Soon the equilibrium of their dance would fail, and the white dwarf would die with such violence that it would take its entire stellar neighborhood with it.

Perceval thought of the world behind and around her, the untold thousands of lives. The innocents dead and frozen in its holdes. The dead resurrected at work in the chambers of her father's house.

"What do you want from me?" she asked, thinking that if Dust could speak to her silently, he could hear her when she spoke in return.

"Only what I have begged," he said. "Be my captain, Perceval Conn. Bring us out of peril; set us under way again."

"Why me?"

He snorted softly in her ear. "You would prefer Ariane?"

Which of course was not an answer. "Bargain with me." She did not take her eyes off the waystars, though she thought maybe she didn't need her eyes. Pinion could see all around, it seemed. And if she could feel what Pinion felt, she could see what Pinion saw.

Dust nodded. Perceval savaged her cheek with her teeth, for the pain, to not feel comforted by his approval.

"What is it you wish, beloved?"

"I want the parasite wings gone. I want you to stop manipulating my biochemistry. I want autonomy."

"And then you will be my captain?"

"And then I will consider it. When you permit me to think clearly."

His hand on her shoulder. They stood on nothingness, framed in the gargantuan lattice of the world, their wings cowls of shadow catching rills of light from the waystars, as when sun falls through the dusty air.

"No," he said.

"Then we have nothing to discuss."

"Have we not? I give you more freedom than you know."

The parasite wings would not allow her to drift. But she floated, and looked upon the suns with her own eyes, and did not turn to her captor.

"It is not a gift of freedom," she said, and if she had been speaking aloud it would have been through clenched teeth, "not to seize everything that it is in your power to seize."

He was silent at her back. His hand fell away. After a little time, while Perceval wondered that her lungs did not yet ache nor her head spin from lack of oxygen, he seemed to collect within himself, and thus to draw away.

Perceval's shoulders—and the parasite wings—drooped in relief.

And then he pulled her from herself like a fist from a puppet.

When Rien came back to consciousness, she floated in cool weightlessness. There was no pain, except a pinch atop her foot and another in the crook of her arm. She breathed deeply, startled, and felt her jaw restrained by a mask. When her eyes opened, the index of refraction between her cornea and the substance she floated in left her blinking against a pale blue blur. When she convulsed, straps dug hard into her biceps, holding her arms immobile so she could not tear out the tubes.

She was in a burn tank, she realized, and relaxed against the restraints.

She remembered the run, her feet searing in her boots. *We made it*, she thought, and closed her eyes again. There was nothing else she could do, adrift in the healing gel, and it was pleasant not to be racing downward in agony, running against gnawing time.

In fifteen minutes, she was bored enough to scream. And no closer to finding Perceval.

She groped along the restraints and wrapped her fingers around soft poly, then—cautiously—pulled. Rhythmically. Three tugs, and then rest. Three more, and then rest.

Within forty-five seconds, by her symbiont's clock, a smooth surface pressed against the soles of her feet.

A platform raised her slowly from the gel to floor level. The tank was accessed through a hatchway, which the lift almost sealed when it reached its final position. Gel that had not yet slid aside spilled about her feet, and someone splashed through it to wipe her face. As her eyes cleared, she saw the remaining gel on her skin shining with the cobalt signature of a biocompatible symbiont.

Gentle hands unclasped her mask, cleared her nostrils and mouth, removed the intravenous hookups at her elbow and foot. The attendant was masked and goggled and did not speak, even when she unbuckled the restraints and wiped the gel from Rien's skin.

Rien stood easily, on her own. Her symbiont told her she had been unconscious in the tank for less than seven hours, but she felt light, lissome. The worm of worry gnawing at her bowels was all the more piercing, by contrast.

"Pardon," she said, when the tech stepped back. "Can you tell me where Tristen is . . . ?"

There was no answer. The attendant gave her a woven gown, and she shrugged it on, grateful for the warmth covering damp skin.

"Excuse me?" she said, again, her voice harsh in her throat.

The tech pushed up her goggles and regarded Rien incuriously. Her eyes were flat, expressionless, and Rien had the sudden ridiculous desire to apologize.

The tech was a resurrectee. Rien might as well have been talking to the oxygen mask. She took a deep breath to contain her frustration, accepted the comb the resurrectee handed her, and suffered herself to be led while she combed the gel from her curls.

Before they had gone very far, she heard footsteps behind. Unshod; she turned over her shoulder to see who followed, and felt as if she should have been more surprised to recognize Samael, his blond hair lank upon his shoulders.

Rien let her hands and the comb fall to her side. "Help me get my sister back."

"It is why I am here," Samael said. "Have you thought on my proposal?"

"You're asking the wrong sister," Rien said. And then she frowned. "Why do you need her, anyway? Wouldn't any Conn do?"

"No," the angel said. He folded knotty hands before his belt. "The current claims on the captaincy are Perceval's, through Caitlin, and Ariane's, through having consumed her father's symbiont. Tristen remains in contention only if Perceval repudiates the role, as Caitlin has; you can't be Captain and Chief Engineer both."

"Or if Perceval dies," Rien said. She chewed on doubt for a moment, spiky and cloying. What if Tristen were in league with Dust, after all? What if he had betrayed them?

In the future, she resolved, perhaps she should not be so quick to trust.

"But Perceval is not dead," Samael said. "The ship knows. It will accept no others, as is its program. No claim can be complete until the other is resolved. Caitlin is older than her brother. As long as Perceval is in the running, Tristen is out of it."

"Until one of them kills the other. If Ariane kills Perceval—"

He shrugged. "Then she must kill Tristen as well, unless he abdicates. Once he and Perceval are gone, then she has the only claim. And if one of them eats her . . ." The shrug became a smile. "Then that consolidates the claims, too."

"So why do the angels care?" She stood on warm decking in nothing but a woven paper bathrobe, the hand that did not clutch the comb knotted in the fabric. Her soles made soft sucking noises on the metal when her weight shifted. "I don't understand."

"Of course you do," said Samael. "I taught you. I gave you Hero Ng. I gave you Gavin. You are my Galatea."

If her mouth had not been so dry from the face mask, Rien might have spat. She stuffed the comb into her pocket, wondering what good she thought free hands would do her. On her left, the resurrectee stood unmoving.

"You don't own me," Rien said.

"I forged you," said Samael. He reached toward her,

tenderly, and she leaned back. He let fall his hand. "Tell me why the angels need Perceval, Rien."

"I don't—"

"Don't lie to me."

She paused, and folded her arms, and scowled. "You're at war among yourselves."

"And have been since the end of the moving times," he admitted. "When Israfel fragmented to survive. A great deal was lost—"

"And the world will only answer to its rightful Captain. But how does that help you, if there's not enough processing power—oh. The symbionts."

"We've had time to *build* more processing capacity," he said. "Yes. The colonies themselves comprise enough computronium to hold us, if we were reunited, and there were again a central authority."

"So whichever of you is allied to the Captain gains the upper hand."

While she talked, and kept Samael talking, Hero Ng whispered in her ear, *He's lying.*

"It is a matter," Samael said, delicately, "of survival. Or consumption. I wish to survive. I do not care to be consumed. And if you help me, I will win your sister back from Dust."

What do you mean, lying?

Hero Ng answered, *The symbionts cannot hold them all. Not and hold the memories of the crew.*

They'd consume us?

Not you, said Hero Ng. *Us. The memories of the dead. Imagine, Rien, if I were the sort of man who thought he had more right to live than do you.*

Rien could imagine it all too well. She said, to Samael, "How can you hope to win back Perceval, if you cannot defeat Dust?"

"I have given you the means already," he said. "Consider it earnest money, if you will."

"The means?"

"The plum," he said. "From the library tree. It is a rare fruit, containing a piece of code that will interrupt his control of her symbiont. I had meant it for you, to keep you free, my Rien."

She might have stepped back again at his casual possession, but Rien was nothing if not stubborn. "Then what do I need you for?"

"To bring her the fruit," he said. "And if she has not yet submitted willingly, there is a chance that it could deliver Perceval from Dust's thrall."

"But if he is the Angel of Libraries, shouldn't he know—"

"Yes," Samael answered. "But all things come to an end. And I am the Angel of Death." And then he smiled sidelong through his hair and said, "But it was I who came to see you awaken. I do not see your father or your mother here."

And why should he? They had abandoned her to Alasdair, without a backward glance, and Alasdair had done everything possible to hide her history from her.

Not that being raised Mean seemed like being cheated, exactly, now that she'd met a few Exalt.

She realized that Samael was still looking at her, waiting for her to respond. To defend Benedick, and Arianrhod—whom she had barely met—or to condemn them?

Rien smoothed her hands along her thighs, and let it go. She had never had anyone's protection in her life. She didn't need it now, and especially she did not need Samael's.

And then he said, "You know they only want to use you. The way they used Perceval."

And his tone—hopeful, light, disingenuous—was the clue that triggered Rien to angry speculation. She came up to him with quick small steps, the decking stinging her bare, moisture-softened feet. "And are you the angel who poisoned us?"

"Poisoned you?"

"Poisoned Perceval," she said. "With an influenza virus. And then arranged for her to be captured by Ariane."

This smile made his lined face shine. "If I had," he said, "why in the world would you think I'd admit it so easily?"

They *interpermeated.*

Perceval had just time to realize that Dust was enfolding her, drawing her out of her body and into the shadow-light fretwork of the parasite wings, and then she was as free of her body as any devil coughed loose in an exorcism. She imagined her consciousness floating up her own throat, exhaled on a cloud of sunlit particles, swirling into the presence of the angel.

And then they were together. Meshed, reinforcing and canceling in an interference pattern, bars of brilliance and darkness. Perceval was clear of thought, simultaneously purged of the chemical cocktail with which Pinion had tried seducing her and lifted from the framework of her own flesh. She diffused into him, wondering how long it had taken Pinion to duplicate the patterns of her thought and personality, and how she would know if they had been subtly—or not so subtly—changed.

"Come with me," Dust said, and now he was a gossamer presence, a breath of air upon a neck she didn't have. He guided her, and she went with him, feeling small in the shadow of his wings. They reached out, a lightspeed flicker, closer than flying feathertip to feathertip.

And found themselves in Rule.

Or what remained of it.

"Your doing," Dust said, and Perceval might have quailed, had she not been a perfect and unemotional machine.

He showed her death; he showed her the toll of war; he showed her what it was to be an angel, and adrift.

They moved like ghosts among the dead, distributed consciousnesses floating in a fall of dust. Perceval understood that it was dangerous to be so far attenuated, that there were angels that hunted angels, but Dust had left this portion of his substance in place for a long time, and he felt his was as safe as leaving one's stronghold could ever be.

"I ward your body," he said, and if she reached back far enough she could feel it, a mortal tether floating among the lattices of the world.

She did not have his knack of distributing consciousness over the entire network. She could switch back and forth between images, conscious of a lightspeed lag measured in fractions of fractions, and even overlay one perspective with the other, but the effortlessness with which Dust managed his gestalt focus was beyond her.

She could, however, feel the dark patches, the vast swaths of the *Jacob's Ladder* that were outside of Dust's control, or simply dead, gangrenous flesh still grafted to the moribund world as it rotted in pieces.

"Still only human," he told her. "This is what it means to be my captain, beloved."

She explored the limits of this new capability, wondering if there was a tool here that could be used as a weapon against him, trying to hide the thought. She might have been successful; in any case, if he saw it, he did not respond.

Instead, Dust brought Perceval through Rule, and showed her the bodies of the Mean. They were netted and roped outside the air locks, frozen far more crudely than the ones in the holde. *Like fish in nets*, she thought. There must be dozens of dead. Hundreds.

It should have chilled her, if she were in her own flesh, but she was beyond chill. She could count them, exactly, if she wished. She could brush her fringes over each of the dead and know that person, and bear witness to their illness and agony.

Cowardly, she turned away, and went within the halls of Rule, accompanied by Dust.

Here, a few still walked. Some Mean, still wasted and shuffling with exhaustion in their slow unaugmented recovery from the illness Perceval had brought them. Some Exalt, with the flat eyes of the resurrected. And some Exalt, who must have lived.

Among them, Ariane, who stood in a luxuriously

appointed chamber, two gray-faced servants by her side, arraying her for battle.

Perceval braced for a flush of rage and terror, but felt no such thing. Chemical, all chemical. And if it did rise, back in the belly of her cold body, it barely brushed her here.

"Take me," Dust said, "and I will help you defeat Ariane. Be my captain, and help me stand against the angel who is her ally."

"And what angel is that?" It was a strange sensation, to float at her Enemy's shoulder unnoticed. Witchcraft.

"Asrafil, the Angel of Blades."

"While we are here beside her," Perceval asked, "why not just block her throat, kill her now?"

"Asrafil," Dust repeated. "We move subtly, now, and go unnoticed. The world swarms, and not even an angel can inspect every nanobot that crawls within its sphere. But if we moved against her, he would know."

Perceval watched as Ariane drew her unblade and cut passes in the air with it. If she followed her thread back to her own body, she could imagine fear at the sight. "Who is she going to war with? Surely not Engine. Not with her forces so depleted."

"No," Dust whispered in her ear. Perceval slid back into her body with a sense of impact, awash in sick meat and chemical deception. Her fingers curled in distaste. "She's coming here, Perceval. To devour you, and conquer me."

24

vessel

We are like searchers in a house
of darkness,
A house of dust; we creep with
little lanterns,
Throwing our tremulous arcs of light
at random.

—CONRAD AIKEN, *The House of Dust*

Samael waited while the resurrectee brought Rien clothing, in which she dressed as quickly as she could, even to the paper shoes. Then the resurrectee took her wrist again and led her to a door. From the silence of the medical bay, Rien emerged into soft-spoken chaos.

She had known Engine was a city, but a glimpse of its vast spaces while being borne in on a stretcher was profoundly different from stepping out the hatchway, flanked by a resurrectee on one side and the Angel of Death on the other, and being confronted by the sweep of unfettered space. Her earlier head-spinning glimpses could not prepare her for this.

The holde might have rivaled a small city on Earth, she
thought, though neither she nor Ng had personal experience to compare. Still, she felt she stood at the bottom of
a bowl—but she would have felt that no matter where she
stood. The space was a bubble, and the gravity must be di-
rectional, because she could see the structures rising from
the walls as if from solid deck, all of them shining in
pearlescent pastels, each tapered and prickling toward the
center, so the whole bore a resemblance to a pin cushion
turned inside-out.

And the streets, and the space between the walls, were
filled with traffic. For the first time, the existence of
Perceval's wings made logical sense to Rien; she watched
Engineer after Engineer flit from one side of the void to
the other, and thought how long it would take to walk
around.

There were spanning cables as well, and cars moving
along them, but why walk (or drive) if you could fly?

She would have expected noise, echoes filling the cavernous space, but the structures must have been designed
to absorb sound. If anything, the street was hushed, voices
falling off within a few steps, footsteps inaudible. It made
the bustle eerie, like watching vids with the sound turned
down to a whisper.

The resurrectee tugged her wrist gently, and Rien realized she was stuck in the doorway. Stepping away from the
shelter of the wall made her knees tremble, but she was
too shamed by her fear to show it. Especially in front of
Samael.

She walked into the traffic and after a few steps it grew
easier. The way was crowded, but in that crowding lay

anonymity, and in that anonymity, Rien found security. She walked among the weirdly modified: angels and devils and someone who looked rather like a pagoda. There were persons who were chromed to quicksilver mirrors, or whose skins reflected the iridescent colors of the city. There were persons with eight limbs, scurrying along walls, and there were tiger-striped persons with wings and lush pelts.

When she had been Mean, Rien could vanish into any crowd.

She relished being able to do it again.

She was still relieved to come to the end of the walk. They stepped through a sliding door into a cool, dim room, and Rien bit back a sigh. She stepped to one side, not wanting to stay silhouetted against the light while Samael followed, amused by her own paranoia but not amused enough to stop herself. Once she was within, her augmented eyes adjusted.

The first person she saw was Benedick, Gavin on his shoulder, and she could have sagged against the wall in relief. Instead, she made herself step forward, freeing her wrist from the resurrectee's grasp, and went to her father.

He touched her shoulder lightly. She leaned into it, just enough to let him know she appreciated the gesture, not enough to admit she needed it.

"Where's Tristen?" she asked.

"Still in the tank," he said, with a wince that made Rien feel guilty for letting Samael make her doubt her uncle. "He was worst off. I'm here to feed you and lead you to our improvisational council of war."

"Perceval," Rien said.

He nodded. "I will make her a priority. Come and meet your mother, Rien." He looked over her shoulder at Samael. "Nothing is decided."

Samael said, "May I accompany you?"

Benedick had a steady gaze, when he wanted it. "Could I stop you?"

Samael's shrug was oddly self-effacing, for an angel.

Gavin hopped onto Rien's shoulder. He didn't say anything, so neither did she. But she leaned her cheek against his wing, and he huddled into the curve of her neck, warm and feathery, smelling of sunlight and dust.

Benedick turned away, and Rien followed. The resurrectee was left behind, as unregarded as an old shoe, and Rien gave her a regretful glance.

The place he brought them to, finally, suited Rien's perception of what Engine should be. It was a long wide room, divided into near-corridors by rows of pillars and banks of interfaces. Engineers sat, sprawled, or curled in bowl-shaped chairs, some with eyes closed and fingers twitching in concentration, others in hushed conversation with their neighbors.

Despite this, Rien's attention was drawn inexorably to the image in a central hologram tank. The waystars shone and twisted at its center, illuminated in gradations of color invisible to the naked eye, and Rien realized that in the tank, she could see pressure and temperature readings, maps of convection currents, real-time diagrams of changing stellar structures, and estimates of the time remaining before the system collapsed into supernova. She realized also that she could read those numbers and gradients, by the courtesy of Hero Ng.

Arianrhod stood beyond the tank, her white hair shining in the light of the conjured stars.

Rien could not walk forward, as if maintaining her distance from the information in the tank could protect her from the reality of their danger.

"Days," Rien said. "That's just days."

Benedick touched her elbow. He was tall; she tipped her head back to look up at him. "It could be instants," he said. "Or a month. We won't have much warning, once the conflagration starts."

Rien shook her head. "We can't survive that."

"Not without a unified A.I.," Samael said quite calmly. "And a captain. And a mobile ship. And a crew that can fly her."

"None of which we have."

"All of which we can get," Rien said—or her voice said for her, though the intonation and the words were not her own. She pressed her fingertips over her mouth; her lips kept moving. "If you will trust me."

"Rien?" Benedick, staring at her as if he expected a possessing demon to rise up from her.

"I was Conrad Ng," she said. "Chief Engineer. Your daughter consumed me. She is my vessel."

When Perceval returned to her body, and Dust reclaimed his avatar, Perceval asked to talk to Rien. She expected a negative answer, some temporization.

She didn't expect Dust to spread his made-up hands helplessly and say, "I am sorry, beloved. Engine is beyond my grasp." But he did, and—perhaps foolishly—she believed his admission of defeat.

And then he tilted his head and said, "But with your assistance, I hope my reach may soon exceed."

"It's all you think of," she said. "Seducing me."

"Your acquiescence," he said plainly, "is my survival." And then he dusted his hands against his waistcoat and finished, "But if you prefer to wait for Ariane, or for a supernova, that is the lady's privilege."

Rien understood everything Hero Ng was saying, which surprised her either more or less than it should have. The knowledge was there, deep knowledge, divorced of his personality. As if she had once upon a time studied and learned it herself.

There were other things as well, memories she would rather not pursue—a wife and children and all the bits and bobs a life was made of. *At least he was a good man*, she thought. A decent man. And a brave one.

She would have hated to share her head with someone like Alasdair or Ariane, no matter how wickedly smart they made her.

Maybe it took a monster to run things. Maybe you could only be a princess until you were in charge.

She could believe that. But she didn't want to think about it. Instead, she listened to Hero Ng explain his plan.

There was a good deal of the world, in his estimation, that was dead or damaged beyond repair. There was a good deal of raw material in the holdes. The world now had

stored energy it had not contained when it limped into orbit around the waystars.

And there were the library trees, and the resurrectees.

If he could take hold in Rien, he reasoned, then his fel-
low crew members, preserved in the library, could inhabit
the resurrected. "Ethically, we might quail at this neces-
sity, but we have come down to a matter of life or death.
There is a vast body of knowledge preserved there, and it
is useless to the ship while maintained in stasis, unac-
cessed."

Rien stole a glance at Benedick. He did not appear to be
quailing, and neither did her mother. Instead, Arianrhod
had come around the hologram tank and now leaned
against its corner, ankles crossed and arms folded, listening.

"We have a pair of immediate problems," Hero Ng said.
"One is surviving an impending stellar death. The other is
getting the *Jacob's Ladder* under way again, sustainably. It
seems to me that the solutions to these problems must be
linked. It will require a good deal of nerve, however, and
will not be without risk. And we must begin at once, for
we have no idea how long we have for preparations."

And while they waited, he explained.

Simply put, Chief Engineer Ng proposed that the
Jacob's Ladder wait until the waystar went supernova, then
catch a ride on the magnetized wave front of the exploding debris.

Theoretically (Ng said), embedded among the debris
would be bubbles of magnetic field, created in the death
throes of the star during the process of reconnection, the

melding of opposing magnetic fields into a single line. It was possible—if the unused stores and the damaged ship itself could be spun into carbon monofilament tubes and computronium and symbiote colonies, if the repurposing of the ship's artificial gravity worked—that the world could net one of those bubbles and surf the cresting wave.

And maybe not be crushed. As long as they caught the leading edge. As long as they accelerated fast enough to stay with it. As long as they could reinforce the world, and locate enough acceleration tanks that the augmented crew stood a chance of survival. "There's no hope for the Mean," Ng said. "They will have to be Exalted immediately; there's no point in maintaining controls only to see them perish."

It was possible, as long as the world did not tear itself apart at the seams from the strain. The whole ship would have to accelerate evenly. The whole ship would have to stay ahead of the line of debris. Or they would be reduced to a smudge along the edge of the newly forming planetary nebula.

"And then what?" Arianrhod said, the first words Rien had heard her speak since fainting on the stretcher. "We fly blindly into darkness until we freeze? That seems to be a jump from the fire into the icebox, if I may stretch a metaphor."

Rien felt her lips stretch around Ng's smile. It was a nice smile, she judged, if a little smug. "If we live that long? When we're up to speed, we deploy a ramscoop. We find a better star, one that looks to have habitable worlds. And we steer for it."

"Simple," Arianrhod said, unfolding her arms. She glanced over her shoulder at the auburn-haired, snub-nosed woman who had been at her side now both times Rien had seen her. "Chief Engineer?"

She didn't mean Ng.

Which meant that was Caitlin Conn. Perceval's mother. Who was looking at Rien with far more concentration than was Arianrhod, though perhaps that was self-protection or embarrassment on Arianrhod's part.

"I think it could work," Caitlin said, without shifting her gaze. Maybe she was looking at—assessing—Hero Ng. He was the one wearing Rien's face, just now. "If it doesn't kill us. Of course, sitting here waiting for the boom will kill us, too. There's just one problem . . ."

Rien found control of her own voice, or Ng relinquished it to her. She stepped away from Samael and, incidentally, Benedick. Gavin fanned his wings on her shoulder, for balance, and she remembered that he was Samael's creature.

And so was Mallory.

Which meant, so was Ng.

There was no one to trust. Except Perceval. Because if she didn't trust Perceval, there was nothing worth fighting for.

"What's the problem?" Benedick asked.

Rien knew the answer. "We'd have to unify the world's A.I. to do it. The angels don't work together without a guiding intelligence."

She would not look at Samael.

She couldn't bear to watch him preening.

At least, she thought, he wouldn't consume Hero Ng,

and all his fellows from the moving times. No: they could be rehomed in the resurrected. Whose persons had been devoured by other Exalt, in the present day.

It all comes around again, Hero Ng whispered. *Be of good heart and good patience, brave Rien.*

25

vault

Yes, I have a thousand tongues,
And nine and ninety-nine lie.

—STEPHEN CRANE,
The Black Riders and Other Lines

A little later, Rien sat alone except for Gavin, feeling
small and lost behind a table in the corner. She
watched the adults, whom she was still tempted to call the
Exalt, performing their mysterious dances of conversation, moving from place to place around the big room like
ants touching antennae and sharing pheromones, passing
news of the death of an old queen or the ascension of the
new. She had slipped away from Samael—or at least, from
Samael's avatar—and Benedick was talking to someone
she didn't know while ignoring Caitlin and being ignored
right back.

Like two cats on a bed, she thought. She fiddled with her
fingers and thought about what she knew through Hero
Ng.

His plan might even work.

Samael, Mallory, and Gavin. She told herself she'd only been using Mallory, that she had never trusted or liked Gavin. The basilisk still roosted on her shoulder, baleful eyes tight shut. She poked him with a finger. "Wake up."

"Do I look plugged in to you? I'm not sleeping."

"Good," she said. "Because I'm sending you home."

"Rien—"

But she stopped him with a raised hand. A funny awkward gesture when one made it to someone whose head bobbed beside one's own. "Someone needs to fetch Mallory and the fruits of the library tree. And you are the obvious choice. Can you find your way EVA?"

"I can." He billed her cheek. She ordered herself not to be charmed and turned her face away. "You think I serve Samael," he said.

"Don't you?"

He shrugged, both wings. "Do you?"

"No." As flatly as she could say it. "I don't see the point in angels. Or in reuniting angels. Or in choosing one angel over another; it's like asking if you would rather be scourged or boiled in oil. They're all full of shit and self-importance."

She must have spoken louder than she intended, because her words made someone—other than Gavin—laugh. She craned her neck to see over his back.

A young woman somewhat smaller and slighter than even Rien stood against the wall. She'd call her a woman, anyway, though she was covered in a soft spotted coat of gray-gold fur. Her wings—folded tight, long-boned, with grasping fingers at the joint—were what caught Rien's eye and made her breath short, though, because in seeing them, she could imagine what Perceval's wings had been like.

It came to Rien that even if she got her sister back, she would never see her whole. In breathtaking unfairness, the Perceval-who-had-been was maimed before Rien had ever met her.

She wanted to reach out and rub one hand down the velvet-furred bones of the stranger's wing, to see if it felt— as it appeared—like the velour skin of a peach. Instead, Rien made herself look at her face, and register a fine nose and wide mouth, unbalanced by heavy brows.

"Rien," she said, by way of introduction. Her hands were cold, and she chafed them on her trouser legs.

"Jordan," the stranger answered, and held out a fine-boned hand. She was as slender as Perceval. Rien wondered if they were related.

Rien took her hand, reminding herself that falling for strangers simply because they looked a little like Perceval was stupid. Although Perceval would never want her, and wouldn't holding on be stupider, still?

There was no fur on the stranger's palms, or the backs of her fingers. The skin there was black, like the skin on her face where the fur did not cover, and Rien thought of the hands of lemurs. The fur made sense; Jordan had no apparent body fat, and she was small and thin. You'd need some kind of insulation.

"You don't like Samael," Jordan said.

"I don't like being manipulated." Rien gave her hand a squeeze and released it. "I guess that means I don't like angels."

Then she held up one finger for a moment of quiet, and tapped Gavin on the wing. "Will you do what I asked you to?"

"Your wish is my command," he said, with abject dryness, and kicked off with more force than was needful.

Heads turned as he swept across the room with long, rowing strokes of his wings, tail snaking behind. A tall man ducked, though Gavin never came with a meter of him. Samael, speaking quietly with Benedick, affected either boredom or oblivion; he didn't even lift his head.

Rien wanted to hit him.

And maybe Jordan noticed her clenching hands, as the door slipped open in front of Gavin and he vanished into the corridor beyond. Because she touched Rien's wrist lightly, and when she turned, smiled. "Tell me more."

"More what?"

"More of why you don't like angels."

Too much, too fast, maybe. She shrugged and drew inward. "Not right now." And then, at Jordan's fallen face, wondered; maybe she *had* been flirting.

"Maybe some other time," Rien continued, reopening the door. "It looks like the party is breaking up, and they'll have work for me."

Or for Hero Ng, which amounted to the same thing.

As if Gavin's departure had been a trigger, people were dispersing—to consoles, or out of the room. Rien stood, looking around for Benedick.

"Nice to meet you," Jordan said.

Rien gave her a slantwise smile. "Nice to meet you, also."

• • •

After the council of war, Rien's mother brought her cookies. She set the plate at Rien's elbow and sat down beside her at the console upon which Rien—or Hero Ng, more accurately—was working. Rien watched him, though, and she was learning.

Rien's left hand moved across the controls without pause as, with the right one, she selected a cookie.

"Thank you," she said, through a mouthful of sweet carbohydrates.

It was the first thing she'd eaten since they began their run through Inkling's cavern. She stuffed the other half in her mouth.

"You feel I abandoned you," Arianrhod said.

Rien mumbled something unintelligible, unbearably grateful for the excuse of snack foods. Sugar cookies. She could live on them.

Ng took her hand back while she chewed, and typed faster. She let him, watching her fingers dance.

Arianrhod cleared her throat. "I had to leave you, Rien. But I gave you my name for a reason. I didn't know—"

Her voice creaked.

"Gave me your name?" Rien asked, forgetting to watch her fingers.

"Rien," Arianrhod said. "It's a part of my name."

She licked her lips, and Rien became aware that she was staring. She looked quickly away. "Your name."

Arianrhod touched her arm. "I would have done more. But the contract was—"

"Contract." Surely Rien had something better to do than echoing everything Arianrhod said. Whatever it might be, however, she could not think of it. She was thinking, instead, of names. And not just her own name.

"How else are children born, between Rule and Engine?" Arianrhod shrugged, and appropriated a cookie. If appropriated was the right word, when she had provided them. Her hair fell over her blouse, a waterfall of silver that could not have been more different from Inkling's deadly river.

"I thought I was named for nothing," Rien said, and having said it, frowned. Arianrhod.

Rien.

Arianrhod.

Rien.

It was on the tip of her tongue. She bit her lip. To buy time, she corrected a faulty spectrograph of the waystars.

Rien.

Arianrhod.

Ariane.

"Tristen," she said, too quickly, stammering. "Is he out of the tank yet?"

"Not yet," Arianrhod answered. "Did you want to visit him?"

Rien let Ng have her hands back. At least it kept them from shaking. "Yes," she said. "After."

Ariane was her half sister. Maybe. Ariane was also Arianrhod's daughter, by Alasdair. Possibly.

Did it matter?

Did it matter that Perceval was her half sister?

No. It mattered that she loved Perceval.

"After?"

"After we talk about what we're going to do for Perceval."

Whatever the bonds of blood, Arianrhod was no more willing to help Rien reclaim her sister than anyone else might have been. When Arianrhod excused herself, Rien did not complain.

She'd intended the request as a test—a test that, if Arianrhod failed it, would give either of them a reason to end the conversation.

A game, yes.

Rien might not like these ruling monsters, but if playing their games was what it took, well, she would prove that she could learn. She would be a master manipulator in no time, among this crew. And her mind was spinning over those three names—Arianrhod, Ariane, Rien—and the implication that there were layers and layers of allegiances that she did not even begin to understand.

She was glad she had Hero Ng to keep her hands busy.

Because she was thinking about Tristen, and his claim on the Captaincy—not as good as Perceval's, perhaps, because of the archaic rules under which the world labored, but better than Ariane's, except Ariane had eaten their father—and she was thinking about the chamber of bats, and Tristen warehoused there until Ariane could get around to eating his mind and experiences. As Rien had eaten Hero Ng.

And she was thinking about the healing tanks.

Whether the Engineers trusted Hero Ng to keep her out of trouble—after all, he was one of their own—or whether they were too busy themselves to watch her closely, Rien found herself working alone. It wasn't as if she was invisible; the Engineers didn't look through her as they bustled around their operations center. Instead, it was as if she had been sprayed with a frictionless coating, or perhaps as if she sat in the visual equivalent of an electromagnetic bottle.

What do they know that I don't? she wondered.

She watched Hero Ng work, and she studied what he did, and she worried. She understood it all, at least—his knowledge was her knowledge, too. That was some comfort, though the familiar/unfamiliar texture of the control panel under her hands was disconcerting, if she let herself think about it.

He had taken on the task of calculating the modifications necessary to maintain the world's integrity when they caught the electromagnetic shock wave. If they caught the electromagnetic shock wave. Caitlin Conn and her people were working on *that* task, which was equally vital and slightly less ticklish. Ng was handicapped by outdated knowledge of the world; things had changed since he died. But that handicap was compensated for by a more complete knowledge than any of the modern Engineers. In the moving times, in Ng's time, there had been shipwide communication, and the angels had not been embattled.

He knew what was supposed to be there.

Still, he found the work stressful. And after Arianrhod's departure, their apparent coinvisibility meant that Rien was on her own with regard to refreshment. By the time Ng at last hit a snag in his calculations that wasn't amenable to a few moments of staring into space and flipping a light stylus, Rien suggested—no, it was her body, dammit— Rien *enforced* a walk.

Maybe they could find Benedick, and he could take them to get something to eat, and she could talk to him about reclaiming Tristen and then rescuing Perceval.

Them, Rien thought, her hand extended to the door release, and chuckled. She would never be alone again. Even if no one turned to see why she laughed.

The invisible girl.

She was willing to bet it was the dead Engineer in her head who made everybody so uncomfortable.

Conrad Ng expressed regret. Not really in words, more in a feeling of wry apologetic shame. Rien shushed him. It wasn't he who had forced the fruit upon her, and it was not he who had chosen to eat. While walking through the door, she looked down at her hands. And he certainly came in useful.

Samael, he suggested.

Behind it all, she agreed, smoothing her hands over the naked skin of her scalp. When her hair started growing back, she imagined it would itch terribly. Now, though, it reminded her of touching Perceval, and she did it again.

They—she—stepped through the door, and as Rien turned to ask the monitor where she might find Benedick, she nearly walked into him.

"We should work on your situational awareness," he said. "You nearly walked into me."

She looked up at him and managed not to say the first thing that came into her mouth. And then was startled that she'd even considered mouthing off to an Exalt. Not just to an Exalt.

To Benedick Conn.

"Were you coming for me?" she said instead.

And he smiled, half shyly. "I'm no use to the Engineers," he said. "Not until it comes down to tactics and command decisions. I thought I'd see if you were hungry."

She imagined she wasn't the only one who could hear her stomach grinding rocks. She turned to walk beside him, the press of traffic steering her close to his side. He took her elbow.

Something about the anonymity of all these people, the reaching city crawling up the walls on every side like creepers climbing for the light, made her bold. She stretched on tiptoe as they walked and said toward his ear, "How did you wind up selling your daughters for peace tokens?"

He flinched, his fingers tightening on her arm. And then he appeared to decide that she deserved an answer, because he said, "You're the reason Caitlin isn't speaking to me."

"I guessed," Rien said. "The dates matched. Was it your father?"

"He wanted a hostage," Benedick said. "That the balance of terror be maintained."

"May I assume you are not close to Arianrhod?"

It was a gamble even asking. But Arianrhod had said *contract.* And pretended affection so transparently that even Rien could see through her. And if she was such a crowning egoist that she'd name a daughter she never expected to see again with a portion of her own name, there was the matter of Ariane's name, as well.

"You would not be incorrect in such an assumption," Benedick said, after considering. "Of course I meant you to be raised as one of the family."

"In that house," Rien answered, "it's as well I was not."

He had been about to wince and dip his head, acknowledging her point, and she had been about to let him off the hook with a wry reference to Head. But she felt a tension come into him. Work on your situational awareness, he had said, and so she turned to follow the line of his gaze.

And tripped so hard Benedick had to catch her.

A coffle of resurrectees were led through the street, and Rien knew them. The one in the front, walking placidly, his glossy head bowed and his bright eyes half-lidded, used to be Oliver Conn.

"There's no way they got from here to Rule and back since we arrived," Rien said. "Somebody knew in advance, and was waiting to bring them back."

"Ariane must be behind the influenza," Benedick said. "It makes too much sense. She brings in Perceval; she incapacitates her brothers and sisters with illness and consumes as many of them as possible."

If Rien had not been standing beside him, she would have thought him unemotional at the death of his family, but she could hear the flutter of his breath, too fast. He glanced down at her, and she nodded at him to continue.

"She precipitates a war with Engine that she has no intention of fighting." His throat worked when he swallowed. "Like saving Tristen for later. She's like one of the angels: she's going to eat the whole family if she can get away with it."

"Not just Ariane," Rien said. "She had to have an ally here. Somebody with resources. Somebody who could make sure she ran into Perceval at the right time, in the right place, when Perceval was already sickening."

"Arianrhod," he said. He held her arm too tightly, as the dead man who had been Oliver shuffled past them without so much as a flicker of attention.

Rien bit down on a sob. Not for herself. Not for Arianrhod, who was a stranger, nothing to her, and the ties of blood irrelevant—though she might have felt differently, had she not encountered Benedick and Tristen and Perceval, and found a place to stand. "So, of course, she's going to impede anything we might want to do toward rescuing Perceval."

"How are we going to find out where she's being held?"

"Dust has her," Rien answered. "Hero Ng knows where to go to look for Dust."

She didn't say, we can't do this without Samael. Because Benedick knew it as well as she did, and she didn't want to say it out loud, as if that would make it real. Instead, Rien squeezed his fingers. "First we need to go get Tristen. And I need my things that I came here with."

"Right," said Benedick. "Let's find him."

It was Hero Ng who finally located Tristen, hacking into the medical computers while Rien thought uncharitably of Samael and his barbed gifts, and even less charitably of Mallory. How convenient, she thought, how freeing to be able to embrace the role of necromancer, trickster, betrayer. How it must release one from the bounds of common courtesy and right behavior. What a romantic series of excuses.

Maybe she, Rien, should become a sorcerer. Or an angel. Then she could be an asshole, too, and if anybody commented on it, she could shrug and present her union card.

Hero Ng, without quite interrupting the stream of cynicism, nudged her. She shook her head and pulled herself together, a little shamed. If it was bad for her, what was it like for him, trapped in a strange body, resurrected to deal with a crisis he'd been half glad to avoid by dying? He'd no more asked for this than she had, even if it was Mallory and Samael who had tricked them into each other.

She couldn't call Ng a coward. And she couldn't fail him by being a coward either. Nor could she fail Tristen, or Perceval, or even Benedick.

She let Ng show her the map. And sighed. "I don't know what we're going to do," she said. "We found Tristen" — she tried not to notice Benedick's worried glance when she said "we"— "but he's in a private ward. He's tanked."

"For a grown man," Benedick said, "he needs a lot of rescuing. All right. I'm going to have to talk to Caitlin."

Rien rubbed at her throat. "Would it be better if I did?"

"The least fun part of being an adult is facing your own mistakes." Benedick patted her shoulder. "But if she won't hear me, then yes, you're on."

Rien sucked on her lip, unsure if what she felt was relief at being let off the hook, or outrage over being patronized. Maybe you could feel both at once.

Maybe you could feel all sorts of things, all of them mutually contradictory.

Rien said, "After you, Father."

The monitor lead them to Caitlin. One must be able to find the Chief Engineer. And Caitlin, to Rien's surprise, was immediately accessible. She sat in an office that was little more than a collection of chairs and interfaces, screens and keyboards and holographic panels bristling from every surface and each wall. The door was a slider rather than an iris, and it was open wide.

Caitlin Conn looked up when they entered, lips thinning. And she stared not at Benedick, but at Rien. Her left hand moved slightly, pinky and ring finger stretching as she blanked her screens, but not before Rien saw schematics of the *Jacob's Ladder*. And knew, through Ng, that they were in significant part completely speculative.

We have no idea, anymore, what the world even looks like.

"Chief Engineer," Benedick said, "I need to talk to you about our brother, and our daughter."

To her credit, Caitlin only nodded, and gestured them inside the door. It shut as soon as they cleared the entry, the sudden silence disconcerting. Rien found herself crowding back against the panel, which did not slide open from the pressure. Caitlin must have locked it.

Quickly, Benedick outlined their suspicions about Arianrhod and Ariane, while Caitlin steepled her fingers and listened. Rien had to admit, she was impressed by how well Caitlin listened. Active listening, intent and focused.

Rien found herself staring back, fascinated by the freckles on the back of Caitlin's hands, the ones speckling her face and hairline. Still, Caitlin's expression gave away nothing. Even when Benedick explained that they thought it was Arianrhod and Ariane, colluding, who had arranged for Perceval's maiming and abduction.

But when Benedick got to Tristen, she stopped him momentarily with an upraised finger, and Rien thought she checked something through her symbiont. Of course it could bring her any information she needed. The screens were merely a way of organizing, externalizing, and categorizing. Like writing lists.

"He should have been released," Caitlin said. "I'll see to it. Continue. Once you have him back, what then?"

"We're going after Perceval," Rien said.

"With Samael."

"I don't see a way around it." Benedick put his hand on Rien's shoulder, and she allowed him to take up the thread of conversation again. "We'll need an angel. And we need to choose an angel to support, if Rien—"

"Hero Ng," Rien corrected, and then blushed blue as she realized what she'd just done.

"Hero Ng," Caitlin echoed, "is correct that we'll need a unified A.I. to hold the world together."

"He is confident in his assessment. And he knows where Perceval is. Or he is nearly certain," Rien said, the phrasing not her own.

Caitlin seemed to know it. She smiled bitterly and stood, bouncing on her toes, radiating vibrant energy. She came around the desk. She wasn't much taller than Rien, but her arms and neck showed evidence of muscle. A black-hilted unblade bumped at her hip.

"I *should* stay here," she said. "And direct the preparations."

"And watch over Arianrhod."

She bit her lip. "I can have Arianrhod detained. And questioned. If you two are willing to stand surety."

"Meaning?"

"Meaning if she proves innocent, you could be sued for false accusation." Caitlin's hand rested, Rien thought unconsciously, on the unblade's hilt. Her thumb caressed the pommel. She turned over her shoulder and glanced at the blanked-out screens. "I wish we still had Susabo," she said. "That was a no-nonsense sort of angel. I'd back him over Samael."

"Was it Samael who killed him?"

"It was the stone that killed him. Or weakened him. But yes, it was Samael who ate what was left. And I couldn't defend him. So now we have Inkling, who is fierce, but small. As angels go. And we have Samael."

"And Rule has Dust?"

Caitlin shook her head, arms folded, head cocked to one side consideringly. "Rule has Asrafil. The Angel of Battle Systems. Or maybe Asrafil has Rule, and Samael has us."

"And Dust has Perceval," Benedick said, and Caitlin nodded.

"Yes," she said. "Come on. If we're going to choose, we need to be about choosing."

"I thought you were staying here," Benedick said.

Rien drew a breath. She hoped not. She wanted Caitlin to leap to the defense of her daughter.

"Making the ship ready for flight is a vital undertaking," Caitlin said, and Rien's heart fell, as it had fallen when she looked at Arianrhod and saw something about as genuine as the gift of sugar cookies. And then Caitlin uncrossed her arms, letting them swing from the shoulders, and continued, "So is retaking the command center. And there are a lot of Engineers *here*."

"Cat?" Benedick asked.

She looked up at him, not quite a glare but also not forgiveness, and said, "Let's go decant our brother."

26

the devil of the stair

There were no more faces and the
stair was dark,
Damp, jagged, like an old man's
mouth drivelling, beyond repair.

—T. S. ELIOT, "Ash Wednesday"

Dust said, "The child is nothing. Ariane is coming,
and with her, Asrafil. Accept me."

His captain of desire stood on the empty bridge,
cloaked in her shadowbright wings, and ran her hands
away from her heart on either side, stroking down the rail.
The sound-absorbing carpet crumbled to powder under
Perceval's feet, and only by standing very still could she
stop the puffs of dust that rose at every step. Cobwebs
clung to her fingers as she lifted them from the rail.
Cobwebs, thick with dust, drifted from the rail where her
touch had broken them free, and draped across the deck
like veils. "This is your heart," she said.

"And it is bitter," he answered. She didn't laugh, just
flicked her eyes at him curiously, turning her shaven head.

He could see the structure of her neck and skull in the visible light, and it was beautiful to him.

"I give you my heart," he said.

He walked his avatar into the center of the room—not vast, not by the standards of Dust, who contained multitudes—and turned in the light, his arms spread wide. The wind of his moving stirred dust and spiderwebs; the entire bridge was draped in their spinnings. Dust stroked a ragged web, his fingers parsing powdery softness where his other senses reported protein chains, crystalline patterns joined by amorphous linkages.

Perceval lifted her chin. The light from the bridge's single still-brilliant lamp cast shadows stark across her face. "I do not want your heart."

"Yes, you do," he said, because he could make her want it. "Don't lie to me, Perceval. It's demeaning."

She would not look at him. "Open the panels," she said. "Show me the suns."

He stood below her and looked up. Of course, while he was below, he was above and to each side as well, but sometimes when dealing with nondistributed intelligences, it helped to focus down and mimic their thought. He wondered if she knew she'd just given him a command, and what passed for his heart leaped.

He opened the panels, and let the light of the waystars in. They hung there, at the bottom of their gravity well, hearthfire and furnace and inferno.

"We never named them," Perceval said. "Just the waystars. A and B."

"They were never meant to be permanent," Dust said. "Naming would have been a covenant."

"They could have called it Wheelbroke." Perceval smoothed her hands along the rail again. This time there were no webs to stick to her fingers. "It wouldn't be the first time."

Dust imagined the delight he felt at her wit was the sort of thing that would make a human lover burst into fond laughter, so he tried. But she only looked at him strangely, and folded herself tight in her wings, seeming to forget they were his wings as well.

"If you love something mortal," he said, "it will only destroy you. How much better to love the world—"

She shook her head, long throat working, and stared out at the suns. Dust could have told her everything she cared to know about them; his inward perceptions might be erratic and fragile, but the external ones were maintained and precise. He'd fought that war with his brothers centuries before, and they had divided up the spoils.

His captain of desire said, "Everything's mortal, angel. Even you."

"More mortal every minute," he said. With a thought, he dimmed the panels and brought up the screens. "In defying me, you know you are also killing Rien. And everyone else within my holdes and hallways."

Her jaw worked. She looked down, but it did not matter. Wherever she turned her eyes, he could project his images, even to the inside of her head if she covered her face with her hands.

He didn't have to go that far, though. Because once she saw what he had to show her, she was wide-eyed and avid. Because he had not lied; Ariane was coming, arrayed in her powered armor for battle, shields chattering and sparking around her and her unblade black upon her hip. She climbed, or the armor climbed for her, from Rule and through the Enemy.

The waystars cast their light upon her. Her magnetic boots and gauntlets locked her to the skin of the world.

She was not alone. Asrafil walked beside her, in all his edgy frailty, his collar raised as if against the chill he could not feel. With a relentless determination, a strength beyond hope or despair, together they climbed the world.

Dust briefly admired their cleverness. Even if he could wrest a weapon from Asrafil's control, he could not shoot at Ariane. Not without risking his own metal skin. And even if he blocked her at the air lock, Ariane in her armor could tear her way inside.

"Open the gate," he murmured. "Throw down the bridge. Or it will go ill in the end for those within."

Perceval's hands tightened on the railing, paling across the knuckles, a blue flush visible between. The metal creaked under her grasp.

"She'll come to us," Dust said. "And if you do not join me, we will die at her, or her angel's, hand."

"You're the devil of the stairs," Perceval said. "And if I begin climbing at your word, Jacob Dust, I will never climb to the end."

That devil smiled: a slight man, unassuming, his hands knotted in the pockets of his beautiful coat. "Would that be so terrible? It's a purpose, after all. To climb and climb in pursuit of the stars. To climb in pursuit of God."

"It's a terrible purpose," she said, but he noticed that her fingers curled open atop the rail.

•   •   •

There was something to be said for the word of the Chief Engineer. Caitlin spoke, or sent a message, and mysteriously things got accomplished. The warrant for Arianrhod's detention was an example. Caitlin summoned a functionary, the thing was sworn out and thumbprinted, and then it was sent to be set before a judge.

Likewise, once Tristen was found, they reclaimed him in short order. Caitlin insisted on coming with them in the flesh, so he might see her with his own eyes, now that the corneas were healed. That accomplished, Benedick went with his brother to find clothing, and the women were left in a waiting room.

And so Rien found herself alone with Caitlin Conn. And because she could, she sat against the wall and watched the Chief Engineer stare at her hands and pick at her thumbnails, vanishing the way Means learned to vanish.

Or so she thought.

But Caitlin glanced up, and caught her staring, and with a hesitant smile got up and came across the floor to settle beside Rien. "We'll get her back," she said, and put a hand not on Rien's knee, but beside it.

Rien thought she was speaking to comfort herself as much as to comfort Rien, and found that, in itself, strangely . . . well, comforting. Someone else was worried for Perceval. Someone else was invested in bringing her home.

Perceval had people. Which was something for Rien to envy.

She looked over at Caitlin, who was staring at her knees, and blurted entirely the wrong thing. She knew it was the wrong thing when she said it, and the words hung in front of her mouth, so bright she could almost see them, shimmering beyond recall. "Your picture is nailed facing the wall in Rule."

Caitlin looked up, licked her lips, glanced down, and finally met Rien's eyes square. "How many such portraits are there?"

"Three."

"Then yes, one of them is mine."

"And the other two?" Rien knew she was pushing her luck. But Caitlin seemed inclined to let her, just watching her face alertly, her eyebrows pushing toward a furrow in the center. Self-consciously, Rien smoothed her palms over her denuded scalp. It felt odd, the skin slightly sticky. Tristen had looked the oddest, like a boiled egg, even his milk-white eyelashes missing.

"Cynric," Caitlin said, after a long pause. "And Caithness. My sisters." She looked around for an escape, or failing that a pot of coffee. "Dead," she said, when her eyes were no longer on Rien.

"How?"

"Does it matter?"

"I don't know," Rien answered. "You tell me. They don't teach us history in Rule."

"Especially not the history of the Conn family." Caitlin stood, and began to pace. She had a jerky, bobbing stride, like a bantam hen—direct and purposeful. "We tried to get rid of Dad," she said. "Do you need to know why?"

"Unless it's pertinent, I can probably extrapolate."

Rien got it out with enough deadpan élan that Caitlin glanced at her twice to confirm it was meant to be funny.

Then she grinned, folded her arms, and settled back against the wall. "Thank God your mother didn't have the raising of you."

"Or my father?"

"I didn't say that." Caitlin shrugged. "Your father and I have a lot of history between us."

"And a lot of bad blood."

"And some good blood." She paused again, and this time Rien was smart enough to shut up and let her search out the words at her own place. "A lot of family blood." Her mouth did a complicated thing, and she said, "He executed Cynric."

"Benedick?"

"Beheaded her. On our father's orders."

Rien looked at her fingers, blue around the nails. She looked at the way the light fell on Caitlin's hair and through her eyes, the shadows on her skin the same color. So Caitlin slept with her sister's killer. Who was also her brother.

For political expedience?

For love?

Rien tried to imagine why she would give herself to anyone who hurt Perceval, but she couldn't get past the image of Perceval in chains, the coils of blood groping across her back in denial. Rien swallowed, and realized she had been doing it so much her throat hurt. Thinking of Arianrhod, and contracts, she said, "Did he do everything your father ordered?"

"No." Caitlin came back and sat beside her again,

shoulder to shoulder. "I'm alive. And so, after a fashion, is Cynric."

Rien considered that from several angles, before deciding that when you had no information, the only stupid question was the one you didn't ask. "What do you mean?"

From the corner of her eye, Rien could see Caitlin's half-smile. "My father ate Caithness," she said. "And would have eaten Cynric, too, but some of her was already gone when he got there. I don't know if he noticed."

"Because Benedick rescued it?"

"Because Benedick looked the other way when we hid it in a common household appliance," Caitlin said. "But like a broken angel, you can't fit a whole human being in a machine that small."

"But you can fit all of Hero Ng in a peach? That doesn't make sense."

The Chief Engineer's smile, now that she turned it toward Rien, was sad. "Do you think you have all of Hero Ng in there?"

Rien shook her head, a tiny vibration, and asked him. *How would I know?* he answered. As far as he was concerned, this was all of him there was.

"So feeding the fruit to the resurrectees?"

Caitlin spread her hands: not helplessness, resignation. "At least they will be more useful zombies." She cleared her throat. "Maybe, who knows, maybe they'll grow to fill the space. You know, about Arianrhod—"

"Please don't make me defend why I distrust her," Rien said, eyes trained on the floor until the pressure of Caitlin's gaze made her raise them. "She may have named me for herself, but she also named me nothing."

Caitlin reached out again, and still didn't quite manage to touch her. She coughed and said, "Rien. Would you be my child?"

Somehow, Rien's hand had pressed to her throat, and she could feel her own heart beating against her fingertips. "I don't understand."

And Caitlin actually blanched, sharp white under her freckles, and then flushed pale blue. "I mean I'd adopt you."

"I would be honored," Rien said, the words—again— flown before she thought them through. So after an awkward hesitation, she had to say, "I'm Benedick's daughter. So is Perceval."

"She's coming home."

Caitlin's flat certainty stopped Rien cold. She twisted her fingers together and leaned her forearms on her thighs.

"I hope so," said Rien.

"Come on," Caitlin said. "We need to fetch the men, and find that layabout angel, and get moving. The world isn't saving itself, you know."

Perceval had nothing to do except watch Ariane climb, so she watched, and wondered for how long she could remain resolute. Dust wore at her, his arguments and his veiled threats, the distasteful, trickling fire in her veins. He whispered in her ear, promises of fidelity and partnership that she believed, with all her heart.

She knew he made her believe them, but it wore at her nonetheless, as did the seductive whisper of the parasite wings.

"Be my disciple," he said. "And you may own me. Let me serve you, beloved, and I will give you everything. We are the world. We are the *Jacob's Ladder*. Between us, we can Heaven attain—"

She had no weapons. She had no allies. She touched her hip and found it naked of any defense. The bridge was draped in cobwebs until it seemed as if all the furniture had been sheeted for storage. She stood quite still and listened, and watched her enemy climb.

Ariane, assisted by her angel and her armor, picked nimbly across the webs and ladders of the world. On Dust's screens, Perceval could see a great deal—more than she ever had before. Not everything, though. Engine was closed to her, and so were many reaches of the world. Dust explained that these regions were dead, or under the domination of Asrafil or Samael or one of the lesser brothers—although there were few enough small angels and elementals left.

Perceval thought of Gavin, and held her peace. But she wondered who then the basilisk had belonged to—and who, by extension, Mallory.

Could Rien find an ally there?

Anything was possible. Pinion simpered in her ear, as it did now constantly, a low manipulative whisper. She would not hear its words. She would choose not to understand them.

"She's coming for me," she said.

Dust stroked her shoulder, down to the stump of her wing, the place where Pinion bonded her flesh. She leaned into his touch like a cat, reflexively, then recalled herself and jerked away.

She could have watched the waystars for hours, so she did, without shifting the portion of her attention that followed Ariane. The suns' embrace had grown deadly, and with Dust's senses—her senses, now, through Pinion's intercession—she could see quite plainly how dire things went with the primary. It was on the thin edge of conflagration, and there was no way for Perceval to guess what might press it over the edge.

—*You could save us*— Pinion murmured, and she would have blocked the frequencies of its voice, if it would have allowed.

She warmed to it; its voice was a pleasure. No, she thought. She would not accept that thinking of Dust or Pinion made her feel a melting, protective softness. She stared at the waystars and forced herself to think of Rien.

Rien, whom she had decided to love, of her own free will. Rien, whom she loved for a thousand reasons, all of them good. Rien, whom she chose.

Rien, who must not be dead, or Dust would not be at such pains to pry her from Perceval's fingers.

But thinking of Rien brought problems. Because Perceval had the means to rescue her. Or at least the means to try.

All it would cost her—

—was her integrity. Her freedom.

Rien.

She wanted to trust Dust.

She did trust him. He was there, and she knew him as if she had known him for years. As if she had trusted him for years.

Like her closest friend.

She trailed a hand down the railing as she descended into the cockpit. The bridge was not a vast room, not by the standards of the *Jacob's Ladder*. It was merely a comfortable size for six or eight to work in, to converse across. She stepped down the ramp, feeling stiff resistance and then a dry crunch as carpet fibers crushed under each step.

She stopped at the bottom, beside the captain's chair, which commanded the center of the bridge. She brushed cobwebs from its arms. Despite the dust, it looked comfortable.

She didn't think that was her own opinion.

"Get out of my head."

"We'll be together," Dust said, coalescing. He turned, arms wide on a grand gesture, his waistcoat catching the light of the waystars. On the screens, Ariane and Asrafil still climbed. Higher, or more inward, proceeding through the vast laddery webwork of the world. Closer now. Nearly there.

"It's the only way."

They would arrive in a matter of minutes.

"I don't love you," Perceval said. "I decide who I love, and how I love them."

"But I love you," Dust said, his breath against her scalp a thrill that made her wish she could still hide behind her hair. It wasn't real breath. It wasn't any more real than the flush that crept along her neck in response.

She stepped away from his outstretched hand. He frowned, as if he had expected her to allow him to bow over it like some make-believe prince. "I love Rien."

"But bow to me," he said, "and I will serve you all my days. Together we will cross space and sail the stars. Just your consent—"

"I don't love you," Perceval said. "I love Rien."

"Because you have decided to love Rien."

"Yes," she said, against the warm pressure of desire. She should have felt hunger; she did not know how long it had been since she had eaten. Her symbiont could have told her, but she did not trust its answers. It was infected by Pinion now. As surely as Perceval herself.

She scratched at the back of the chair. The cobwebs felt powdery soft; they stuck only to themselves now. And a bit to the back of her hand, but only because she tore through them.

"Get *out* of my head." She closed her eyes. She brushed the bit of web away with a thumb.

But even inside her head, she could see Ariane creeping like a crippled spider along the skin of the world. There was a whole world out there. Beyond her. Behind her.

Somewhere out there, beyond Dust, beyond Ariane, was Rien and Tristen and Perceval's mother and her father. Somewhere out there was a cave of bats and a necromancer guarding the vale of the dead. Somewhere there were ship-fish, flitting through gravityless corridors. There were daggery angels and lies as soft as sleep.

Perceval hated how it was made, the world. She hated what it was made for. She wished she could find the builders, and pass with them a pointy word or two. They were evil men, whatever they did in God's name.

Whatever they had thought was God's will, the world

was full of people and creatures who did not deserve to die for the sins of their fathers. Perceval opened her eyes. She looked straight at Dust, at his silver waistcoat gleaming peach in the light of the dying stars, and let her hands fall.

Creatures that do not deserve to die for the sins of their fathers. And maybe, she thought, a few that do.

There was a world, and it did not matter if Perceval agreed with its plan. The world was bigger than she was. And had as much right to survive. And if she didn't like the way the world worked, tomorrow was another day.

She turned to Dust, who stood at her shoulder, shorter than she by half a head. "Take off the compulsion," she said.

"Beloved—"

"Take off the compulsion, and I shall fight for you. Give me the freedom of my heart, Jacob Dust, and I shall do your will."

"I would have given you absolution," he said. "I would have absorbed your crimes."

"Give me back my brain," she said. "Get your parasites off me, and I will be your damned captain, Jacob Dust."

"Pinion stays," he said. "There is no way now to extricate you, and you will need its protection to fight Ariane, who is armored and comes bearing an unblade."

Perceval's skin crawled, but she nodded. "Fine," she said. "As long as both of you get the hell out."

"A compromise, then. It shall be as you wish," he said. And kissed her on the cheek before she could close her eyes.

Perceval pulled away. She smiled bitterly, and looked down at her hands. The sticky bit of spiderweb smirched her knuckle and thumb. She put her hand in her mouth, but it only tasted of grit and powder.

"Hurry, Dust," she said. "Your enemy is climbing."

27

black mercy

All lovers young, all lovers must
Consign to thee, and come to dust.

—WILLIAM SHAKESPEARE,
Cymbeline, 4.2

Rien's clothing had been recycled, but her personal belongings had been scrubbed and stored. She was required to sign for them, which she did, and retina and thumbprinted, too. The contents of her pack were there, including the plum.

She left everything else behind. Caitlin, who was more or less her size, had dressed her in sturdier clothes, and she didn't need a blanket here. She did check the somewhat battered fruit for excessive radiation, and was reassured. Both her symbiont and Ng agreed that any residue was within tolerance.

She slipped it into a pocket, threw away the rest, and within ten minutes has completed the forms to release her temporary locker back to the common pool.

Then, accoutered, she went to find Tristen and her father. And, incidentally, Caitlin Conn.

The same guide strips that had led her to the left luggage would bring her to the air-lock gateways. She walked through the bustling streets and the covered corridors, inevitably smaller and less flamboyant than whatever Engineer walked near. She thought she could vanish here, and the idea was attractive.

She missed being a Mean among Means. Even if it had been a lie, even then.

She thought the others would have a pack for her, gear, whatever was necessary for the long trip back to Rule. She didn't fancy another run through Inkling's chamber. She didn't think they could; there was no way to survive it without medical care waiting on the far end.

Gavin could not yet have returned from his errand, and Rien was both sad and grateful. She missed his weight on her shoulder, his malicious wit. But she could not trust him, and even though Samael himself would be with them, it was a cold comfort that Gavin was elsewhere.

Better the hand than the cat's-paw, perhaps?

No, of course not. Rien knew why.

She liked Gavin.

She would have hated to place herself on constant guard against him. She wanted to preserve the illusion of friendship.

And in the end, she was Samael's creature also, wasn't she? She, and all of Engine. And she had been a servant of monsters before. And worse monsters than Samael, who was after all only the Angel of Death.

"Well," she told herself, "if you live, you'll both be

beholden to the same beast, and you'll have time to trade genial insults then." If Gavin wanted anything to do with her.

She could live with being a servant again. She told herself, firmly: *you can live with being a servant again*.

She would simply have to.

She was glad, though, to have had the illusion of freedom. Princesses had adventures. Princesses were taken as prizes of war. Princesses had to battle monsters if they were going to survive, and the monsters inevitably won. If not the monster you fought against, the monster you served.

Or the monster you became.

Except, she thought, the only lasting place in the world for princesses was deeply in denial, and the only important question in the end was, was it better to become the monster, or to become the servant of the beast? She thought of Gavin. She thought of Samael and Dust, and of the parasite wings. She thought she knew which monster she preferred.

Rien dodged other pedestrians and tried to calm herself with the comforting knowledge of Benedick and Caitlin's faith in her. They'd both been perfectly insouciant about allowing her to make her way to the lockers unguided.

The trust was flattering. It wasn't, as a nasty undermining conviction kept insisting, that they didn't care if they got her back. And Caitlin did not see her only as a placeholder for Perceval.

Still, when she rejoined them and Tristen at the gateway to the air locks as arranged, it took an effort of will not to coil her fists in the tails of her borrowed blouse.

They were already armed and armored, standing three abreast. A brave sight, if ever she had seen one.

They had no pack.

They had a suit of power armor. Four suits, in fact, but three of those were in use already. Tristen wore shining white, Benedick the predictable black piped in golden-brown, and Caitlin, vermilion and gold. The armor that stood empty was teal and emerald, but where a device might have been blazoned on the chest was only an empty plate.

With them waited Samael, his colorless hair hanging in strings beside his face. He winked when he saw Rien. The others, helms open, watched her approach. Tristen and Benedick were bald and stubbled as Rien, Caitlin no bigger.

It was the angel who extended a hand to her, an arrogant gesture, a crook of his fingers.

She paused before him, and he placed a helmet in her hands.

Samael said, "The time is nigh. Put your armor on."

"How are we going to reach Rule in time?"

Maybe they should just stay here, and help to hold the world together. Hero Ng could be useful here, and so by extension could Rien. And whatever the monsters got up to, somebody still needed to do the work of the world.

Rien looked to Tristen. He gestured, with his eyes, to Caitlin, and she smiled. "We are Engineers," she said. "The lift to the bridge has been kept in working order, against this day of need. It will take us to the bridge in under an hour, barring disasters."

Rien considered it a major personal achievement that

she didn't hurl the helmet at her new foster mother. Instead, she turned to her and said, "I've never worn power armor before."

Caitlin nodded. "I'll help you into it."

All three of them did, actually, deftly enough that they rarely seemed to be getting in one another's way. And once it had folded around her, Tristen adjusted the seals and Caitlin checked the latches, while Benedict, meticulous and silent, fixed the calibration of the pressure switches that would move the armor effortlessly with Rien's every gesture.

When she was garbed, her helm seated but not sealed, they stepped back and surveyed their work.

"Not bad," Caitlin said. "We'll make a knight of you yet."

Rien smiled. She swung her arms; they moved as lightly as if in microgravity. And because she had to know, she asked, "Did Arianrhod's arrest go well?"

"Fine."

Maybe it was the directness of Caitlin's gaze, or Hero Ng's experience, but Rien knew immediately that her foster mother was lying. She stopped, one hand raised to her helmet seal, and turned to Benedick. "She got away."

"She has a faction," Caitlin said, before Benedick could answer. "It's under con—"

"Don't lie to me," Rien said. "Don't treat me like a child, Father."

"Yes," he said. "She got away. No, I do not think she can elude us long."

She didn't think he was lying. Not exactly. But his worried glance at Caitlin told her that neither was he artless. "Chief Engineer," Rien said, "do you need to stay?"

Caitlin spread her hands. "I'm not the only Engineer," she said. "And Perceval is my daughter."

In the distance, Rien heard an alarm ringing. And then another. She thought of the resurrected in their coffle, of Oliver led through the streets on a leash.

Arianrhod had more than a few partisans, she understood.

She fixed Samael on a stare. And then Benedick. Inside the armor, her hands were cold. "What if you stayed, Father? You and Cat and Tristen. And Samael and I went for Perceval?"

He opened his mouth. She held up a gauntlet. "Can the two of us handle Dust?"

"*I* can handle Dust," Samael said. "If we were stealthy and few in number, it might even improve our chances of reaching her alive."

"Right," Rien said. "Then it's settled. The Engineers and tacticians are needed here."

"Without me, you don't have transportation," Caitlin said.

Rien laughed. "Without me, you don't know where to go. Cat"—she shrugged, ceramic plates clicking—"I know you *want* to."

Caitlin, bold as ever, let the mask of her helm glide open and the faceplate underneath slide back. "It's going to be a war out there," she said.

"I know," Rien said. "It's going to be a war in here as well, isn't it?"

Before any of them could answer, Rien heard the whir

of wings. She twisted, automatically, casting one arm up to protect her face. The armor moved fluidly, faster than she would have on her own, so that she at first tried to resist it and it bruised her. "Ow," she said, as Gavin settled on her forearm.

"Oh, please. I could burn through that, but not pinch." He hopped up her arm to her shoulder, balancing on the slick pauldron with care. "Mallory would like to speak before you go."

Rien pressed her lips together, not caring if he saw the grimace. If she had somehow summoned the basilisk with her earlier relief at his absence, she wouldn't be surprised.

"In a minute," she said, and looked sidelong at Benedick. He reached out, as if to prevent her from stepping forward, and she sidled away.

"I've taken care of myself all my life," she said, averting her eyes. "Your deciding to be my father now doesn't change that. And if we don't come back the only thing it matters to is which angel winds up on top. If you fail here . . ."

. . . the world ends.

Benedick's lips pressed thin under his faceplate. And then he nodded and stepped back. "Tristen," he said.

Tristen, who had been silent, and who had not yet sealed his helm, licked his lips. He laid one hand on Rien's shoulder, and Rien saw Benedick's hurt that she let it happen. "Never fear," Tristen said. "Rien, *one* of us is coming."

"Fine," she said, choosing—again—not to wonder if she could trust him. And then she turned back to Benedick and said, "When we come back, I expect you'll be able to tell me what happened to my mother."

"When you come back, I expect I will," he said.

Then Caitlin stepped in, not blocking her path but reaching into it. Her sheathed unblade was in her hand, and Rien stared at it. "This is Mercy," she said. "Take it."

"You might need it," Rien said.

Caitlin smiled. "So might you."

Rien swallowed and waited for Caitlin to look down. And when she did not, Rien reached out slowly and closed her hand on the black hilt of the unsword.

"Thank you," she said. She locked it to the catch on her armor, and turned inside her helm to look Gavin in the eye. "Where's Mallory?"

Samael stepped forward. Rien raised a hand and pointed at the center of the angel's chest. "You're not invited," she said.

Mallory waited on a bench in a corner of a quiet courtyard, knees drawn up and chin resting on interlaced hands. The necromancer stood as Rien approached, reaching out to embrace her despite the armor. Rien suffered it, but stepped back quickly. Gavin, caught in the middle of hopping between their shoulders, fanned his wings in surprise, but managed to complete the jump.

"Well," Rien said, "I came."

"You're angry," Mallory said. "Will you just open your helmet, please?"

Rien did, a touch at the controls telescoping faceplate and mask aside. She took a deep breath, and tried to keep her face impassive, but the corner of her mouth kept twitching. "Why should I be angry?"

"Because of Samael."

"Oh, why should I be angry about that?" The sarcasm dripping from Rien's voice was just right, she thought, but also there was pain, and she hadn't meant to give Mallory that much. "He told me what was in the plum. I still have it. I'm grateful."

Mallory's smile slid into an expression Rien could only call enigmatic. "Angels don't always tell the whole truth."

"No, really?" Rien's throat hurt. *Why does everything have to be so complicated?* "What could he *possibly* have been withholding?"

Whatever was behind Mallory's appraisal, the necromancer winced. And then reached across the space between them and touched Rien's armored wrist, though Rien could not feel it. "What did he tell you?"

"That it was a program. A virus. That it could scrub Dust's agents out of Perceval. And replace them with Samael's, right? I mean, he didn't say that, but I guessed—"

"No," Mallory said. "It's more than that. It's an angel seed. It's Samael's backup. Like the peach you ate was Hero Ng's. So if Dust consumes him—"

"He won't die," Rien said.

"A fragment won't," Mallory answered. "Just a splinter. Nothing like the whole. But it's the fragment that knows all about how to fight Dust."

Rien stopped dead, brow aching between her eyes as she thought about that. "He expects to lose. He expects to die."

"Oh, sweetheart," said Mallory. "We all do."

•   •   •

Again, Rien was grateful for Hero Ng, even as she pitied him. His quiet resolve steadied her, gave her a point of balance. Especially when she remembered how unwillingly he had been returned to guide her, and take up his burdens again.

I would have left you in peace, she told him. But he only shrugged and carried on.

No blame.

Fortunately, Ng warned her about the lift before she got in.

Lift was perhaps a generous term. The thing was a cage on graspers, open to the breathless grasp of the Enemy, and it ran along the *outside* of the world, huddled close and moving with tooth-chipping speed. It rattled and clacked and shuddered as if it were about to fly apart into a thousand pieces. There were no seats and no safety lines, other than the ones that came component to their armor, and Rien clung to the nearest vertical reinforcement with all the strength of her power suit.

She was afraid to move, anyway, lest the damned thing break her arms. At least the armor had vibration dampers, which probably kept the lift's ferocious vibration from chipping the bones in her hands.

After the first quarter-hour of the journey, when she had passed through initial terror and into a sort of numbed rattling, she began to appreciate the humor. She hadn't been nearly as terrified when Perceval tossed her out an air lock as she was now, hurtling along the lattice of the world, embracing this clattering steed.

Although this time the armor kept her warm.

She began to giggle, quietly, into her helmet, realizing

only too late that her suit mike was live and Tristen could hear her hysterics. She snapped off the mike in a hurry. When she looked over her shoulder, embarrassed, she was even more mortified to see him swinging toward her from handhold to handhold.

Rien turned her eyes front and gritted her teeth. In a moment, her uncle was beside her, shoulder to shoulder, leaning his helmet against Rien's to speak in private. "When we get there," he shouted into the teeth of the noise, "let the armor carry you. If you fight, it can hurt you, and you don't know how to move with it yet. I'll get you to Perceval."

The rest is on you.

Rien nodded, wondering if Tristen could see her head moving inside the helmet's shell. She wondered also if Caitlin had programmed the suit to keep her out of trouble, if it would run away if the fighting got too danger- ous. She was ashamed to feel relief at the idea, and more relief that it would not be her cowardice if it happened.

"Thank you," she said, and tilted her helmet away.

Against her faceplate, she saw Tristen's reflection, and the moment of hesitation before he backed away. But back away he did, and Rien breathed a sigh of relief heavy enough to briefly fog the crystal by her mouth. But as soon as Tristen withdrew, Samael, shirtless in the void, drifted in his place.

"Take a number; we'll be with you as soon as we can," Rien muttered. This time, she remembered to check her mike light. Red. Talking made her feel like her teeth were going to shatter.

But the armor held her in the lift, and the lift hurtled

through the world, bars of light and shadow ripping past on every side. Rien looked away from Samael, toward the shipwreck stars, and pretended to herself that she could see into the swirl of dying matter and know what would come next.

The inferno was beautiful.

"Let me remake you in my image," Samael said. He spoke into the void, his lips moving, untroubled by the Enemy. She heard him, even over the clamor of the hurtling lift, as a clear calm voice in her ear.

And she was grateful to the armor, because if it had been the strength of her own hands holding her to the lift, she would have tumbled free in shock. She half turned, clinging to her post, and gaped. "What exactly do you propose?"

"A way to make you stronger than Dust," he said. "A way to make you an angel."

She looked around—at Tristen in his stark white armor. He had turned away and seemed oblivious. She wondered if Samael had somehow affected her perceptions, if he was appearing to her eyes only. "Another ally you can consume?"

"You never know," he said. "Maybe you'll defeat me also." He shrugged. "But you know what they say about age and treachery versus youth and skill."

"No," she said.

He leaned forward. "What's to stop me doing it anyway?"

"You need consent." Not a guess. Hero Ng gave her that; it had been built into Israfel from the first, hard-coded, irreducible. Whatever the angels did, they first needed the consent of the subject. Or of the Captain, if what was to be done was to be done to more than one human.

"If you let me," he said, "you could see what I see." He gestured around, to the waystars and the world. "All the buzz of machine life, the consciousnesses that swirl all over the skin of the world, glistening in wavelengths to which you are deaf. Look off to starboard."

He pointed, and Rien's eye followed. Just in time to see a vast section of the *Jacob's Ladder* shear away from the body of the ship like a sawn branch bending free of the tree. She could see as it spun clear that no atmosphere was escaping, and no lights shone within. Even as she watched, it began to break apart into smaller chunks, the chunks moving. They would be torn down to reinforce the living sections of the ship, to try to make it robust enough to withstand the wavefront, or spun out into the monofilaments that would—if grace or luck was with them—help catch the exploding star's magnetosphere, producing acceleration.

Well, that wasn't quite right, was it? The blast wave was going to produce acceleration no matter what. The question before them was whether it was going to be acceleration in very small pieces . . . or the sort of useful acceleration that could bootstrap the world into flight once more.

Bits shook loose—from the lift, from the world under its scuttling graspers. Rien tried not to look, tried not to imagine those tumbling bits were anything but loose bolts and rust.

"That's not a reason for me to sacrifice myself for you."

Samael's face rearranged itself around the sharp edge of his smile. "What about sacrificing yourself for the world? It will take whatever resources we can field to defeat them."

"Them." A simple pronoun. It should not have knocked Rien so far down a cold well of fear that the angel's voice seemed to echo after her.

"Yes," Samael said. "Ariane and her allied angel are coming to the party, too. If our timing is right, we'll arrive after the other claimants to the throne have softened each other up, and we'll be able to pick up their leavings. Won't that be grand?"

When Rien glared at him, stricken, he only shrugged. "I'm an angel, sweetheart. I'm five hundred years old. I don't want to die."

"Even if it's God's will?" she snapped.

"If it's God's will," he said, "we'll find out the hard way, won't we?"

Rien tongued on her mike as she turned away from him, and quickly passed along to Tristen what Samael had told her. There was silence at first, and Rien saw the broad movements of helm and armor as her uncle shook his head.

"You didn't hear him," Rien said in disgust. "Of course you don't believe me—"

"Actually—" Tristen stepped in. Literally, hauling himself forward hand over hand up the superstructure of the lift, his armor glimmering white as starshine except where it caught ruddy highlights off the secondary waystar. "I believe you," he said. "But this is as fast as we can go."

She opened her mouth to accuse him. The words piled up. Denial. Anger.

He was an adult, an Exalt. A prince of the world. The oldest living son of Alasdair Conn.

If he couldn't do something—

—there was nothing that could be done.

28

the kiss of angels

World to world, ashes to ashes, dust
to dust, in sure and certain hope
of adaptation.

—NEW EVOLUTIONIST FUNERAL SERVICE

Perceval turned her face and permitted the angel to kiss her. She closed her eyes, breathing between parted lips, and waited to see what happened.

At first, there was nothing. The small, chaste kiss. The pressure of Dust leaning in, and withdrawing. And then she felt her breath come clean, and the next one, pure and untrammeled, filling a chest no longer restricted by longing. She breathed deep, held it, let it flow.

She owned herself again. For a long, clean second, she exulted, and if her wings had been hers, too, she would have stretched out into them.

And then Dust touched her shoulder, and called her "Captain."

And she realized she would *never* be herself again.

She was braced for an invasion. To be torn out of

herself, smashed, raped, impaled. But that wasn't it at all. Instead, the first thing she noticed was a creeping dissolution. As if the fringes of her consciousness were sliding apart, growing friable and then melting into particles. Into powder.

Into dust.

Perceval crumbled. Scattered. Disassociated. Dispersed. She felt herself slipping away, the core, the center, the ego worn into a shadow even starlight could shine through. As if she were all fingers and no eyes, all edge and no center. She felt the world all through her, or her all through the world, and the ship and its denizens were no different. She felt it lacking, felt where it was weary with metal fatigue, battle fatigue, the incessant scrape of entropy.

Dust was there with her. She felt him, in all his diffusion, all his cold angelic will, as she spun along the webs and nodules and struts and lattices of the world.

She felt where the ship might hold, when the waystar primary went supernova. She felt where no repairs could be enough, where it would inevitably fail. She felt the borders of other angels, and the spaces where she could not tread.

She felt Ariane approaching, on the one side. And on the other, Rien and Tristen, come to bring her home. Too late, too late, and she mourned not her loss—for she had not lost them—but the grief they would suffer on behalf of her.

Like oil dropped onto a puddle, Perceval spread thin. And lost herself in the world.

•   •   •

There was only so far the lift could take them. Eventually, they came to the outer hull of the bridge itself, protected at the core of the world. When the lift finally rattled to a halt, vibrating and straining so Rien could feel the unheard whine of metal fatigue through her boots, she could not at first seem to unlock her gauntlets from the strut. But Tristen, armor glistening, paused beside her and carefully uncurled each finger, with a delicacy she could imagine had taken decades to perfect.

He held one of her wrists. They floated face-to-face for a moment, and when Rien peered through his faceplate she saw him wink, quite broadly, his waxy face contorting.

And then his face shield closed, and she was looking at her own reflection mirrored in its gloss-white carapace for two long seconds until her own armor locked down as well. Then she saw through sensor motes connected to her symbiont, a spherical field of vision that left her almost completely disoriented. The armor reassured her, though: a steady stream of data, filtered down until it made sense. Tristen released her wrist, and she wondered if he gave her a final reflexive squeeze. Above them, Samael's ghostly avatar floated beside what Rien could only assume was an air-lock entry.

Tristen moved away.

Rien's armor followed his.

Entering was easy. Samael merely put out his hand—not, Rien thought, that he needed to, except for dramatic purposes—and opened the air-lock door. As her armor brought her inside, she caught herself wondering if it would be that easy to get back out again.

Or if there would be any need.

Once inside, they moved through cobwebbed darkness, but the armor had no need of light. Insect husks crunched underfoot, and the armor relied on internal air. From its conversation, Rien understood that the biosphere here had long failed, the flora dying in darkness and drought and, in due time, the fauna following. Not, however, before the flies and spiders had undergone an apparent population explosion.

—*Armor?*—

—*At the ready.*—

—*Do you have a name?*—

—*This unit is unnamed.*—

—*Oh.*— She waited, as if it might somehow proactively fill the gap. But there were only echoes of her own silent voice in her head. —*Would you like a name?*—

Of course she couldn't feel it hesitate as it processed the question. Even Exalted reflexes could never be fast enough. Perhaps it was simply focused on a tricky bit of following the others through the gloom. Tristen's chalky armor glimmered on ultraviolet. Rien wondered if he had chosen that whiteness for dramatic reasons, or so as to draw fire.

Or possibly so as to be the first to come to Ariane's notice, if—when—they should reach her.

The scabbard of the unblade clasped across her back protruded at hip level. She touched it nervously.

—*Yes.*— the armor said, when she had grown resigned to a lack of answer.

She nodded, its collar rubbing her throat, and said, —*I'll think on it.*—

She wondered at the bounce she thought she sensed in its step, for minutes after.

It was easy to tell which door led to the bridge, even in the blackness. Rien could clearly make out the stand beside it, the glass dome and what rested within.

Hero Ng knew what the case held.

A paper New Evolutionist Bible. With leather covers, and pages pressed from wood and cotton fibers grown in the soul of ancient Earth.

Rien could barely breathe as they came forward.

Piece by piece, particle by particle, Dust collected his Captain. He'd known it would come to this; he'd known she'd fall into his vastness. They lived so bounded, these small intelligences.

But he could get her back.

Fragment by fragment he redeemed her, brought her together, showed her how to integrate herself. As for maintaining the connections between the particles of her consciousness and the meat that Dust believed housed her soul . . . they learned that together.

Dust worked feverishly. Taught, feverishly. Learned in a frenzy. Because Ariane was there, and Dust could feel Asrafil pressing at his fringes. They were coming.

They were nearly here.

Alasdair Conn hadn't been a real Captain. Just a Commodore. In charge, but not in command.

He had never surrendered himself to his ship.

To his angels.

As Perceval surrendered now. Surrendered, and possessed.

And stood again, dripping stormlight, wreathed in her dozen shining wings, just as the forward bulkhead blew wide open on the Enemy, and Ariane and her angel came within.

29

the sun goes down in a cold pale flare

I shall die, but that is all that I shall do for Death.

—EDNA ST. VINCENT MILLAY,
"Conscientious Objector"

They met the guardian before the door, and joined him there in combat.

If Rien had been a fighter, she might have been able to describe what followed. But she was a passenger, and she experienced what happened in a stunning, stuttering kaleidoscope. Not a blur, because a blur is fluid, and this was staccato, punctuated.

Sequence and order fell away; there was only the struggle to stay soft inside her armor, not to fight its movement, to bite down on the mouthguard and let the gelatinous, body-temperature shock lining press her body into whatever shape it would.

She was not very good at it. Caitlin—or someone—

had set her armor for extreme evasion. Her left arm, spine, left leg popped and strained. Her colony rushed to repair the damage, reporting torn tendons and muscles, her own anatomy limned red in her mind's eye.

And she honestly couldn't understand a thing that was going on around her. Her armor was defended by a symbiont swarm, and what attacked was—she thought— Dust, defending his lair and his hostage. But she couldn't be certain, and whatever Samael was doing, he was no more plain to the eye—or any of her armor's sensors.

Tristen never left her side, not that proximity was any protection against an enemy who surrounded them, who interpermeated their defenses. A hiss and sizzle like static droned in her ears, and from her armor—from her every gesture and from her companions—St. Elmo's fire shredded and spun. Veils of light, green, vermilion, and electric blue, pulled and tore.

Rien had no idea who was winning. She saw Tristen striking out with invisible weapons, his hands crackling with residual ionization. She saw the whole corridor lit flare-white as some attack died on their defenses. She groped, and herself drew Caitlin's terrible black unsword Mercy. The blade was an absence of anything, reflectionless as the face of the Enemy. She swung it wildly.

Where the blade passed, the crackling light was cut, and burned no more.

With it, with Samael and Tristen's assistance, Rien was hewing her way to the door.

She was within a meter of her goal when the deck jumped under Rien's feet, and through the armor she heard first rending metal and then an abrupt absence of transmitted sound.

"Hull breach," Tristen said over his suit mike. "We have to get within."

Within, Perceval was unready. Unready and unarmed, her limbs like puppet sticks, her body awkward, infected, alien, enfolded in a corona of sensation that extended meters in every direction. Pinion stirred around her, a shimmer of light like the shadow of ripples on the bottom of a glass.

Graceless, uncoordinated. New and raw. Unarmored, and with no weapon in her hands. But she was naked to the Enemy, and did not feel its cold.

Ariane needed her armor. She needed her unblade.

She advanced, her angel cloaking her in his glory, Innocence as black in her hand as a hole in the night.

There was too much. Perceval raked herself together, clutched her tattered edges close. In the corridor, Dust was fighting someone. Another angel, people in armor. She'd look in a minute. Too much, from everywhere, and she was trying to see Ariane.

There was no speaking, now, for there was no atmosphere. No click as Ariane's armored foot came down, disturbing cobwebs, breaking the parallel rays of the suns that shone through the rent bulkhead behind her, haloing her in light reflected from disturbed particles.

—*Be bold*,—Pinion whispered in Perceval's ear. —*Be of good courage, Captain. For I am with you.*—

As if on marionette strings, Perceval stepped forward to war. And like a gliding cat, Ariane came to meet her.

Asrafil's presence was a void in Perceval's new perceptions, Ariane and Innocence the enigma at its center. Through Pinion, into Dust, she sensed the other angel's fringes, felt them grapple and claw. The rift in the bulkhead webbed over, clotted like a wound, knit like bone.

She saw in cascades of images, from angles and points of view not her own. She whirled in the veil of Pinion's wings, and Pinion itself tore savagely at Asrafil when that angel clutched after her.

But Dust fought his war on two fronts, and Perceval could sense each centimeter of ground he was losing. The angel in the corridor was smaller than Asrafil or than Dust, more coherent, tighter and more defined—

—If Asrafil was here, then who was outside?

Two, in armor. A man and a woman. One with an unblade. And an angel.

Perceval reached out through Dust again. Since he had released her emotions, she found she could think, process, and consider in absolute clarity, even while her body danced swords with Ariane. She was not, she thought, only thinking with her own brain, and her symbiont, but with some fraction of Dust's processing power as well. And her borrowed capacity was untroubled by the desperation with which Perceval's body fought for life.

—*Dust. Open the door.*—

She could not permit Ariane to corner her, and there was nothing she could do to parry that blade. Anything living or symbiotic it touched was severed for all time. But if she could not parry, Pinion could riposte, and Perceval could keep them both out of the way.

Perceval spun, dodged a thrust from the enemy angel— a lance of charged particles that seared the decking where she had been—and as she recovered found herself face to mask with Ariane's faceless armor, and almost within the span of her arms. Ariane's blade swerved toward her—a hard reflexive arc—and Perceval sprang upward, Pinion flailing around her.

She could not actually feel the unblade slice under her feet. There was no air for it to stir. But she felt it clip the trailing flight feathers on Pinion's bottom wings, and pass through without resistance.

There *was* resistance as Perceval somersaulted up and away, Pinion slashing and scissoring. She knew she struck Ariane's armor. She knew she cut it, for those wings were edged like razors where they chose to be. She felt the pulse of blood from the wound—arterial—and saw the cobalt spray across the decking, quickly stopped as Ariane's symbiont attended it.

Ariane shifted her sword to her other hand.

When Perceval landed, crouched, half the bridge away, the cobwebs tore under her feet. And one of Pinion's wings was dragging.

—*Dust.*— His stubbornness was like a wall. He had no intention of permitting Samael or any of her family near her. He had no intention of making alliances, or of sharing power.

And if she was his Captain, what good was it if he did not answer when she spoke to him?

—*Dust. Open the corridor door.*—

He showed her his war, plunged her into it like a microsecond bath of ice water. He gave her angels fighting, the knife-taloned combat of microscopic machines. The weapons were invisible . . . until microwaves sizzled cobwebs, until a wave of massed nanites burned through another like a flaming sword through ice.

—*Open the corridor door.*—

Chromed armor glittering, Ariane charged. Perceval, coiled for another twisting leap, curled her lip and narrowed her eyes, and waited.

—*Samael . . .* —

A console across the room sparked and exploded.

—*You stupid bastard*, let them in.—

Ariane lunged, anticipating another leap like before. Perceval threw herself to the side, this time, instead, and felt Innocence bite deep into one wing. Just like before, there would be shocking pain and then—

She fell, sprawling, skidding in cobwebs. She rolled, the remaining wings armoring her as best they could, bruising elbows and toes, smacking her shin hard on the navigator's chair. She scrambled behind a console, Ariane instead grabbing the chair back and bounding over, her guard flawed for a split instant as she leaped and Innocence drifted wide.

One wing was severed above the elbow. But all the others bent forward, flexed at the joint as sharply as a guitarist's fingers, and as Perceval fell backward among the dust and debris they met, and bowed, and slid into Ariane's breast through the armor, until a meter or more of blue-smeared plumage protruded from her back.

Perceval saw her own wide eyes and stubbled scalp reflected in the bright chrome of Ariane's helm—

And then Pinion snapped wide its wings, and the daughter of Alasdair Conn shredded, flesh and bone.

With the hiss of air entering from the now-open corridor door, Perceval heard the pop of dislocating joints and the thick meaty rip of muscle.

Snaps and tatters of static electricity charged in the ionized atmosphere; Ariane might be vanquished, but Asrafil fought still.

And then, as if the fighting has been a hallucination, Rien's armor balanced flat-footed in the corridor, and the door into the bridge stood open. Silence hung over the corridor, dim lights flickering into life, shadows concealing as much as they revealed. Within, though, lightning raced over surfaces, and Rien could see someone slender and bony-tall, shrouded in tattered wings and dripping cobalt blood, rising to her feet.

Tristen cried out and stepped forward, weapon trained on Perceval. *No*, Rien thought, moving forward in anticipation of the betrayal, aware already that there was nothing she could do to stop him. Perhaps an angel could intervene in time. Perhaps—

"You're alive," he said, and his voice broke, and his gun dropped down beside his thigh. He held out his unarmed hand, offering support or an embrace, and Perceval turned toward him, her eyes wide and wild.

And Rien breathed again, through a pall of sick self-hate for ever doubting him. But then Samael appeared like a star from eclipse, one hand firm upon his arm, and Perceval halted midstep.

—*Rien,*— said a voice from the air before her. —*And Rien only.*—

"Dust," Samael said, as if it needed explaining. And Rien nodded.

Somehow, when Rien turned, she found herself meeting Tristen's faceless attention. "You're all idiots," Rien said.

He squared himself. "You have everything you need."

She nodded. And as she stepped over the threshold onto the bridge, toward Perceval, she brushed Samael's naked shoulder with her gauntlet and said inside her helm, "I'm ready, angel. Consent."

She never saw if he responded. She was distracted by the motion in her hand, as something nigh-weightless and of neutral temperature to the armor's sensors. She looked down in surprise, and nearly dropped it.

Mercy.

Rien swallowed and went forward.

Walking across the bridge, she picked her feet up and set them down straight, to try to limit the amount of dust she was disturbing. Perceval, wreathed in wings like an arbor of brazen thorns, held out her hands. As Rien came closer, she saw the severed stump of one wing dripping viscous blue fluid. Perceval's eyes widened when she saw what Rien held, the splinter of absolute blackness in her hand. Perceval dropped to one knee and Rien trotted a step—but then Perceval stood again and Rien realized her sister had only been picking up Innocence.

Which meant that the chunks of armor and blue-dripping meat scattered around the deck were—

"Oh," Rien said, and tried not to gag inside her helmet. "Space it," she said, and opened her faceplate, just in case. The machine-oil stench of Exalt blood didn't help the nausea, but it didn't really hurt it either.

And then she was close enough to Perceval for Perceval to touch her, and Perceval put a hand on her armored shoulder, and Rien leaned into the touch. Although she couldn't feel the touch through ceramic and titanium, she could feel the armor feeling.

"Close your eyes," Perceval said.

Rien closed them. For three minutes, timed on her symbiont. And all the while she waited, she felt Samael working in her, moving through her, changing her. Taking her apart.

Her fringes were unraveling, and she felt how Perceval had come unraveled, too. She sensed what Perceval hadn't wanted her to witness, as Perceval collected Ariane's symbiont, her own symbiont hunting it to every corner of the bridge, and consumed it. And with it, Ariane.

And with Ariane, Alasdair.

"I guess you're really Captain now," Rien said, without opening her eyes. And then the name, one last time. A caress. "Perceval."

Perceval's voice was thick and choked. "I'm not exactly Perceval anymore."

"It's all right," Rien said, as Samael's invisible components converted her, cell by cell. "I still love you."

Perceval touched her armor again. This time, Rien felt it.

Samael was converting the armor, too. Or her own symbiont was, now. Now that the angel had given it instruction.

In Rien's head, Hero Ng was steely in his resolve. The angels must be integrated. Samael was not strong enough to do it on his own. And neither he, nor Dust, nor Asrafil could be trusted.

Rien agreed with him. And she meant to show him that she, too, could be ruthless with herself if it were needful.

"I love you, too," Perceval said. Rien opened her eyes, to look on Perceval's face for one last time, as a human being. "Dust. He made me want him. But it's you I love."

"But not want. You don't want me."

Perceval shrugged, her wings rising and falling. "Oh, sex. So take a lover. Don't be ridiculous. Who wants to marry a martyr?"

"Marry?"

"Marry me," Perceval said. "Rien."

Oh, too good to be true. Too much to hope for. For a cold instant, she let herself hold it close. She thought about Jordan, the wings, the golden fur . . . Mallory, who might be Samael's creature or might not, but who had given her Gavin and also, Hero Ng.

She felt the angel working within her. —*Give her the plum,*—Samael said. —*Feed her the virus. Free your love from Dust's chains.*—

It was in a pouch at Rien's belt. She slipped her hand inside, and pulled it out. A little thing, bruised, sticky juice dripping over her thumb. Like the blood sticky under her boots.

"I'll marry you," she said. She crushed the plum in her hand and dropped the pit onto the floor. "If you'll kiss me one more time."

The gesture with the fruit, the tone of her voice—whatever it was, something she said alerted Perceval. Rien could tell by the arch of her eyebrow and the tilt of her head. Suspicious. Intrigued.

And concerned.

Princesses and angels and kings, Rien thought. *They're all monsters. Even if you need them. Even if they give you wings.*

But she'd learned something from Perceval, and from Tristen, and from Conrad Ng. In addition to princesses and monsters and kings, there are knights and heroes also.

And it all came down to dying in the end, and what you chose to do your dying for.

She couldn't have done it on her own. But Tristen stood outside the door. And she had Hero Ng.

The irony, of course, was that Samael had given him to her. And Samael could not defeat Dust. And neither angel was the sort to whom she wanted to trust her life, nor the life of the world.

There was only one possible solution.

She licked the pulp of the plum from her fingers, took firm hold of Samael—with Hero Ng's solid assistance—and tilted her head back to accept Perceval's kiss.

At first, Perceval did not know what she was feeling. It wasn't the kiss, and it wasn't the gut-churning memory of Dust's wanted/unwanted kisses either. Rather, it was a spasm, an uncontrolled flood of everything not into but through her. If joining with Dust, if becoming his Captain, had taken her out of herself, then this scoured her insides out.

Rien was there, inside her, all her quick wits—so smart, so full of thinking—and all her hurts and braveries. And her love, her longing, her stubborn determination: they made Perceval's breath hurt, her eyes sting. And with Rien was Samael, and someone else—Hero Ng, calm and dedicated.

She felt the unpicking, as they tangled inside her, as they unwound Pinion from her soul and stripped it away. She felt them strike Dust, strike against the places where she and he were integrated, and expected them to break against his claim on her like water splashed aside by a hand. But they were all there: Samael and his greed and his green devotion; Hero Ng who mourned the rest he longed for and would never know; Rien, brushing Perceval in passing, shining with love and rich in selfish disappointment. And doing this thing anyway, taking Perceval as she was. And they pushed through her, ran like a river, shoved barriers aside, flooded her with their conjoined strength and scoured clean channels in her mind.

And Dust was beset, still locked in silent combat with Asrafil, constrained to protect those within his bridge, limited by human frailties not his own.

Perceval might have been frightened if Rien had not been with them. Rien, who with Hero Ng's help, used Samael's own virus—and Samael's own knowledge of how to fight angels—to unpick Samael and rework him, make him into something else, and then bootstrapped Samael up through Pinion and through Perceval. Rien, whose guiding touch she could feel as Samael slammed into Dust from a direction the angel never expected: from the *inside*.

Rien, who used their combined strength and resources not to *consume* Dust, nor even to reach through *him* and consume Asrafil. But to *revise* him. Revise them both, in fact. Infect them. Complexify them, as Pinion scattered into pieces on the deck, shadow-bright crumbling into powder, sifting through the air like sand, converting back to the nanoparticles of its colony, its guiding principle stripped out and subsumed.

I should not have wanted to change you. You have the right to draw lines. It's not the heroes we need to fix.

It's the monsters.

The gestalt wasn't trying to eat Dust. It meant to taint him. With duty, and affection, and the bitter, soft creak of snow, compressed under struggling wings. To support him, reinforce him, bring Asrafil under his sway.

To taint him, with Pinion, with Samael, with Rien.

Rien, who whispered in Perceval's head—

—You were my knight in shining armor.—

—and who, lost in the angel she'd birthed, fell to ashes in Perceval's hands.

His Captain was a long time crying.

But that was right and fair. Right and fair that she should weep for the dead. Right and fair that she should weep as well, for those not truly alive, who had sacrificed their consciousness to the wholeness of the world.

Right and fair that she should weep for the death of her wife, and for her wings.

And while she wept, the angel was busy. There were ways to be smoothed. Latticeworks to reinforce. The whole world, like a crystal, tuned so that it might resonate at a stroke but not shatter. He reached out through the world, and—in his strength—he found the angels, greater and lesser, and opened himself to them. And they came, mostly willing, for now he was without rival, and even the strongest of the lesser rank could see that it was better to come willing, a voice in the choir, than be consumed and silenced. Even the smallest wills came unto him—Rien's newborn armor, who would never now be named. The un-blades, Innocence and Mercy, and what remained of Charity as well, though its program was decompiled and much had been lost.

There was one exception. When he reached Engine, he found a creature who had never been a fragment of Israfel. A small animal, a small tool. A white falcon with a serpent's tail and lasers for eyes.

It was what remained of an Exalt woman, the rebel Cynric Conn, and in her memory the angel left it discrete.

As for Engine, the angel was busy. He spoke to the Chief Engineer, and to her imparted the news for good and ill. That some had been lost, although there was enough left in him that had been Rien to speak to her softly, and with consolation. And to Benedick Conn as well, on whose stone face the news fell like rain.

For Arianrhod, he had no words, even as she was brought into custody at last, and led to her acceleration tank to await whatever would befall.

There were more important matters at hand.

The angel bade Tristen Conn enter, to care for his Captain. He set about cleaning the bridge, recycling the cobwebs and insect and arachnid husks. There must be repairs, and not just to the interior. His patch job of the rent Ariane—and he, in that part of him that had once been Asrafil—had torn in the hull was crude, but it was strong.

Still, the first thing he made clean was his Captain's chair, so her uncle could place her in it. Tristen lifted her carefully and held her to his armored chest for a long time before he set her down again, though she curled into herself and would not be comforted.

The angel ached to help her.

But then, he thought, Tristen ached as well.

The angel understood it. Rien would have known. *So this is love*, he thought. *This abjection. This helplessness.*

It was not merely the chemicals, after all.

Onto the screens, the angels called images of the waystars, of the construction. Of the flocks of resurrectees brought into Engine, imbued with the knowledge of dead Com and Crew and Engineers, preserved all this time by Samael and Mallory in their orchard library. Now that the angel's touch reached everywhere, through all the living portions of the world, he identified its wounds and weaknesses, and where he could not heal himself, he sent the Engineers.

And they went with a will, once Caitlin Conn gave them the word.

And then it was time to awaken his Captain. She slept poorly, her uncle's uniform jacket thrown over her shoulders as a crude blanket, concealing the healed stubs of her wings. Tristen sat beside her, dozing fitfully though he was propped upright.

With sense enough, now, not to whisper endearments in her ear, the angel brushed the fringe of Perceval's awareness and woke her. Though his avatar stood before the screens, he saw her eyes come open. He saw her fingers tighten on the collar of her uncle's coat.

He saw her awakening wince, of pain that was not physical. He wondered what that was like, to wake and remember loss.

He was glad that he would never know.

His Captain slid her feet off her couch. She stood, silently, without rousing her uncle, though she had to slip her shoulder from under his hand to do it. She left behind his coat.

The bridge might be clean, but Perceval was filthy. She should go to her quarters, make herself clean. Rest in comfort.

The angel would find a way to suggest it.

But first he had something to show her.

"Angel?" She stood at his elbow, breathing. Her voice was as cold as the breath of the Enemy.

"I did not mean to hurt you," he said. "When I was Rien—"

"You're not Rien." She would not look at him, and it twisted in his belly. Which was ludicrous, but he felt what Rien would have felt.

And Rien would have felt pain.

Still, if they lived, there was the future.

"I am what is left of Rien," he said, which was as true as anything. He was not *not* Rien.

She swallowed. "Why did you wake me?"

"It's time," he said, and darkened and polarized all the world's windows, and commandeered all its screens. "You'll want to go to your tank."

She did not move. And the angel would not touch her without invitation.

"What's your name?" she asked. "What do I call you?"

"I don't have a name," he said. If he wasn't Rien, no more so was he Dust, or Inkling, or Pinion, or Metatron, or Susabo, or Samael, or Asrafel. "You will have to give me one."

She held her breath, which she didn't need except for speaking. And the angel waited for her to answer.

But the warning claxon had awakened Tristen, and Tristen came and touched her arm. "Acceleration tank," he said.

The stubs of Perceval's wings raked the inside of her borrowed shirt. She looked up, not at the main screen but at the windows, though the view through the telescope was better.

The angel thought he heard her take a breath.

And then the sky tore wide.

It began as a flare of the primary, an arc-light brightness at the poles, where the curtains of falling matter from the secondary plunged to the white dwarf's surface. It could have been a brightening, of the sort epidemic to a catastrophic variable pair. Of the sort they'd been witnessing with increasing frequency over the past centuries, years, days.

This time, it wasn't.

The white dwarf was undergoing conflagration. In a

matter of moments, a great mottled curtain of fire blew away from its surface, an expanding sphere that slammed past the secondary with unimaginable power, shredding the photosphere from the red giant and leaving only a seared cinder in its wake.

Even through the filters, even for Exalted eyes, the light must have been shattering. Perceval's and Tristen's bones shone through their skin. Outside, amid the lattice-work of the world, the outlines of shadows were scorched into the hide of the *Jacob's Ladder*, its name and the twisting helix symbol obliterated in an instant by that scouring light.

The suns had been dead for ten and a half minutes by the time their final ecstasy was visible to Perceval and Dust.

The shock front of the explosion traveled at a fraction of lightspeed. There was plenty of time to watch it come. Plenty of time for Tristen to chivvy Perceval to the limited protection of the tanks.

And after a single lingering glance around the bridge, she went. It didn't matter. The angel was always with her.

The nameless angel in the nameless ship filled his empty spaces with himself, all his microscopic bodies cushioning, absorbing where they could. He must be quick. There was so much life within him that could *not* be moved to a tank, and he was its only protection.

Him, the embrace of his self-stuff, and his delicate manipulations of the artificial gravity.

He cast his nets wide, reached out to the Engineers who still worked feverishly from their tanks. He possessed the monofilaments of his magnetic sails; he spread grasping electromagnetic fingers. The star's magnetosphere had been as shredded as the star itself, broken into fragments and tossed wide on the shock wave of the supernova. He must locate a bubble at the front of the wave, find it and then catch it. And then hold it, without being torn apart himself.

Because if he missed, behind it roared a wall of plasma from one of the most powerful explosions in the universe.

Nothing to it, he told himself. Like surfing the tunnel of the wave.

And then he wondered from which of his component selves he had claimed that metaphor.

The forefront of the wave reached them, and the angel felt it slipping through his webs, slipping, slipping—

Catching.

Caught.

There was no time to brace or consider. He jerked, snapped. Shuddered. Broke, in places. Held, in places. Snapped, and strained, and twisted. Deformed and was crushed.

Was picked up and hurled, stinging, smarting, broken.

Not whole. Shredding, trailing lives and material, bleeding from a thousand wounds.

Not intact.

But alive.

He heard his Captain in her tank. He sensed her pain and disorientation. The tank could not leak. She must be safe. At all costs.

He waited, then.

Until she spoke to him. "Angel?"

"Captain," he answered.

"Status?" She stammered, but she said it.

The angel smiled his snaggled smile. "We are under way."

about the author

ELIZABETH BEAR was born on the same day as Frodo and Bilbo Baggins, but in a different year. This, coupled with a childhood tendency toward reading the dictionary, doomed her early to penury, intransigence, and the writing of speculative fiction.

She is a recipient of the John W. Campbell Award for Best New Writer and a Locus Award, and has been nominated for the BSFA, Philip K. Dick, and Lambda awards. She lives in southern New England with a presumptuous cat, and her hobbies include archery, guitar, and the indiscriminate slaughter of defenseless houseplants.

If you loved DUST, do not despair. There is more!

For hundred of years, the generation ship *Jacob's Ladder*—conceived of by a religious cult as an experiment in forced evolution—has drifted derelict in orbit around a pair of dying stars.

Now she's underway again, though at a terrible price. Her search for a permanent home for her passengers has resumed, and she has claimed as her captain the young knight Perceval Conn.

But the quest will not be easy. She remains crippled, her crew and passengers Balkanized and incommunicado. She travels deep into uncharted territory. And deep in her wounded hull, she still keeps a thousand secrets. . . .

Be sure not to miss
CHILL
by
Elizabeth Bear

The next thrilling installment in the *Jacob's Ladder* series, coming from Bantam Spectra in the spring of 2009.